Thunderbird Studios Presents

WELCOME TO SAN CICARO

EXPLORE. EXPERIENCE. ENJOY.

Edited by A. R. Aston and James Fadeley

A Thunderbird Studios Publication

Welcome to San Cicaro Copyright © 2019 Thunderbird Studios Limited Liability Company.
All stories contained within this book are the property of the respective authors.
All rights reserved.

Cover Image and design by Manuel Mesones (https://herearedragons.uk/)
Book design by James Fadeley (https://jamesfadeley.com)
ISBN 13: 978-1-946289-03-2
ISBN 10: 1-946289-03-5

Follow Thunderbird Studios at their website or on social media at:

https://www.tbirdstudios.com
Twitter: @tbirdstudios
Facebook: www.facebook.com/ThunderbirdStudiosLLC

Table of Contents

The Siren of Gatsby Rock

Ichabod Ebenezer

"Why'd you want to meet here?"

Manny Cargille looked up from his phone to see his partner, Jason Burbank standing at the edge of the booth. "Oh, hey. Sit down. Did you get us rooms?"

"Yeah, at the Royal Embassy Hotel," Jason said, sliding into the bench opposite Manny.

"Really?" Manny asked, impressed.

"Hell no. Best Western. And we could barely afford that, so don't drink too much." Jason slid a room access card across the table. Manny accepted it with a scowl. "So, why are we here?"

"Look," Manny started. "This is our chance to make it back to the big time. I'm surprised that the place isn't crawling with paranormal investigators, but I'm not looking a gift horse in the mouth. We are here first so we have to move quickly."

"No, I didn't mean San Cicaro, why are we here, in this bar?"

"That's easy. There's all sorts of news about San Cicaro, like that corpse that just got up and walked out of the hospital morgue. Or the sixteen total strangers who simultaneously won the lottery, to the snowfall in July, to the ghost ship in the harbor with a couple dozen witnesses. The problem is, we can't investigate the whole city, and we can't hope to be somewhere before it happens if we don't know where it's going to be. That's why we're here. We're going to talk to some people, and collect some local knowledge. We find somewhere with a lot of activity, we get some of it on camera, and we're gold. Once we put that up on YouTube, TLC is going to be calling *us* about doing a series."

"Alright. But you talk to them. I don't want to get recognized," Jason said with a sigh. "I'm tired of being laughed at."

"You know, you're gonna have to get over that at some point if you want to be famous," Manny replied. He looked Jason in the eye as he finished off his beer.

"I don't want to be famous. I just want proof."

"Proof. Right. I'll stick with fame." Manny chuckled as he slid out of the booth and knocked twice on the table, pointing at Jason before heading toward the bar. He pulled out his wallet and removed a few business cards, riffling through them for one that wasn't too dog-eared.

There were eight people at the bar in ones and twos. Manny selected a young blonde woman standing on her own with something pink in a martini glass.

"Hi," he said to her with a bright smile. As she turned toward him, he flicked out two fingers with the business card wedged between. "Manny Cargille, P.H.a.N.T.o.M. Investigations. I was wondering if you've seen anything odd recently."

She looked up from the card, then looked him up and down. "Look, no offense? But, bite me."

With that she turned back toward the television on the side of the bar. A soccer match was on, which gave him very little to run with, so he turned toward the man on his other side. He too was looking up toward the TV rather purposely.

Manny insinuated himself in the man's line of sight. "Hi! I'm Manny Cargille, paranormal investigator. I'd love to buy you a beer if you have any interesting stories about the recent claims."

"Sorry, pal. Now, could you move?" The man flashed him a look of annoyance and moved his head to see around Manny. After a moment, he put a hand on Manny's shoulder and gently ushered him aside.

Manny sized up the bar patrons again. Just past the blonde girl there were three young men, probably from the nearby CSUSC campus, who were talking amongst themselves rather than watching the match. Maybe he'd have better luck with them.

"Hey, guys. Quick question: Have there been any reports of paranormal activity on campus?" He held out his business card hopefully.

The three turned to face him. One of the boys, shorter than the other two but with a linebacker's shoulders, took Manny's card and looked it over. "You mean like at the Delta Omega Alpha fraternity?"

"Could be," Manny said, pulling his notepad out of an inside jacket pocket. He patted about himself to locate his pen, and once found wrote down D.O.A. "Why, what happened there?"

"Well, they say that every time they throw a party, a girl goes missing. They also say that the fraternity president has been a senior for as long as anyone can remember, and he doesn't age or go out during the day."

Manny clicked his pen again without writing anything. He looked up at the trio suspiciously. "No, I get it. D.O.A. Dead on arrival. Very funny."

The three kids erupted into laughter and clinked their glasses together. Manny tried to snatch his card back, but they held it out of his reach.

Dejected, he moved on to the man next to them. A businessman who was playing a game on his phone while nursing a scotch and soda. He'd have to go with his second best card. "Hi. My name's Manny Cargille. I'm with P.H.a.N.T.o.M. Investigations, and I'm looking for anyone who's seen something strange in San Cicaro. "

The man sighed and glanced at his card, though Manny was reluctant to let go of it. The man met his eyes, and opened his mouth to say something, but one of the college kids spoke first. "Hey! Didn't you use to have that YouTube channel?"

Manny closed his eyes, let his breath out in one long Zen exhalation. He replied without turning around.

"Yes, actually. Still do. We had thirty million views on our last video," he said proudly. He quickly returned his attention to the man in the business suit. "You were saying…?"

"Oh my god, you're right! It's them!" It was the other of the college kids, who barely avoided spraying beer out his nose as he said it. "You're the guys that faked that video!"

Manny sighed. He couldn't go anywhere anymore without this happening eventually. "It was a re-enactment! It wasn't fake! The cameras and equipment all malfunctioned when it happened, so we recreated it exactly like it happened before."

All three of them were laughing now, and the businessman was smiling broadly too as he handed back the card. "Little bit of advice. When it's a re-enactment, you should say so before you show it."

The shortest of the college boys clapped him on the back. "It also looks bad when you deny everything until the video editing guys proved it!"

All four of them were laughing now. Manny snatched back the other card while they were distracted. The YouTube response from the forensic video specialist had gotten twice as many views, and within hours of it going up, TLC had pulled out of talks with them for a series.

"Okay, have a laugh! But I'm serious about catching San Cicaro's ghosts on tape."

The bartender called out to him. "If you're going to order something, be my guest. But leave the other customers alone, alright?"

Manny shook his head and walked back to the booth where Jason was waiting, out of sight of the bar patrons.

"That went better than in my imagination," Jason said as Manny slid back into his seat.

"Yeah, yeah. I think I almost had that last guy before the meatheads recognized me. We should try another bar. Maybe we'll have better luck somewhere that the game isn't playing."

"You're asking the wrong questions," said a gruff voice from the next booth over.

Jason turned around to see the face of a bearded old man hovering over the divider.

"Oh yeah?" Manny said. "What questions should I have been asking?"

The old man came around to stand at the end of their booth. The rest of him was in line with what they had seen so far, flannel shirt and suspenders over jeans and workman's boots. The smell coming off of him was of stale cigarettes, and his hands were more callus, scars and liver spot than skin. "You're asking where weird things are happening. The question you should be asking is, why has it all changed?"

He sat down at the booth, forcing Jason to scoot over. "San Cicaro has always had an otherworldly presence, just nobody used to talk about it. People have taken notice lately, maybe because it's all gone evil."

"You mean that some sort of evil influence has moved into town?"

"I don't know nothing about that. You lot are the experts, maybe you can find something? I'll tell you what I do know, and maybe you can start from there."

The old man leaned in over the table, and Manny had his pen and notepad out again. *Click!*

"When I was a younger man—this was before the big tech boom, but things were already starting to go well for San Cicaro—I served on board a fishing ship called *The Lassiter*. Sometimes we'd spend an entire week on the open ocean, and we were used to bringing in our catch in the pre-dawn hours. By then, there were brokers at the dock, loading fish into freezer trucks to be flown all over the U.S. We were making good money, but at the same time, we worked eighteen-hour days to do it.

"Anyway, coming in at that time of day, we relied on the Gatsby Rock Lighthouse to lead the way past the treacherous shallows beyond the harbor. But on one particular day, a storm blew in out of the north, and the swells were twenty feet high! It was all we could do to maintain course, but we knew that once we reached the harbor, the seas would calm and we'd be safe.

"So, we stuck with it, using the steadfast lighthouse as our reference, when a bolt of lightning lit the sky like daylight! When it passed and our eyes adjusted, we couldn't find the lighthouse. Our beacon was gone. The compass spun, useless in the swells, and we soon lost all confidence in our position. The only thing we knew was that the shallows were all around us, ready to slash our hull and drag us down to a cold, unholy death.

"Even the captain, as steady a man as you'd ever meet, was near panic. He called for us to drop anchor, but I knew that could mean our death as sure as the rocks, and I held the winch. Other crew thought me mad, and had their filleting knives out, ready to gut me and throw my body overboard in the hopes of saving themselves. But just then, there was a blinding white light. We went back to being crewmen instead of mutineers and murderers, and sought out the source of the light. And there! Off the starboard bow we recognized the cliffs of Gatsby Rock where the light was coming from. We knew again where we were, and how to get into the bay safely."

He leaned in even further, and spoke barely over a whisper. "Once we were in the calmer waters of the bay, we looked again at where the light was coming from, because we knew that no one could have repaired the lighthouse in that short time. Then the captain pointed out how it didn't spin around like it should. No, it shone in all directions at once. I got out my binoculars and saw that the beacon wasn't coming from the lighthouse at all, but from a woman standing on the cliffs and looking out to sea."

The old man met each of their gazes. Manny swallowed and glanced up from his notes, eager for more. Perhaps convinced of his audience, the man continued.

"It was the Siren of Gatsby Rock. Many a mariner has told tales of the Siren. They say she was the ghostly widow of a sailor lost at sea during a great storm. And for almost as long as there's been a San Cicaro, the Siren has been seen on stormy nights, haunting the rocky shore, singing to her husband to bring him back home safely. God only knows how many of us would have joined her husband at the bottom of the ocean if not for the Siren."

Manny looked up from his frantic scribbling. "Wow. That's fantastic."

"You say that it's all turned evil now?" Jason prompted.

"Well what would you call it?" The old man gestured to Jason and Manny. "Those people in the ICU claiming their attacker was a beast that walks on two legs, stalking them through Sentimental Pines Park? Or those insect swarms appearing out of nowhere up in the heights and razing houses? The things in the sewers, snatching bodies?"

"Well, what about all those lottery winners?"

The old man sat back, chuckling dryly. "What do you get when you split 1.3 million sixteen ways? After taxes and all that? A lot of those folks went right out and spent like they were getting the whole amount, and now they're in bankruptcy."

The man slid back out of the booth. He stood facing them for a moment longer, an ancient and indistinct tattoo poking out from beneath both sleeves. "Not so lucky after all. You boys figure out what's made it all go bad, you'll be heroes around here, even if you don't get your show."

Manny was back on his phone, frenetically tapping away.

"So, do you think there's anything to that story?" Jason asked, keeping his voice low in case the old man could still hear them.

"It's the best lead we've got, and man, wouldn't that be a fantastic visual for the cameras? Widow woman glowing white, against the crashing waves of an angry sea?" He turned his phone toward Jason. "And, bam! There's a storm tonight. Hot damn!"

The two of them looked at each other for a moment longer, then raced to get to the van outside. The first drops of rain were hitting the dusty windshield and evaporating almost instantly. Jason got behind the wheel and called out, "How do I get to the lighthouse?"

"Find the PCH and head north!" Manny said while looking through their equipment in the back of the van. He found and opened a new package of batteries. "Let me know when we get that far, and I'll direct you from there."

He quickly swapped out the batteries in the Mel Meters and the REM pods, grabbing hold of the shelving momentarily as they tore around corners in their haste.

"Okay, where to next?" Jason called from the front.

"Hang on a moment." Manny put one of the voice recorders under his arm, half way through replacing the batteries. He glanced at the map on his phone. "We should be passing Howard Avenue now. Turn left when you get to Phillips Drive! It will wind around a bit from there, but it's on that street, and there should be signs."

Two minutes later, they pulled up to the lighthouse with the wipers on full. Jason came around the van and opened the back. Manny handed him a vest covered in pockets that were pre-filled with a Mel Meter, walkie-talkie, flashlight, and a still camera plus a backup battery for it. Jason slid his arms into the vest, and Manny handed him a pouch that contained the REM pods.

Manny stepped out of the van with an identical vest, two video cameras, one running and one backup, plus a helmet equipped with a GoPro. They spent a quick second in the pouring rain, verifying all the pockets on each other's vest. Then, in a moment that seemed almost ceremonial, each zipped up the other's vest and clapped their partner on both shoulders, before Manny closed the van. The two ran toward the shelter of the lighthouse.

Jason rattled the door. "It's locked."

"Well, of course it's locked," Manny said, stopping the recording.

"Wait, shouldn't we get a permit or something?"

"Dude. How often do you think they get storms around here? If we go looking for a permit now, assuming they even grant us one, the ghost could be gone for years! No, tonight's our only chance, and we're taking it." With that, he produced a set of tools and began picking the lock. Three minutes later, he turned the knob and pushed the door open.

"Okay, now, let's do this for real." He indicated the knob, then took a step back and lifted the video camera.

Jason took the handle and waited for Manny to push the record button, then slowly pushed the door open and clicked on his flashlight. He looked back at the camera.

"We're entering the infamous Gatsby Rock Lighthouse. According to reports, this location is haunted by the widow of a lost sailor. On stormy nights she appears physically to guide sailors safely into the harbor. And, as you can see—" As Jason paused, Manny panned the camera around to take in the rain forming a stream in the new mud just outside. "—Tonight, we've got one hell of a storm. Let's go inside and look around."

Jason stepped inside and shined his flashlight around. The room they were in had a small shelf full of books and postcards, and several tables covered in t-shirts, sweat shirts, snow globes and other items for sale. To his right was a long counter with a cash register, and overstock behind it. To his left was a gated-off iron staircase leading up, and a large poster board depicting the lighthouse and a few paragraphs about its origin.

Jason turned back around, waving the fingertips of one hand back and forth across his neck. Manny stopped recording and lowered the camera. "What's up?"

"Dude, she appears outside during storms. And the lighthouse gift shop is not the spookiest place to find EMF spikes."

"Well, I didn't know it would be a gift shop, did I? And we need some establishing shots before we get to the ghost. If our video is just, 'hey look, there's a ghost' and it's over, we won't get any likes."

Jason spread his arms and looked around the room again. Then he pointed the flashlight up, where the beam disappeared in the distance. The stairs continued around the inside of the lighthouse like the threads on a screw. He spread his arms again and turned back toward Manny.

"I know. I get it. But how about I film you from a low angle. We won't get any of the tables, and no one will know it's a gift shop. You call out 'hello' a few times, we get some footage of you on the stairs, maybe some close ups of the Mel Meter, then we go look outside. Okay?"

Jason sighed. "Fine. You know, sometimes I think you care more about making a show than proving ghosts are real." He took his Mel Meter out and switched it on, holding it out near his flashlight.

"Man, it ain't even close. Okay, rolling," he said before Jason could respond.

"Hello?" Jason called, then under his breath, "zero point two... zero point three..."

They got the required footage, and were preparing to go outside, when Manny suddenly lifted the camera back up. "Jason! Did you hear that?"

"Shh, shh, shh," Jason responded, holding a hand near his ear.

They stood silently, with the pounding of rain and the occasional roll of thunder in the background. Then softly, during a momentary lull in the storm, they heard a woman's voice.

Jason began jumping up and down, a broad smile on his face. He let out a string of expletives that Manny made a mental note to bleep out later. "That's a voice!"

"It's singing isn't it?" Manny asked. Jason took on his listening pose again for a few moments.

"It's coming from outside," he said after a moment, and headed for the door.

Manny followed him, and Jason pushed the door open, running outside. Both paid the downpour no mind as they looked in all directions for the Siren. Neither one saw her immediately, so Jason shielded the screen of his Mel Meter with his hand and turned slowly, looking for a spike. In a few moments, he pointed off in one direction and started walking.

He wiped his soaked bangs out of his face. Thunder rumbled loudly overhead, and lightning lit the sky more than once, but he was on a mission. They went around the lighthouse to the cliffside, and stopped short.

There she was.

She was clearly visible, yet so were the rocks and the sea beyond her. There was a glow coming off of her as she sang, but it was faint—nothing like the beacon the old man had described. Her long silvery hair and the nightgown she clutched to her chest blew in the wind, giving her a sense of presence that went away as soon as Manny noticed that the rain wasn't drenching her.

Manny could practically smell the money he'd soon be rolling in. This was the Holy Grail of paranormal investigation. People could hunt ghosts for a lifetime and never see a full-body apparition that lasts for more than the blink of an eye. This specter was just standing there!

Ever the professional, he made sure he had her center frame, but kept Jason on the periphery as he turned excitedly to the camera, holding a finger up to his lips. They could only see the back of the Siren's head, but they could make out the sound of her voice. And she was definitely singing! Damn this rain for drowning out the actual words.

"We need to get closer!" Manny said in a loud whisper.

Jason gave a thumbs up, and turned back toward the Siren, crouching down and moving slowly. Manny had a moment of clarity as if looking at his life from the outside. *Oh my god, we're sneaking up on a ghost!*

A few more steps and Manny felt they were close enough. She filled enough of the camera frame that no one could claim this was just an actress. They could see straight through her! But Jason kept edging closer.

"Jason," Manny whispered. His partner either didn't hear or ignored him, so he tried again, louder, "Jason!"

Jason turned, motioning impatiently at Manny and whispering, "I want to know what she's singing!"

Manny took another couple steps, but that was as close as he was willing to go. Every horror movie he'd ever seen played in his head. He tried again. "Jason!"

Jason turned angrily and mouthed the words, "Shut up!" then turned back, edging closer.

As a film production specialist and a camera man, Manny wanted to get closer. But as a human, aware of his own fragile mortality, he just couldn't make himself do it. Finally, he took the spare camera from around his neck.

"Here! Take this!" When Jason turned around, he threw it to him.

Jason caught it and swung out the view screen, then gave a thumbs up and turned back around.

The Siren faced them.

Jason jumped, and Manny let out his own string of expletives. But a few moments later, when the ghost neither attacked nor vanished, they relaxed a little.

She was beautiful. Manny didn't know what he was expecting—something ethereal anyway. And she looked frightened at first, but Jason held out his hands in a calming gesture and took a few tentative steps toward her. Thankfully, he remembered to keep the camera pointed in her direction.

Her features calmed, and she even went back to singing. Manny still couldn't make out the words above the sounds of the storm, but Jason kept moving forward. Later, when they got his camera hooked up to Manny's computer, he might be able to play with the ranges and isolate her voice better. He'd be just as happy to hear it then.

Jason continued on. There was being brave, and then there was this. Manny was growing concerned. His steps were no longer tentative either. He was still moving slowly, but confidently as if he knew she wouldn't harm him. Manny wasn't so sure.

"Jason?" No response. "Jason!"

The Siren's face was kind, smiling even, gazing into Jason's eyes. She held her arms out toward him, and Jason continued toward her, mere feet away, entranced.

"Jason!" he tried again, but his friend didn't so much as look around.

It's all turned evil now, the old man had said. At the time, Manny had thought he meant the newer phenomenon. But now he suddenly felt like he meant the things that used to be good were now bad. This spirit who used to guide sailors to safety might now just lure them to their doom!

"Jason!" he screamed at the top of his lungs. Lightning lit up the clouds overhead, and the thunder drowned out his scream. Jason was in front of the Siren now.

The lightning showed something under her transparent face, the skull beneath was visible for a moment, and when the light was gone, so was whatever illusion there had been. Her clothes were torn and wet. What hair remained on her decaying head was plastered to her rain-slick and greying skin. One eye was missing from its socket, and the soft tissue around her nose and mouth had receded, leaving a rictus grin.

Jason screamed and stepped backward. Yet the Siren lunged and wrapped her bony arms around him. Suddenly she launched backward into the air, cackling madly and carrying the struggling Jason.

She paused in mid-air with lightning bouncing across the clouds overhead, and Manny screaming below, before she simply disappeared.

The skies were dark again. Manny could see nothing, but he could clearly hear Jason's screams descending from high above, and passing below him. Once his eyes adjusted to the darkness just enough, he ran to the cliff's edge and looked over.

Jason's shattered body lay upon the rocks below, repeatedly swallowed and then regurgitated by the turbulent surge.

The windshield wipers hammered back and forth, vainly trying to displace enough rainwater to see by. Manny was driving too fast. He glanced down at his phone again. Still no signal. "Come on, come on!"

He looked up to see the guardrail just in time to wrench the wheel to the left. The van fishtailed loudly, but stayed on the road.

He wasn't sure how long he'd been driving. His only thought when he'd left the lighthouse was to get away before the Siren killed him as well. Was Jason really dead? Manny had never seen a body before, but he sure looked like it. Only, he couldn't even think of his best friend as gone. He kept imagining a pair of paramedics crouching around Jason, telling Manny that he would be just fine. Ever since then, Manny'd been trying to call for help, but he couldn't get through.

Did the entire city lose signal? So much for the high-tech capital. He thumbed out 911 again and jammed on the send button. The alternating short and long tones told him there was still no signal. He threw the phone at the passenger side door where it bounced off into the wheel well. He gripped the wheel with both hands and stepped harder on the gas pedal.

He needed to find a landline. He just caught a neon sign for The Silicon Ship passing by on the left, and he slammed on the brakes, spinning out in the middle of the deserted road. It was the bar they'd been at earlier that night, and he was pretty sure he'd seen a phone behind the bar. He gunned the motor, running up half-way over the curb in his haste, and parked in a fire-zone just outside the door to the bar.

He left the van, slamming the door and paying no attention to the buzzing noise that told him the headlights were still on. He ran through the rain with his camera slung over his shoulder.

"Someone call 911!" he said as he burst through the door. Conversations stopped, and the group at the bar turned toward him. One of the bartenders, whom he recognized from his earlier visit, went to the phone.

"Whoa, whoa, whoa. Just hold on a moment here," said the other bartender. "Just come inside a moment. Let me pour you a drink, and you can tell me what your emergency is."

Manny headed straight for her. "My fr—my partner—"

"You just hang on. Take a seat over here and calm down. There's no reason to freak everyone else out, they've all got their own troubles. Now. What'll you have? It's on me." She nodded toward the other bartender, and he picked up the phone to start dialing.

"Beer. IPA," Manny said, mounting a stool at the end of the bar. He looked over the patrons. The business man and the college kids were still there, and they were watching him with looks of amusement. The other patrons were new.

The bartender set a coaster in front of him, pulled a pilsner glass out of a fridge and carried it over to the taps. "Alright, mister. Let's start with your name. You aren't hurt, are you?"

She brought the full glass over to him, and leaned over the bar, waiting.

"Manny. Manny Cargille. No. I'm not hurt. Just shaken. And soaked."

"Good, Manny. I'm Amy," she said with a smile and a little shimmy. "Now drink up and tell me your story."

He opened his mouth to speak and she put on a stern expression, pointing to the beer. Annoyed, he took a couple good swallows and put the beer back down. She smiled.

"My friend is dead. He was killed by the ghost of your lighthouse."

"Okay, that sounds pretty serious. We're a long way from the lighthouse though. Why'd you come here?"

"I don't know really. I didn't mean to come here, I just had to get away from there. I needed to tell someone, and we were here before we went there. I guess that's why."

"Telling someone is a really good start. Did you call 911?"

"I don't—" He looked down at his hand, realizing he'd grabbed his camera when exiting the van, but his phone was still there, probably with a cracked screen. "I couldn't get a signal."

"Are you sure about that? We've usually got pretty strong reception in San Cicaro. Take another drink?"

He looked down at the beer. It wasn't what he wanted right now, but Amy could be pretty insistent, so he drank.

"Good. Now, are you sure your friend is dead?"

"You have to make me say it again? Yes, dammit! I saw his body on the rocks at the base of the cliff! The way it bent all at odd angles! It must have been a hundred-foot drop for god's sake!"

"Okay, okay. Have another drink. Now, emotions run high in cases like this, and things get exaggerated. I'm not saying you're doing it on purpose, but that's what people do. It just so happens I know that spot pretty well, and those cliffs are no more than forty feet at their highest. It's possible he could survive that if the ambulance gets there fast enough."

"You're not listening to me!" Manny said, slamming a fist on the bar and regaining everyone's attention. "It was the ghost! She grabbed him and flew off with him! Then she just dropped him. He didn't just fall off the cliff, he fell from the sky!"

Amy took a couple steps back, raising her hands placatingly. "Tommy, those cops on the way?"

"They should be here any minute," the other bartender said.

Manny looked around at the other patrons. Everyone was looking at him, but no one was talking. There was no sympathy in their eyes, no understanding. He saw skepticism and even pity. He looked down at the camera still at his side. He had proof.

He stood up on his barstool and leapt over the bar. Amy ran to get out of the way, and Tommy ran toward him. Manny stood up and faced Tommy. He took a swing and got the bartender full in the jaw, taking him down. He opened the door behind the bar that held their satellite equipment and pulled the box forward to access the wires behind it.

Tommy started to get to his feet, and Manny pulled back his fist warningly. Tommy put up his hands and stayed down. Manny turned to look for Amy, but she'd vacated the bar.

He went back to the wires, pulling them out of the receiver box and plugging them into his camera. The screen behind the bar went blue, and Manny rewound the tape in the camera. When it finished, he pushed play.

"We're entering the infamous Gatsby Rock Lighthouse," Jason said on screen. Manny slammed his thumb on the fast-forward button, and he watched them go in double speed through the gift shop and briefly up the stairs. They returned to the gift shop area, then Jason jumped up and down, and they ran outside. Manny hit play.

He stood up and watched the bar patrons. They were watching his video. Now they'd see for themselves. Even Tommy got back up, and was craning his neck around to watch. Amy was nowhere to be seen, but Manny didn't care. He watched the video with them, waiting for his vindication.

Jason was running around the side of the lighthouse now. Manny found himself admiring his filming. There was none of that shaky-cam that was so popular today, and yet looked so unprofessional. He didn't even use a gimbal, that was all him.

And there she was. It brought a smile to his face despite what had happened. He had been a bit worried that she wouldn't show up on film or something, but there she was.

Undeniable proof.

Jason was sneaking toward her. He heard himself call out to him several times, and saw Jason's impatient waving away. Finally, he tossed the spare camera to Jason, and this time Manny could see the Siren turn around. At the time he'd been watching Jason, but now he saw the look in her eyes, and it sent chills down his spine. If he'd seen it then, in time to do something, he would have warned Jason away—hell, he would have dragged him away. That look was pure evil.

But he could no longer stop it, and the scene played out. Her expression was one of fear and innocence by the time Jason turned around. He walked to her and she changed. She grabbed him, and she was gone. This time the camera lost her, the two of them just sped off-screen. But he found her again, far above and tiny against the raging storm clouds. Each time the lightning brightened the background, the camera tried to refocus, and they disappeared. After the second time, the auto-focus failed to find them.

Then he heard Jason's scream again and had to close his eyes. Even still, it doppler shifted toward the camera and away again and Manny could see him falling with perfect clarity in his mind's eye. Then the scream came to an abrupt end.

When he opened his eyes again a few seconds later, the camera was looking over the edge of the cliff at the shattered remains of his partner. Manny hit stop.

"Oh my god," said one of the college kids. Manny stood up and turned toward him. "That was so fake!"

The three boys started laughing and Manny was too shocked to respond. The man in the business suit saw his expression. "Oh, come on. Your actress was supposed to be standing there in the storm, but her hair and dress weren't even wet."

"If I'd *had* an actress, she *would* have been drenched. The *ghost* in the video wasn't wet because the rain went right through her!"

"Seriously?" The shortest of the college students said. "So, rain goes right through ghosts, but the wind doesn't?"

"Yeah," said one of his friends, "why don't you just admit it's fake? It's funny. And funny's good, right?"

"*Funny?* My partner died today!" He launched across the bar at the kid that said it.

Amy came back into the bar with two policemen in tow, just in time to see Manny take a swing at the kid. One of the cops got on the radio while the other ran toward the melee.

Seconds later, the cop was dragging Manny across the bar and pushing him to the ground. He cuffed Manny's hands behind his back. "You have the right to remain silent."

"Backup's on the way," said the other cop as the first one finished telling Manny his Miranda rights. "Alright, who can tell me what this is all about?"

"My friend—" Manny started.

"Not you, Mr. Cargille!" the cop said, holding up a warning finger.

Tommy came forward, holding a bar rag full of ice to the side of his jaw. "This guy was in here earlier asking about ghost stories, and I made him stop bugging the customers, so he left. Then a couple hours later he comes in raving about a dead friend, and claims a ghost did it. He jumped over the bar and punched me, then showed this totally fake video as proof."

"It's not fake!"

"Mr. Cargille, I'm warning you," the first cop said. Then he turned back to the bartender. "He said a ghost did it?"

"Yes. That's right."

The second cop leaned into the first. "Third one tonight. I'd blame the full moon, but there isn't one."

The first cop didn't respond. "And you say he had a video?"

"Yeah. Here. This is his camera."

"Saunders, you wanna take that as evidence?" the first cop said to the second. "And how do you know the video was fake?"

"Uh, because ghosts aren't real, for one?" said one of the college kids.

"Here, look," said another one, holding up his phone. "There's this video where this dude debunks one of their old videos. It's kind of why they're famous."

Manny controlled his urge to comment while the police watched the video.

"And Mr. Cargille," the officer said once he'd seen enough, "where is your partner now?"

"That's what I've been trying to say! He's dead! The ghost dropped him off the cliff right by the lighthouse!"

"So, you came here looking for ghost stories, and sometime later, you were asked to leave here. Then, you heard about the lighthouse, and you and your partner went there, where he died. Correct? Where was he while you were here, looking for stories?"

"He was here in the bar with me!"

The cop looked around at the bartender and the patrons. The bartender finally said, "I only saw him."

"He was here. With me. We sat at that booth in the corner." He tried to point as best he could with his hands cuffed behind his back.

"Did anybody see his friend?"

No one said anything for a while, and finally the short college kid said. "Look, when I saw him, he was alone."

The businessman cleared his throat. "What if he set this whole thing up as a cover story? Maybe the two of them had a falling out after their video went viral for all the wrong reasons, and he killed his partner, and now he's staging all this to cover it up."

Manny charged at the man despite his bound wrists, but the cop caught him first.

"Alright, that's it. You're going to the station." He grabbed Manny by the cuffs, and walked him toward the door. He leaned in and spoke more quietly. "You aren't helping your defense, you know. We've seen how violent you can be here tonight, and fleeing the scene of your friend's death could be looked at as an admission of guilt."

As they neared the exit, Manny caught sight of the old man who had told them about the Siren, standing near the booth where they had first seen him. "That's him! He's the one who told us about the lighthouse! He can tell you! He saw Jason here!"

The police stopped leading him for a moment. "Alright. Who are you talking about? If there's someone here who can back up your story, now's your chance."

He struggled to get a hand to where he could effectively point, and ended up indicating the old man with his elbow. "Right there! The guy with the beard! Tell them! Tell them you saw Jason!"

The cops followed his gaze, but after a moment exchanged glances.

"Ah, Christ," the second cop said. "He's trying to set up an insanity plea, talking to people in empty spaces. Hey, pal, who do you see? Is it Abraham Lincoln?"

"But he's standing right there," he said, staring at the old man. Manny's face fell as he began to doubt his own mind.

The old man looked back with a smile. He shook his head and said, "Yes, sir. Didn't used to be evil. I told you. I don't know what changed. But we did."

Missy's Diner

Evan Purcell

My stomach gurgled. I needed something fast, cheap, and starchy. I also needed a shower to wash off all this blood and filth, but the starchy food would have to come first.

After crawling out of the sewer, I headed down the street to Missy's, the diner on 96th. It was open this time of night and, more importantly, it didn't have the sort of clientele who would look twice at a grimy-looking derelict like me.

The outside of Missy's was a typical, 50's-style eyesore, with a flickering neon sign and the sort of asymmetrical architecture you'd expect from a retro bowling alley. The fifties look was undermined by all the garish posters for shows and concerts, at venues I'd never heard of, plastered up one wall. Each overlapped one another like some madman's collage. I had no idea what exactly a "Golgonooza" was supposed to be, and I wasn't in the frame of mind to find out.

The parking lot was empty, aside from a single station wagon with a cracked windshield.

I pushed through the glass doors, forcing a bell to jingle half-heartedly. No one was inside, so I chose the biggest booth. Just for myself.

I waited.

Not for long, though, because a thirty-something waitress walked out of the back and nodded at me. She smiled pleasantly, obviously using a bit of effort to ignore my filthy appearance.

She was pretty, even with that cold sore, and the lopsided application of eye shadow. Nice, reddish hair. Narrow face. Very pleasant. She seemed to fit inside the diner, as if she were always here.

I had picked the booth against the front window. It was roomy and, more importantly, it would give me a good view of the street outside. If I paid attention, maybe I could spot more of those creatures out in the street. Of course, I probably wouldn't. They lived underground.

Whatever. I had to try. They were still dangerous, and they still had my daughter.

The waitress walked toward my booth with a single menu under her arm. As she slid the menu in front of me, she looked right into my eyes, and it seemed as if she knew me.

My reputation preceded me, apparently. Or my smell. Or the dirt streaks on my face. Or my torn clothes. I knew I looked like I'd just survived some ridiculous fight, which I had.

"What can I get ya?" she asked, as civil as possible.

I looked into her eyes rather than her cold sore and ordered a breakfast burrito and Diet Coke. Extra cheese and sour cream.

She smiled—God, it was hard not to look at that cold sore—and said, "Will do. I'll have a physician ready in case of heart attack."

Then she left. She seemed like the perfect waitress, personable and to-the-point. In a way, she reminded me of Tina, of my daughter. Just last week, she went with me to some diner and warned me about my eating habits.

She wasn't annoying about it, just concerned. At times, she acted more like a parent than I did.

And now she was gone.

I sat alone by the window. Waiting. It was just me and my thoughts.

Just an hour before, I was walking through the seediest area of the city, just a few blocks away from this diner. I was looking for any signs of Tina, though most of my hope was already gone.

It was dusk, a bit cold, when I saw someone scurrying down an alley.

The figure was not Tina's boyfriend. He looked a bit smaller and more stooped. Still, he walked with the same jerky movements, the same almost-limp, and I knew they were related. The same species.

Whatever that meant.

The figure looked around. He didn't see me. Stooping onto one leg, he slid open a manhole cover on the sidewalk. He lowered his twisted body into the sewer. Disappeared.

As the manhole cover loudly clattered back into place, I waited. No one else was around, human or otherwise. The sun dipped behind the crumbling apartment buildings to my left, slipping the alley into shadow. The darkness should've put me on edge, but I wasn't afraid. I was driven.

The streetlights clicked on, all at once. I took that as a signal to keep going. Carefully, I slid open the manhole cover and lowered myself into the sewers. I used my crappy cell phone for light, but it wasn't much. All I could see were shapes and shadows.

I charged forward, my boots making muffled noises in the sludge. The figure I had followed was long gone at this point. The sewer tunnels ran in either direction, but I knew he must've gone to the left, where the tunnel sloped deeper into the ground. Whatever he was, whatever they were, must've lived as far away from the surface world as possible.

Without hesitating, I headed deeper into the darkness. Again, I wasn't scared. There was a level of repulsion rising inside me, but it wasn't fear. Not at all.

I shined the dim glow of my phone across the floor. It didn't take long before I saw a moving shape up ahead. It was small, hunched over, wearing a cloak. It skittered into my tunnel, turned to the side, and disappeared down a smaller passage.

I followed, not bothering to stay quiet. My trudging footsteps echoed, but it didn't matter. When I rounded the corner, I saw the creature. No. Two creatures. They stood together and watched me.

The tunnel ended in a stone wall, which meant I had them cornered. I slid the phone into my pocket.

The creatures were both in hoods. Swaying. Twitching. Waiting for me. Maybe one of them was the thing I followed into the sewers, or maybe not. They all looked the same.

"Who are you?" I asked.

No answer.

"Where's my daughter?"

The creature on the left tapped himself right on the nose. Three times. The other one didn't move.

"Where is she?" I asked.

They both looked at me. Synchronized. They froze, aside from a bit of shaking from the one on the left.

"Where. Is. She?" I demanded.

"You don't belong down here," both of them said. They shared a voice, cracked and low, almost a whisper but not quite.

I stepped forward and attacked. I didn't have a weapon—just my bare hands—but they were enough. I grabbed one of them by the head and twisted. The other jumped onto my back. I shook him off and slammed him against the wall.

It didn't take long for me to tear them apart. They didn't give up. Just kept jabbing with their elbows and slashing with their fingertips.

One of them scored a punch right on my jawline, but that didn't stop me from grabbing his arm and twisting it off his body. The twitching limb popped off without making a sound.

As they whimpered at me, I disassembled them. Piece by piece, until they were nothing but piles. I could've tried harder. I could've gotten more answers out of them, but once the violence started, I couldn't stop myself.

As I left them there and reentered the main tunnel, I thought I heard one of them moan for help. I looked over my shoulder and saw one of their heads, sitting at an angle on the ground, as it opened and closed its mouth. He was trying to get my attention.

But I kept walking.

As the memories flooded my brain, I leaned against the glass window next to my booth. It was cold. I could hear the neon sign buzzing through the glass. I could *feel* the buzzing through the glass, like a warning, like something was going to explode.

Less than five minutes later, the waitress came back and slid a plate onto my table. It must've been waiting under a heat lamp. It didn't look particularly good, but I wasn't particularly picky, either.

"Extra cheese and cream. You must've earned it tonight," she said. Clearly, she was talking about my disheveled appearance. Maybe my smell, too.

Probably both.

"Yeah," I answered.

The waitress started to leave, but she stopped herself. She looked at me for a long moment. I could tell she was arguing with herself about something. She should've left, we both knew that, but she leaned closer and asked, "You okay?"

"Yeah," I lied.

"I know this is a tough neighborhood," the waitress said, "so it's not surprising if you... found trouble."

Trouble was an understatement. I stared at the burnt edges of my burrito. I suddenly wasn't feeling hungry. Not right now.

"I'm okay," I admitted. "Stood up for myself."

The second part was true. The first part, not so much.

She forced a smile. "Are you looking for someone?"

I watched her for a long moment, forcing myself to focus on her eyes and not on the cherry red cold sore on the edge of her upper lip.

What did she already know? Did she see those... things too?

I didn't know if I should tell her the real reason I was here. She might be able to help, or she might become an obstacle.

"My daughter was taken," I said flatly.

Everything started two weeks ago. In my house. At the time, I knew something was wrong. I should've done something then and there. I should've...

I was watching a basketball game when Tina ran into the room. All smiles. God, she looked so young when she smiled.

"Daddy," she said.

I stood. "Someone's having a good day."

Her smile was a bit nervous. She said, "Daddy, I'd like you to meet someone."

And then the stranger walked in.

He waited in the doorway, rubbing his arms and smiling. Then he stepped forward. When I first saw him, I thought he was normal. As he got closer, though, I knew that he was... wrong. Something was wrong with him. Off-centered.

He offered his hand.

When we shook, I could tell that he was trying to squeeze as hard as he could, but his grip was weak. It almost felt like I could tear his hand right off his body. His skin was warm, though.

I turned to Tina. "Is this your...?"

"Boyfriend," she answered. "Tommy."

The stranger smiled at me. He half-waved, which basically meant he jiggled his fingers in the air. He didn't say anything.

I didn't say anything.

He had striking green eyes. Their color was beautiful, a deep emerald with flecks of gold. But there was also something unnerving about them, like the eyeballs themselves were too big for his face. Like they'd been meant for a different skull.

"So... um," I started. The silence stretched between us. I knew I needed to say something, to offer a bit of small talk, but I had nothing to say.

"Dad," Tina said. We were standing in the middle of my living room, and I knew Tina wanted me to ask them to sit.

I didn't.

"How did you two... meet?" I asked.

The stranger considered his answer. Finally, he spoke. "In the city."

That wasn't much of an answer. There were a lot of dangerous areas in the heart of San Cicaro. Places for upstanding citizens to avoid at all costs. I stared at him, waiting for him to elaborate.

"It was by that amazing ice cream shop. You know the one, Dad," Tina chimed in, to fill the awkward quiet developing between me and the boy.

"Yeah, I know it, all right..." I hadn't taken Tina in some time, but I couldn't help this feeling of our memories together being intruded upon. I was going to ask him for more details, but instead I told him, "It's a pleasure. I know you'll treat my daughter right."

That last part was more of a threat than anything.

"Of course," the stranger said. He looked at Tina and they exchanged a quick smile. "She deserves it. She has a very bright soul."

Weird comment. The words made my skin crawl.

Back then, I didn't know that my daughter would disappear. I didn't know that the next time I saw this man, I'd be bludgeoning him to death.

But I did know, and I'm not sure how, that he was planning to take Tina away from me.

The neon sign flickered just a bit louder. It filled the silence.

"Your daughter," the waitress said. Not a question. "I'm so sorry."

With a grunt, she slid into the booth and sat across from me. No invitation. She smiled, but it was a gesture of sympathy, not happiness.

I knew I shouldn't get this stranger involved. This was my mission. I had to kill those things by myself and I shouldn't unload this burden on some minimum-wage stranger. Still, she lived here, and she'd seen something. I knew it. I also knew that she wanted to talk to me, so I said, "You don't sound surprised."

"What do you mean?" she asked, almost cagey.

"I mean, this happens a lot, huh? People are taken?"

She looked away, her eyes focusing on the dark streets outside. She rubbed her hands together as if she were cold.

She wasn't. If anything, it was hot in here.

She wanted to give me information about those things. That was obvious. All I had to do was continue the conversation.

"Be honest with me," I said. "You're…"

"You went… down there," she said. She pointed toward the floor.

The sewer tunnels were below us, dark and narrow. And I saw those creatures again. So close to being human, and yet… not quite. They moved like dolls, as if their arms and their legs each had different people controlling them.

No use beating around the bush.

"They attacked me. I fought back," I said. "I…"

"What do you know about them?" the waitress asked. She was still rubbing her hands together, perhaps nervously.

"I know everything."

Thirty minutes before, I was still in the dim light of the sewer. I still had blood on my face and hands from the two creatures I'd killed. It wasn't a lot of blood, though. They were almost dry on the inside, and I took that as yet another sign that they were very, very inhuman.

I'd been wandering through the tunnels for a while now, fully aware that I'd get lost if I wasn't careful. Thankfully, there were manhole covers every twenty yards or so, which meant I have several escape options if things got too dangerous.

I followed skittering and muttering noises down another tunnel. This one was slightly wider than the others.

And I saw them. There was a cluster of those creatures, all huddled around a metal barrel. Each of them was reaching into the barrel, rifling through its contents.

With a gulp, I realized that its contents were body parts.

Human body parts. Arms. Feet. Ears. So many pieces. And what were they doing with them?

I stepped closer, accidentally knocking a tin can with my foot. It rattled loudly.

They all turned at once, as if governed by a singular will.

There were seven of them in total, all about the same size and shape. Two of them hissed at me. A few more clicked their tongues. One of them opened and closed his jaws in a sign of intimidation.

But the last one on the end didn't react at all. He just stared with a blank face and unblinking eyes.

Green eyes. Green eyes with flecks of gold. Green eyes too big for his face. This was Tina's boyfriend.

Bile rose up the back of my throat. Without thinking about the danger, or anything aside from the glaring flashes of anger, I dove toward him and grabbed his shoulders.

The others scattered to the corners of the tunnel. They watched as I shook their brother and screamed into his face, "Where's Tina?"

"Uhhh," the thing said.

I grabbed him by his thick throat, holding him in place.

"You..." he sputtered as he squirmed. "You found her. You found... her."

"What?" I screamed into his face. "Where is she?"

He tried to say something, but the words couldn't get through his throat.

Still, I squeezed harder. Kept squeezing.

"You..." he struggled.

I relaxed my grip, just a bit.

"You... dark soul," he rasped. "Dark soul."

I didn't get it. It sounded like he was cursing me or something. Like he was... I don't know.

"Where is she?" I tried again.

His mouth opened and closed, fishlike.

In a single motion, I pulled his head forward and then pushed back. His head slammed against the stone wall behind him.

I knew it would cause damage, but I didn't expect his head to shatter like that.

After the remnants of his skull finished their gradual slide down the stone wall, everything went still. Silent. I looked around, and the other creatures were gone. They'd fled.

A single ray of light streamed down on me from above. I looked through the vent over my head and saw the flickering neon of a diner. I even smelled a whiff of fried food, though that might've just been my imagination.

It was time to get out of there.

"Tell me," the waitress said, her eyes narrowing. "Tell me exactly what you know."

"These things live below us," I said, shaking my head. "They use us. They use our parts."

"What do you mean?"

"I couldn't figure it out at first," I explained, "but all the answers I needed were in their movements. I should've figured it out before. They... they take us and replace their body parts with ours. Arms, legs, eyes, whatever. This guy... one of his arms was more muscular than the other. His eyes were the wrong size."

"And there was this line right here." I ran my finger across my own neck. "Like his head had been sewed on."

She nodded, forcing a smile even though moisture was welling up at the corners of her eyes. She knew exactly what I was talking about.

"Have you seen them up close?" I asked.

"I think so," she answered. She was keeping something from me. That was obvious. The way her eyes darted around the diner... the way her smile didn't touch the rest of her face...

Whatever. I didn't really trust her, but I still kept talking. "This week... Tina left, and she didn't come back."

"You think she was taken," the waitress said.

"I know she was." I had to stop talking for a second, so I took a big bite of my burrito. It was warm except for the sour cream. It tasted good, even with the low-quality meat.

The waitress looked at my arms, which were coated with grime. "You went down there tonight," she said. "You went to save her."

I shook my head. "Save" wasn't the right word.

"I think she's gone," I said. "I think she's already been... disassembled. It's like... this feeling. I'm a father. I can tell these things."

The waitress reached across the table to hold my hand. It was clearly a sympathetic gesture, but I wasn't interested. She took the hint and withdrew her hand.

"I killed three of them," I said, answering a question that had gone unspoken. "I followed them down there, got lost, and three guys went after me."

"What did they look like?" she asked.

"They wore hoods and cloaks," I explained. "Their clothes were scraps. Their proportions were all wrong, and their faces were mismatched. They were fierce, horrible things."

"And they attacked you," the waitress said.

"Yes," I told her, even though I knew that wasn't completely true. I had gone after them first. I had made the first moves.

"Well, that explains your appearance," she said. It wasn't meant to come across as insulting.

"Yeah," I muttered. With a napkin, I wiped at my cheek. It rubbed off a bit of the grime, but not much.

"Listen, I'm really sorry about what you went through." She slid her arm across the table once more. She tried to hold my hand again, but I shifted out of the way. Looking disappointed, she pulled back and clasped both hands together in her lap.

"The last creature…" I started, forcing my voice to go flat. I didn't want this woman to hear the pain in it. "The last creature, I recognized him as Tina's boyfriend. The one who drew her into that world."

The waitress didn't say anything.

"I killed him," I said flatly.

"So you got your revenge."

"Hardly." I took a long, tasteless drink from my Coke. It didn't quench anything. "My daughter is still gone. And who knows where the rest of her is."

The waitress sank deeper into her side of the booth. She looked around. We were still the only ones in the building.

"I probably shouldn't say this," she whispered, "but those underground people… They're closer than you know."

Her customers? Was she talking about the typical patrons of this diner?

I didn't want to think about it, but the diner was the only restaurant in this part of town that remained open at night. It would be the perfect place for those things to skitter out of the shadows and order hamburgers or something. Maybe she had a deal with them? Maybe she knew what they were, but she turned a blind eye?

The front door jingled. There was a bell just above it. I looked over my shoulder just as a short man in a hoodie walked in.

"Mornin'," he said to both of us.

The waitress ignored him, cleared her throat. She wanted to pull my attention away from him, because she knew he was one of them.

I did, too.

It was those movements. Those jerky, off-centered movements. Other people would see him and think that he was a junkie, or maybe someone with a limp. But I'd been down there. I'd seen them gather together and charge at me. I knew a creature when I saw one.

"Mornin'," the man tried again.

"Morning," the waitress returned, but her eyes didn't leave mine. It was like she was begging me to ignore him.

He smelled like the sewer, too. I knew I probably smelled the same.

The waitress kept talking to me, asking me about my daughter, about what her life was like before. While she talked, that man sat at a table in the other corner. I didn't look at him directly, just through the edge of my vision.

He sat and nudged the metal napkin dispenser toward the center of his table. He acted so casual.

"Excuse me for one second," I told the waitress. I slid out of the booth.

"No. Wait," she said. She reached toward my arm but didn't grab me.

The man didn't notice that I was walking toward him. He was too busy getting comfortable in his seat, adjusting and readjusting that napkin dispenser.

"Excuse me? Sir?" The words came out of my mouth before I could stop them. I waited about a foot away from his table, smiling patiently.

The man looked up at me. His face was lined with age, and streaks of grime accentuated each wrinkle. Up close, he looked more vulnerable than I'd expected.

His left eye was brown, and his right was a dull gray. But it was more than that. It looked like one eye was bigger than the other. Even the shape around them seemed off. The brown eye seemed almost Asian while the smaller gray eye had an extra crease of skin along the top.

As he looked up at me, I grabbed the napkin dispenser off his table. It was rectangular, made of cheap metal, and about half-filled with napkins. Its corners were sharp.

"Yes?" the man asked.

In a single motion, I slammed the metal into his face. It struck him directly in the nose, making a loud crunch noise. Bone. Cartilage. Pushed to the side.

He rose from his chair, seeming ready for a fight, so I struck him again, this time ramming the metal against the side of his head. He spun in a half circle, his mismatched legs wobbling under him. He crumpled onto the tile.

As he cowered under me, one hand on the floor and one hand shielding his face, I slammed the napkin dispenser against his temple. Again and again. Each time, he grunted and sank lower to the ground.

Speckles of red dotted the black and white floor, leaving designs almost like decorations on a birthday cake.

With a crunch, his shoulder split apart. His left arm didn't completely detach, but it dangled there and spilled open long strands of reddish noodle stuff. Like the others, he was coming apart at the seams.

With his shoulder spread open, I now had a new target. Using the corner of the metal box, I struck at the wound at least six times. Honestly, I lost count.

His arm slid off his body. Of course, it wasn't even *his* arm in the first place. With a *thwump*, the arm landed on the floor, twitched once, and was still.

I knew what I had to do. I had to go for his neck, hack it open just like his arm. From what I could tell down in the sewers, there really wasn't any way to destroy them. All I could do was tear them into smaller and smaller pieces. Until they were harmless. Until they were piles.

I raised the napkin holder once more, muscles tensed, readying myself for the killing blow. I stopped.

A hand grabbed me from behind. Long fingers with sharp nails dug into my arm and wouldn't let go.

I looked over my shoulder. I wasn't surprised to see the waitress holding me in place. I was surprised, though, to see that she looked worried. Not angry.

Not insane. The expression that crossed her pretty-ish face seemed full of concern… for me. She was worried about me, about what I was going to do.

She squeezed even tighter.

I felt something more than just the warmth from her hand. I felt… I couldn't quite explain it. I felt a surge of recognition. I felt Tina.

Instantly, I dropped the napkin holder. It clattered onto the tile.

I looked at her hand, still gripped tightly around my arm. She had long fingers. Pale skin. Her nails were painted a pale rose color. She had a single freckle on the edge of her index finger, right on the knuckle.

Then I looked into her face, and she nodded.

This was my daughter's hand. Maybe her whole arm.

Below us, the man moaned pitifully. He tried to say words, but what came out was little more than a cracked noise.

"I live down there, too," the waitress said. She still held me with my daughter's arm.

"But…" I started. "But… but…"

"Don't make this difficult," she said.

"But you're so…"

"I take care of myself," she said. "I use only the best pieces."

I felt hot vomit rise up the back of my throat. Burrito. Bile. Stomach acid.

"I have a piece of your Tina," she said, her voice shaky. "It explains why I felt such love for you when you walked in. It's not just an arm, Dad. It's your daughter, living through me."

"No," I spat.

The waitress looked at me with genuine warmth in her eyes. It disgusted me.

"Tina lives on in a dozen different bodies," she explained. "You should take comfort in that."

This was wrong. It was twisted and wrong. These things killed my daughter, tore her up, and now they were spinning things, making it sound like something beautiful and natural, making it sound like something other than murder.

"It wasn't her choice," I shouted. "You killed her."

"She's not dead," the waitress said, and the cadence of her voice was very much Tina's. Finally, she let go and my arm dropped to my side. "There's a brightness in her soul. That's why we chose her. And why she chose us."

I heard scraping noises. Sneakers against tile. Just below us, the man scurried out the door. He didn't stand, perhaps he was too weak. Instead, he crawled with his butt in the air, pushed the door, and disappeared into the night. He left his arm behind.

I didn't stop him.

"Here," the waitress said. She slid her hand… Tina's hand, into mine. She had a hopeful look on her face, her eyes wide open. "Look."

I did. I looked at those long fingers, the perfectly colored nails, the freckle. This was Tina's hand, now and forever, and it was still pink with life. It wasn't the cold blue shade of dead flesh.

I think the pinkness was the worst part.

"She didn't want this," I said.

"How would you know?" the waitress argued. "She lives differently now. Not worse, just different. She's one of us now. But…"

"She didn't want this!" I shouted again. My voice cracked.

The waitress looked at me, a little sympathetic and a little fearful. "Tina didn't donate her parts. Tina joined us. And now she's spread all over the city. Pieces of her soul are…"

"Shut up!"

"She has such a bright soul, Dad," the waitress said.

Dad.

I waited.

She waited.

The diner was silent and empty.

The neon sign buzzed.

Slowly, I smiled. It stretched across my face and stayed there for a long moment before I realized it was even there.

A real smile.

A genuine smile.

"Good," the waitress said. "You're understanding."

I didn't say anything.

"It'll be okay," the waitress said. *It* would be okay. What was *it*?

I knew what I had to do. "Give it to me."

"What?" she asked.

I grabbed her arm, Tina's arm, and started pulling. "This," I said. "Give it to me. Please."

"But…" she screamed in both shock and pain. "No… I…"

I pulled hard enough to hear a tearing noise.

Harder.

Harder.

It would've surely come off at the shoulder, except the waitress grabbed that napkin dispenser with her other arm and slammed it into my head. Its corner connected with the edge of my eyebrow. The contact didn't quite register as pain, just a jolt. My vision sparked with colors, like reflections off an oil slick, and I blacked out.

Raindrops.

Cold water fell in thick drops, pelting my face and waking me up.

I was outside the diner, stretched across the sidewalk, my body twisted and my arm hanging unnaturally over my head. I looked around.

The waitress, or friends of hers, had taken me outside. Not to the front of the building, but around the back. By the dumpsters.

The diner was closed and dark. Even the constantly flickering neon sign was out. This was a 24-hour establishment, but I guess tonight they made an exception.

The rain got worse. It almost never rained in San Cicaro, but when it did, the rain was always thick and angry.

Cold.

With a grunt, I pushed myself into a sitting position. My joints were sore… my *everything* was sore. But I was otherwise okay. I looked at my sneakers. They were both there. My hands. They were there, too, though my left pinkie was clearly broken.

I was all here. I wasn't missing any parts.

They didn't want me. The waitress and the other creatures… they left me here without taking anything.

I guess my soul wasn't bright enough.

Mr. McGarry's Basement

Jonathan Ward

"What do you think?"

Chris squinted at the screen of the smartphone being offered to him. It was another hot day in San Cicaro. The sun beat down mercilessly from a clear blue sky, bleaching the color out of everything and reducing the screen's display to a blurred smear.

"Er—"

Julio sighed, snatched the cap from Chris' head, and held it over the smartphone to blot out the sunlight. "There. Better?"

"I guess." It *was* a lot better; he could see it was an article now, from the Channel 5 news site. He scrolled through the story quickly: something about a gas explosion in the commercial district near the Tesla Museum, talk of a whole area being cordoned off, disruption to travel and so on. Bland statements from the Fire Department and City Hall. In short, boring.

"*This* is what you wanted to show me?" Chris asked, taking his cap back and cramming it over his unruly mop of blond hair once again.

The museum was the latest target of Julio's conspiracy theories. He wasn't going to drop it.

Julio rolled his eyes. "Didn't you look at the pictures?"

"What? Why would I?"

"Fine," he sighed, holding his smartphone out again. "I'd tell you to look on your own, but..."

Chris plucked the phone from his friend's hand, trying not to show how that little jibe had irritated him. His *own* phone was in the left pocket of his pants, feeling like a brick and about as useful. After his mom discovered the picture on his phone, she had enabled parental controls or something like that—he wasn't sure what she'd done exactly to be honest. All he knew was that his brand-new phone was only good for texts and calls. *All he needed* according to his mom. But compared to what the other kids his age had access to he might as well have been a caveman or something.

He could still her voice in his head. *"Eleven-year-old boys shouldn't be looking at things like that! You want the internet back? First you have to prove you're responsible enough for it."*

It was so unfair! It wasn't as if he'd searched it out either. The picture of that woman wearing... well, not much... had appeared as a pop-up on an online game site. He hadn't even *meant* to screenshot it.

He shook his head and focused on the pictures accompanying the article. Cordoned-off streets, a building that had basically been reduced to a pile of rubble, a lone fire-fighter caught clambering up a heap of concrete and twisted girders.

"So what? I'm not seeing anything."

"Seriously?" Julio held out his hand, and Chris returned the phone. "How could you miss it, man? Was supposed to be a gas explosion, right? But where are the fires?"

"The fire-fighters must have—"

"They didn't put them out already," Julio interrupted. "Where's the charring? The pools of water everywhere? This was no explosion, I'm telling you!"

"Right," Chris murmured, already losing interest. Julio was a good friend, probably the best one Chris had if he was brutally honest, but his dad was a real cospina... *conspiracy* nut, or so Chris' own father had said. Julio tended to parrot whatever his dad said to him, which was pretty embarrassing when he did it around Chris' other friends. *At least he's not as bad as he used to be*, Chris supposed.

"Come on, let's get out of here," he said quickly, hoping to switch Julio's focus. "It's too hot now and it'll be time for dinner soon."

Julio glanced at the display on his smartphone again before slipping it into his pocket. "Yeah, I guess you're right."

Both boys got up off the bench. One of their usual spots to while away the hours, the seat overlooked a playground with swings and a slide, with a fenced-off basketball court behind it. Now and again their parents would let them stay out until almost dark, watching the older boys play, but the oppressive heat had kept them away for once. As they set off, Chris caught Julio glancing almost wistfully at the swings, but didn't comment on it. They'd last been on them a few months ago, when a group of passing older girls had laughed at them. Neither of the friends had known who the girls were, and never saw them again, but it didn't matter.

After all, they were both eleven. They weren't kids any more.

They crossed the road and cut down an alley that ran between back gardens fenced off by chain-link. Most were empty during the day—the whole suburb basically occupied by families who worked closer to the center of San Cicaro. Yet a few had people in them, watching the two boys pass with varying degrees of disinterest. Both Julio and Chris quickened their pace as they passed a fence hung with **BEWARE OF DOG** and **TRESPASSERS WILL GET BIT** signs. Fortunately, Rambo was in his kennel, tongue hanging out, showing utterly no interest in them.

Across another road, round the next corner, then another right. In a few minutes Chris would be home. The idea of an ice-cold glass of lemonade before dinner was burning itself into his thoughts so strongly that his mouth was watering a little. His attention elsewhere, Chris almost yelped when Julio grabbed his upper arm and dragged him to one side.

"What's the mat—"

Julio frowned, jerking his head frantically farther down the sidewalk. "Watch where you're going man, 'less you want to get run over!"

Noticing who approached them at a rapid pace, Chris quickly stepped out of the way. First came the old shopping cart, half-rusted wiring wrapped around with rags and old newspapers, all four wheels squeaking at a pitch that cut right through him. The cart itself was overflowing with boxes and bags loaded with old junk, cans, ragged clothing, half-filled bottles of who knew what, a pair of old TV antennae. Basically, anything that its owner had seen and liked the look of for whatever wacked-out reason.

Pushing the cart was a figure wrapped in at least three layers of clothing despite the heat, making her seem much fatter than she really was. Scrawny hands tightly gripped the cart's handle, fingers jerking convulsively in an irregular pattern. Her brown and grey hair was a tangled lattice of knots that made Chris' look immaculate by comparison. She was not that old, though her cheeks were sunken enough that she appeared ancient. Her eyes…

Chris could never look at Flo's eyes for long.

"It sees you, you know," she said, almost but not quite looking at the boys. "The glow watches you even now. Watches me. The others would know what to do. I have to sleep but I can't because it doesn't."

Chris started to respond, despite not really knowing what to say, but Julio frantically shook his head and clamped his mouth closed. Flo didn't seem to notice, one hand releasing the cart and shifting through the gathered junk as it screeched past the boys.

"Always watching, always. It won't stop, maybe it can't but it should fucking well try I—two dollars ninety-nine for a tin of lima beans? Crazy. Used to get them for..."

Chris was too busy hurrying after Julio to hear what the price had used to be. They left her waving an empty can in the air and hurried along the block, slowing down when they were only one street away from Julio's house.

"She's *loco*," Julio said. "Maybe she's like those homeless in the sewers downtown. The ones on that video I showed you? Someone should do something about her."

"Like what?"

His friend glanced around for a few seconds as if the answer was spray-painted on the sidewalk somewhere.

"I don't know. *Something.* I hear her shouting sometimes at night when I'm trying to sleep. Stupid crazy cat lady."

"She's not a crazy cat lady, man. She... um... doesn't have any cats..."

"You know what—"

"Anyway, Mom says she used to be a scientist. Real big name in all the papers a few years back. Archaeology or something but she had, like, a breakdown. Dad says she's just sick in the head, same as getting sick anywhere else."

"Yeah but—"

"Christopher? Christopher, is that you?"

Both boys looked round. They had stopped outside Mr. McGarry's yard without realizing it. The man himself was slowly getting up from his porch swing with the faltering aid of his cane.

"Yeah, it's Chris," he shouted back. "You okay Mr. McGarry?"

"I'm fine sonny," the old man replied, finally succeeding in standing up. "Just need a quick word if you don't mind waiting there a second."

"Sure thing!"

"Come on Chris, let's get out of here," Julio said. "Forget him."

"What's your problem?"

The other boy frowned. "He's the one who has a problem with Latinos. You know he doesn't like me."

Chris shook his head. "He doesn't not like you for being Latino, Julio. He doesn't like you because you broke his window with your basketball last fall and never said sorry."

"Whatever, man," Julio said, already backing away. "I'm off home anyway. I'll message you later, *Christopher.*"

Chris made a rude gesture, but his friend had already turned and headed off. Smiling to himself, he waited for Mr. McGarry to make his way through the yard to his back gate. The house was a two-story place like so many in the area, with a basement underneath. A short flight of stairs led to an expanse of decking that ran the full length of the house's rear, the roof extending out to shield it from the elements. Mr. McGarry could often be found sitting out there, usually engrossed in a book.

The yard was almost fifty feet long, with flowerbeds bordering the fences and lawns covering the rest of the space either side of the path. He had vague memories of it being quite pretty, as far as gardens went, flowers of all different colors arranged in neat rows. These days though, it was mostly just overgrown. Watching the old man limp down the path, leaning heavily on his golden-brown cane, it wasn't hard to work out why.

Still, it wasn't the worst thing in the world. For him, anyway.

"What can I do for you, Mr. McGarry?"

The old man halted on the other side of the white-painted wooden gate, taking a moment to get his breath back.

"Same as ever, Christopher." McGarry swept one hand out, gesturing at his lawns. "Grass is getting tall again. Ten dollars for the lot, same as usual. Interested?"

"Of course!" Chris got money for doing chores around the house, of course, but his mom wasn't exactly generous about it. At least not compared to the parents of most of his friends. Another ten dollars now and again was always handy. "No problem, Mr. McGarry, only..." He hesitated, a trickle of sweat down the small of his back reminding him of just how hot it was.

"Only?"

He shifted uneasily. "Does it have to be this afternoon? I want to, it's just a little, well..."

"Hot?" McGarry chuckled to himself. "Trust me Christopher, I feel it more than you do these days. Tomorrow's Sunday so how about ten in the morning? I'll even bake some cookies for you."

He smiled broadly, nodding so enthusiastically that his cap almost slid off his head. "Yes sir! That would be perfect!"

McGarry chuckled once again, though Chris wasn't exactly sure why. "Alright then. Have a good evening Christopher. I'll see you tomorrow."

"Sure thing. Bye!"

Chris turned and walked away, thoughts already turning to what he would spend his money on. Candy was always an option, but then there was that new water pistol... a lot more expensive than ten dollars, but he might have enough saved up. Still, the old man would probably have more garden work that needed doing, and the money was good. McGarry was decent for an old guy, even if he did insist on calling him *Christopher* all the time.

He slept uneasily. In his dreams he awoke in darkness, save for shifting colors playing across a narrow band of his bed, shining through a gap in his curtains. Each time he rose and went to the window, pulling back the curtain to get a better look. Lights pulsed in the distance, towards the city center. They flickered and fluctuated like firelight, yet no fire came and went so quickly, nor burned in shades of blue and purple. And all the time the wind *screamed*. It was like something in pain, though the branches of a nearby tree didn't move, and all else seemed still.

And then it happened again.

And again.

When Chris woke up, for a moment he wasn't sure if he was still dreaming. Only the color of the light shining through the gap in the curtains convinced him that what he was seeing was real, confirmed a moment later by the wailing of Sarah, his six-month-old sister. He yawned and rubbed his eyes, the dream starting to fade from his mind as such things usually did, and got out of bed.

His parents were already at the kitchen table, his father pouring coffee while his mother sat a little further back, breastfeeding Sarah. She looked up and smiled distractedly as he pulled a chair out and sat down.

"Morning sleepyhead. That was good timing, your dad was about to come wake you up."

"Sorry," Chris mumbled automatically, though he didn't *feel* particularly sorry about it. He reached for his usual cereal as his dad chuckled.

"Go easy on him, Maria. I bet that wind woke you, huh?"

Chris looked up. "Wind?"

"About three in the morning. Howled for like five, ten minutes, then stopped. Weird storm or something."

"Oh. No, I slept right through it." Chris thought about mentioning his dream, but that seemed stupid even to him and probably would to them as well. Instead, he made himself a bowl of cereal, and began working his way through it.

"Oh yeah, I'm going to cut Mr. McGarry's lawn for him," he said, "around ten. I'll be back in time for lunch." He hesitated as he saw his parents glance at each other.

"Actually," his mother replied, "I was hoping you could walk to Tandy's and pick up some food for us? I'd go but your sister's acting up right now."

Chris made a face and flung a desperate look at his father. "Can't *you* do it, dad? Tandy's is *ages* away and the place smells!"

"Sorry son, got to head in for a meeting. No idea when I'll be back."

"But Mr. McGarry's—"

His dad raised a hand. "It's fine. You can get the food *after* you mow the lawn for McGarry." Chris saw his mom open her mouth as if to object but seemed to think better of it. "You made a commitment, you've got to keep it."

"Fine," Chris said, injecting the single word with as much frustration as he could, hoping that it would somehow cause his parents to change their minds. As usual, it did nothing of the sort.

After breakfast he took a few minutes to message Julio about what complete *dicks* his parents were being, but got no response. He was probably in church, considering how religious his family was. None of it had really rubbed off on their son but his parents kept making him go, probably exactly because of that. Shrugging to himself, Chris filled up an empty bottle with water from the kitchen tap, tossed it in his backpack, and set off.

The streets were fairly quiet at this time on a Sunday, and though the sky was free of clouds the sun wasn't quite as hot as it had been the day before. *At least not yet*, Chris reflected. It would probably be scorching right about the time he was lugging shopping back from Tandy's for his lazy parents.

When he reached Mr. McGarry's, he was a little surprised to see that the old man wasn't on the porch, sitting in his usual spot. He had been every other time that Chris had mown the lawn for him. The blinds were down across his windows as well, and the small basement window at ground-level to the left of the porch steps was completely dark.

"Oh man," Chris muttered. "He'd better not still be in bed."

Wood creaking beneath his feet, he clomped up the steps and knocked twice on McGarry's door. Nothing happened for perhaps ten seconds. He sighed, knocked again. More seconds passed. Still nothing. Chris swore, though force of habit made him keep it so quiet that it was little more than a whisper, and started to turn away. If McGarry wasn't going to answer, then he could mow his own lawn. At least now Chris could—

A thought struck him that gave him pause. What if something had happened to him? McGarry was old, like, *really* old, and wasn't exactly stable on his feet at the best of times. Maybe he'd fallen down in his bedroom and couldn't get up? Maybe he was lying at the bottom of his stairs, head all bleeding, half out of it, not even knowing where he was? He could be *dead*.

The rattle of a chain sliding back made Chris jump out of his skin, and something that was mortifyingly close to a squeak escaped his lips. By the time the door swung open, he was grinning goofily at his own foolishness.

Mr. McGarry stood there, cane gripped loosely in one hand, its tip off the ground. He looked down blankly at the boy, with no sign of recognition in his expression. His hair, usually so neatly-combed, was tangled and out of place. He *had* been asleep then, Chris realized, his grin slowly fading as the old man continued to stand there, nearly motionless.

"Mr. McGarry?"

Silence. Feeling increasingly uneasy, Chris fought the urge to take a step back.

"It's ten o'clock," he prompted. McGarry's head tilted slightly, but the blank expression remained. "You wanted me to mow your lawn." Chris glanced back for a second, at the white wooden gate that had swung invitingly open. "Are you... okay?"

Silence for a few seconds longer, then the old man's expression abruptly altered, as if he hadn't really been paying attention until right that moment.

"Oh yes. The grass. Of course. My apologies, Christopher. I've only just woken up."

"That's fine," Chris said, unsure but doing his best to hide it. McGarry didn't *sound* particularly sorry. If anything, it was like… he wasn't sure what it was like. As though he was reading his words from a script.

"Good." Pause. "I'll get the mower for you. Just a second."

Chris stood aside as McGarry walked down the steps and across to the small shed adjoining the house. He emerged a few moments later holding the mower. Without apparent effort, McGarry moved it onto the lawn and plugged it into an extension cord, which he then ran into the house. His cane was tucked under one arm the entire time. Chris watched all of this with faint amazement, remembering how heavily the man had been leaning on it the day before.

He was probably on some new pills.

Shucking his backpack from his shoulders and leaving it at the bottom of the steps, Chris set to work. The grass was high and thick enough now that pushing the mower through it was a bit of an effort, but nothing that he couldn't manage. He even started humming as he worked, though the roar of the mower's motor was loud enough that he couldn't actually hear himself.

It took perhaps fifteen minutes to do the first of the two lawns. After he'd pulled the mower back to catch a few long stems that he'd missed the first time around, Chris released the button in the handle and the noise of the motor died away. He removed his cap to wipe the sweat from his brow, winced as the sunlight lanced his eyes, and quickly replaced it. It was lucky that he had thought to bring a bottle of water. Usually Mr. McGarry would have made lemonade for him by now, but today the old man had disappeared inside and closed the door. But then it didn't really matter, so long as he paid up once the work was done.

Chris took a long drink from the bottle, immediately feeling a lot better, then returned it to the backpack for later. He was about to get back to mowing when he caught sight of something.

Flo stood on the other side of the road that ran along the back of Mr. McGarry's property, facing the house. She seemed to be staring straight at him, completely motionless. Chris shivered, but told himself he was being stupid. Deliberately turning his back towards the road, he grabbed the mower's handle and carried it across the path to the other lawn. After he had set it down and pulled its electrical cable out of the way, Chris straightened up and looked round again.

She was still there.

He couldn't tell if Flo was looking at him or at the house, but either way her constant staring was freaking him right out. Doing his best not to think about it, he started the mower once again and set to work on the second lawn. He kept his gaze on the ground as the first pass took him towards the fence, only looking up quickly as he turned to approach the house. She *still* hadn't moved.

"Creepy bitch," he muttered.

He went up and down the lawn a few more times, deliberately not looking at the road any more. Let her do what she wanted; soon he'd be done and out of there. Halfway across the lawn, though, heading back towards Mr. McGarry's house, he noticed something odd.

The basement window was almost directly in front of him now. Normally he would be able to see everything inside: the ping-pong table folded up against the wall that probably hadn't been used since before Chris had even been born, a few chairs stacked one atop another, suitcases, boxes with labels bleached clean by years of sunlight. Even the single bulb hanging from the ceiling. Today though, he couldn't see anything.

It was dark in there, completely dark in fact. The closer he got, the more confusing it was. He should have been able to see *something*, but somehow couldn't. At first he thought Mr. McGarry had put up blinds or curtains, but there was no sign of that. The sunlight shone on the wall of the house, the decking, the ground beneath, illuminating everything it touched. All except for the window, and the room beyond.

Chris shivered, feeling suddenly cold for no reason he could think of. This was *stupid*, all of it. He'd get the mowing done, get his money, and get out of here. Even the thought of shopping in Tandy's was appealing right about now.

It took him another few minutes to finish, and when he was done he let the mower handle fall and left it on the grass. Carefully avoiding looking at the street, he walked up the steps, across the decking and knocked on the back door. This time it opened almost immediately, the old man looking down at him with actual recognition. Chris could see something else though, something different about his features. Were his wrinkles... smoother than before?

Shut up, idiot! Get the money!

"All done?" The old man asked, his tone friendly enough. Chris nodded rapidly. "Yes sir, all finished."

McGarry glanced at both lawns, down at Chris, then back in the house briefly. "While you're here I've got a few more chores that—"

"I can't," Chris said hastily, before remembering both his manners and that he hadn't been paid yet. "Sorry, but... well, my mom needs me to pick up some food for her. Maybe another time?"

Once more the old man looked behind him, and when he turned back his face had regained the blankness Chris had seen earlier.

"Of course, that's not a problem." He groped in his pocket for a moment, his hand emerging with a crumpled bill clutched between his fingers. "Your money."

"Thanks!" Chris took it as quickly as politeness allowed, and immediately retreated down the steps, pausing only to grab his backpack. "See you later, Mr. McGarry!"

Chris heard the door close when he was halfway down the path, and had to bite back the impulse to sigh from relief. He was being stupid, he knew it. Mr. McGarry was just having an off-day. And so what if it had been dark in his basement? What the hell did it matter? He'd got his ten dollars. His mood lifted further when he looked across the street and saw that Flo had disappeared.

As he opened the gate, he pulled his phone from his pocket and checked the time. Mom had texted him a list of what she wanted. If he was quick he could get to Tandy's and back within an hour.

Only as the gate clicked shut behind him did he look across the street again, and realized that, whilst Flo was gone, her cart full of junk was still there. Flo *never* abandoned that cart, it held everything she owned. Which meant—

A hand clamped tight around his right wrist, fingers like twigs digging into his flesh as he was hauled round. Chris let out a strangled cry that died in his throat, coming face to face with the homeless woman. She *stank*: a cocktail of dirt, alcohol, sweat and body odor that together formed a reek so overpowering his stomach lurched in protest.

She stared at him with such intensity that Chris wanted to avert his gaze but couldn't. He could see something burning in her eyes—it held him transfixed, though not so completely that he couldn't see her cheek twitching in spasm. Her breath came in quick pants, like an exhausted animal. He heard himself whimper, despised himself for it, but still could not look away.

"It sees you," she said, so calm compared to her usual self that for a moment Chris couldn't even make sense of her words.

"It sees you, it sees me. It knows what you've seen, that you've seen *it*. You shouldn't let it see you but then we don't always have a choice, do we?" Her expression altered, becoming like his mother's face when she'd learned that *her* mom had died. "No choice, no choice. We live our lives, all of us, and it sees it all, it sees *it* too, do you see? It's watching and *it's waiting*. Stay away!"

Her grip tightened, and this time Chris couldn't keep from yelling out in pain. Absurdly, Flo looked baffled by this. In a moment of desperate inspiration, Chris shifted his posture and kicked her shin as hard as he could. The homeless woman let out a yowl like an injured cat and immediately released him. Without hesitation he twisted and flung himself the other way, accelerating into a full-on sprint.

Chris dashed the rest of the block and across the next road without slowing, sparing only a quick glance either way to ensure he wasn't about to get flattened. Only when he reached the opposite sidewalk did he stop and risk looking back.

Flo seemed to have no interest in pursuing. She'd crossed back to her cart, and once more appeared to be standing in place, staring at McGarry's house.

"You crazy bitch!" Chris yelled, though not loud enough that there would be any danger of her actually hearing it. A passing woman frowned at him, and for an instant he felt almost ashamed. But the pain from his wrist soon smothered that. Wincing, he lifted his hand up to get a better look. Fingermarks stood out prominently against his pale skin, and half his arm was aching. It would undoubtedly bruise.

"Stupid bitch," he said, but to himself this time as he turned away. She might be crazy, but that was no excuse. He'd have to tell his parents.

"We should call the police!"

"It won't do any good," his dad replied. "She's long gone by now. Did you see her on the way back, son?"

Chris shook his head. He'd been on the alert as he returned from Tandy's yet saw no sign of her. She hadn't been outside McGarry's house either. It should have made him feel better but didn't really. At least when she'd been standing out there he'd known where she was. Now, she could be *anywhere*.

"Won't do any good? She could hurt someone else!"

"I know that, Maria," his dad said in the flat tones that meant he was pissed off and doing his very best not to show it. "And if we see her again, we will call the police straight away. Chris, you should warn your friends, too."

"What?" Chris looked round. His attention had strayed to the TV in the other room; a news feature was running about a company called Radnitzky Pharmaceuticals, something about revolutionary new drugs aiding in tissue regeneration. There were before and after pictures, the former being fascinatingly grisly.

His dad saw what he was looking at and sighed. "Pay attention. I said you should warn your friends."

"Already have, dad."

He'd thought of that just as he had left Tandy's and texted every contact in his phone to tell them what had happened. Some hadn't answered, a few had expressed skepticism. Mikey, who was notoriously a bit of an asshole, had even made fun of him. Most, though, had been sympathetic, and promised to look out for her.

Julio had sent him a lot of messages. Chris had told him basically everything, leaving out the detail of the dark basement, or that Mr. McGarry hadn't been himself. It had seemed unfair to him, somehow. Still, it had been nice of his friend to be concerned. He'd even mentioned that he might wander past McGarry's place and see if Flo was there. That was also a kind thing to do, though Chris suspected Julio was interested more in the possibility of getting money for chores than anything else. *Good luck with that.* After all, he doubted McGarry had forgotten about the broken window.

"Good. That's basically all we can do for now," his dad said. He shot a warning glance at his wife when she looked ready to add more. "Why don't you go and relax for a bit, son."

Chris was happy to take advantage of that, disappearing into his room before his parents could think of any work that needed doing to keep him occupied. He spent the next few hours watching movies in his room, and was engrossed by Bruce Willis crawling through a ventilation shaft when his phone started to ring. The number on display wasn't saved in his phone, and didn't look familiar. He glared at it for a while, willing the caller to hang up. When it became obvious that the phone wasn't going to stop ringing, he picked it up and answered with a hefty sigh.

"Hello?"

"Hello, is this Christopher?"

He frowned, and considered ending the call right there, but the voice sounded familiar.

"Yeah, it's me. Is that Julio's mom?"

"Yes, that's right. Is Julio with you?"

Chris paused for a moment. "No, sorry. I haven't seen him today."

Something that might have been a curse in Spanish was faintly audible in the background. "Are you sure? He said something about speaking to you today."

Oh wait here he is, hiding under the bed, Chris thought, but carefully didn't say. Julio's mom was quite intimidating. "We texted, but like I said, I haven't seen him."

"Okay, right. Probably his phone is out of battery again, he never does remember to charge it. Any idea where he is?"

"Mr. McGarry's, maybe, he had chores that needed doing and Julio said he might stop by there."

Another curse word in Spanish, and Chris had to put his hand over his mouth to keep from laughing.

"Look. Could you do me a favor? I'm not home for an hour and I need him there when I get back. Would you mind seeing if he's at this McGarry man's house? I don't know where that is."

"Well..."

"I can make fajitas for you next time you're over if that helps?"

That sealed the deal. Say what you like about her personality, Julio's mom was easily the best cook Chris knew.

"Sure thing. I'll go have a look."

"Thanks Christopher."

He ended the call and pulled his shoes on. Probably best not to tell his parents where he was going. After what had happened this morning, they would only worry. Instead, he made his way to the back door as quickly as he could, aware of his parents in the lounge but not daring to look at them properly.

"Just heading out for some fresh air," he shouted. "Back in a few minutes!"

To his relief, neither one saw anything suspicious in this, his mom contenting herself with a simple "Ok, have fun!" That was fine, of course. There was nothing to worry about. It would only take him a few minutes to see if Julio was at McGarry's. Flo probably wasn't anywhere nearby.

Definitely nothing to worry about.

Even so, he found himself increasingly anxious as he drew closer to the old man's house. When he rounded the last corner and it came into view, Chris found that his heart was racing.

"Don't be an idiot," he told himself. "It's fine. It's fine."

Even so Chris remained where he was for a good two minutes, checking each road and sidewalk in view for any sign of Flo. Nothing. No crazy woman, no cart. She wasn't there.

Shaking his head at his own foolishness, he crossed the road and jogged along the sidewalk until he reached McGarry's property. The back gate was slightly ajar. After a moment he spotted Julio's bike on the old man's porch, leaning against the wall, next to the back door. He couldn't see his friend in the back yard, nor McGarry for that matter. Both were probably inside, then.

Only when he had pushed the gate wide and taken a few steps into the yard did he finally spot Flo.

A flicker of movement drew his attention and he turned, staggering as he realized what, or rather *who*, he was looking at. Flo was already inside the yard, crouched low next to the fence, shielded from view from the street by a large bush. Chris wanted to run, but hesitated as he noticed that the homeless woman didn't pay him the least bit of attention. Her gaze was fixed on the house, one hand outstretched towards it, fingers jerking convulsively, as if trying to grasp hold of the air itself.

"Can't go in," she murmured, barely loud enough for Chris to make the words out. "Can't. It's awake now, it's hungry. The glow sees, it sees it all. It wants this, can't, can't. Burning, burning so bright, blinding without light. It's so hungry."

With inhuman swiftness her head snapped round. She stared straight at Chris.

"He's in danger."

Before he could think to respond she twitched back round, her gaze locked on the house once more. Chris couldn't help but notice that while one hand constantly groped towards the structure, her *other* hand was wrapped around a fencepost, so tightly that her knuckles were white. Her whole body jerked towards the house, as if something intangible was pulling her away from the fence.

He backed slowly away, wanting nothing more than to run for his life. Only two things stopped him. The first, which he was slightly ashamed of, was the knowledge that running for the gate would mean getting closer to Flo. An idea he found terrifying. The second though, was something that she had said. *He's in danger.* She was crazy as fuck, that much was obvious, but what if that part had been true? What if Julio or Mr. McGarry needed help? He had his phone—he'd be able to call an ambulance for them if they needed it.

He needed to make sure they were okay.

Slowly, casting frequent nervous looks behind him, Chris walked down the path and up the porch steps. He lifted his hand, trying and failing to stop it from quivering slightly, and knocked quickly on the door. Immediately he cast a glance behind him, suddenly convinced that Flo would have somehow sneaked up behind him while his back was turned. But she was still where he had left her.

His nervousness subsiding a little, Chris turned back to the door. "Julio? Mr. McGarry? Everything okay in there?"

Something *thumped* inside the house. A door slamming? There was no mistaking what came next, though—the start of a shout, cut off so quickly that Chris almost missed it, so muffled that he couldn't tell who had made it. But then, it didn't matter. Something was wrong. He couldn't just wait outside, could he?

Almost without thinking, Chris tried the door handle. It turned easily, and the door swung open.

The kitchen was deserted, though the presence of a plate of cookies on the table, along with a full glass of lemonade, suggested that it hadn't been that way for long. Another glass lay on its side by the back door, its contents sprayed widely across the floor. *An accident,* Chris told himself, doing his best to ignore his mounting unease.

"Julio?"

Another sound, from deeper in the house. *A scraping noise,* he thought, though it was faint.

"Fucking hell," Chris muttered, and stepped forward, his sneakers splashing through the spilled lemonade. A doorway led through to McGarry's lounge, which was chock-full of furniture. The walls were lined with bookcases, shelves bowed under the weight of enough books to fill a decent-sized library. The blinds were down over the front windows, but there was enough light for him to see that this room was deserted as well.

A doorway in the left wall of the lounge led to a foyer. From there the front door was on his right while to his left a staircase led up to the next floor. Beside it was another door that probably led down to the basement. The door shuddered just as Chris looked at it, as if something had bumped against it on the far side.

"Mr. McGarry?" Chris heard the quiver in his voice and hated it, even as he felt his unease grow even stronger. It was the house: silent, seemingly deserted, dimly-lit. And something else too—a feeling of pressure in the air, as though a storm were about to break. He found himself breathing quickly, his fingers trembling as he reached out to the basement door.

A single lightbulb hanging from the slanted ceiling illuminated the horrifying scene that lay beyond. McGarry was halfway down a short flight of wooden stairs that led to the basement, and he wasn't alone. The old man had looped his arm under Julio's armpits, half-carrying, half-dragging him down. Chris' mouth fell open as he struggled to make sense of what he was seeing. Julio was almost limp, one hand thumped slowly against the man's back but there was no strength to the blows. McGarry barely seemed to notice them.

Chris screamed. He couldn't help it. As the sound of his terror echoed through the house, McGarry paused and slowly raised his head to look at him. The light from the bulb cast his features into stark relief, bleaching the color from his face. Despite that, Chris could see that he had changed. The wrinkles lining his forehead and around his eyes had all but gone. His hair was almost completely black, with only patches of light grey clinging on at his sideburns and temples. He looked years younger, if not *decades*. And yet... he stared at Chris with unfocussed eyes, looking at him with bleary incomprehension.

"Necessary," he said slowly, as though trying out each syllable for the first time. Drool trickled from the right side of his mouth, apparently unnoticed. "The price must be paid. They made it that way, it knows nothing else. And in return..." McGarry's voice trailed away, and he slowly started to turn towards the basement. Chris' gaze strayed past him.

The door at the bottom of the stairs was wide open and in the basement beyond... darkness. Yet it was *moving*, impossibly. Twirling around a central point suspended between floor and ceiling, a whirlpool turned on its side. It made no sound at all, yet the atmosphere practically flickered with energetic flashes. He could barely make sense of it. And as the midnight currents swirled into the depthless void at the heart of the presence, he looked into that abyss and saw... he saw...

Chris tore his gaze away, his eyes feeling as though they were burning inside his head. Someone was screaming, and it took Chris a second to realize that it was himself. His heart pounded wildly in his chest, breath coming in gasps as though he'd been running for ages. Nothing made sense about this—this was *crazy*. McGarry took a step down the stairs, pulling Julio along with him. Chris understood then what the once-old man had been saying. His eyes met Julio's and he saw the helpless desperation there. The thought of McGarry throwing his friend into the... he couldn't... he...

Before he was even conscious of what he was doing, Chris stumbled down the stairs, closed both hands around Julio's left arm, and pulled as hard as he could. McGarry jerked to a halt, shifting back slightly before he regained his balance. Chris tugged frantically, but the old man's grip remained tight around his friend. Nothing he could do would break it. McGarry looked straight at him, and behind him Chris saw the darkness ripple, as if a stone were cast into deep, black waters.

Abruptly, both of Chris' hands were torn away from Julio's arm. His feet were off the ground. He was flying, no, hurtling, backwards. He opened his mouth to yell, but the breath was driven from him when his shoulder collided with the door frame. He dropped sharply, skidding halfway along the hall before he finally came to a halt.

McGarry hadn't even *touched* him.

Chris whimpered, clutching at his shoulder. He felt tears streaming down his face but couldn't find it in himself to care. He slowly got to his feet, not knowing what to do now. He could just see McGarry look at him for a moment, then slowly turn away as if Chris wasn't even worth bothering with. And he was right. He had no idea what to do and there was nothing he *could* do. He had never felt so helpless in all his life.

A shadow fell across him, and a familiar smell reached his nostrils.

"It can't be helped," Flo said, standing in the lounge doorway. "It sees it now, you see? The glow. It can't be allowed. It must go hungry... it must be *denied*. Things are changing, so much is at stake. Eating all the colors. You understand?"

Chris shook his head, wishing he could look away from her, but found himself unable to. Her expression was calm, but there was something else... something behind her eyes. A light. Even as he watched it bled from her, haloing her pupils, slowly staining her cheeks, pushing her features subtly out of focus. He could just about see her smile through the distortion.

"It can't be helped," she repeated, sadly this time.

Flo turned, accelerating towards the basement doorway in a blur. He dismissed her freakish speed as a trick of the tears still brimming in his eyes. He blinked them away even as curiosity drew him forward. She disappeared, and he heard a *thump* so deep, so intense, that he felt it reverberate in his bones. The house seemed to shiver around him, a rumble like distant thunder splitting the air.

Julio sailed through the air, somehow landing on his feet, staggering a few paces before Chris caught him. Even so the jolt of impact nearly knocked him off his feet, and he only kept his balance with an incredible amount of effort. His friend stared at him from a distance closer than Chris had ever wanted him to be, before abruptly springing to life, like a switch had been thrown somewhere inside him.

"Chris? What the fu—?"

"Run!" Chris shouted, pushing him towards the lounge door. Julio looked confused but obeyed, lurching through the doorway. Chris was about to follow but something held him back, made him take those extra few steps to the top of the basement stairs. He was just in time to see Flo, wreathed in lambent light that streamed from her skin, her arms wrapped tightly around a struggling Mr. McGarry, throwing herself down the remaining few steps and into the basement. The formerly old man's eyes met Chris'. What he saw in them would haunt him for years to come.

Flailing wildly, both figures vanished into the darkness, which began seething… churning. The whole house shook, plaster dust cascading from the ceiling. Something in the darkness unleashed a mournful wail, so loud that Chris could feel it boring deep into his head. In the next moment the light bulb shattered, and the door to the basement stairs slammed shut.

Chris ran.

Terror lent speed to his exhausted legs and he careened through the house, ricocheting off furniture without slowing. Shrieking cries of the damned chased him even as he emerged into the sunlight, flinging himself down the porch steps. Julio was at the end of the path, hunched over, tears streaming freely down his face as he stared back at Chris with an expression that—

When Chris came to, several hours had passed. His parents were by the hospital bed, his sister sleeping soundly in his father's arms. He had never been so glad to see them all. It was only when they began to look concerned, did he realize that he had started crying again.

It was a gas explosion, they told him, or so the firefighters had told *them*. Her eyes brimming with unshed tears, Chris' mom clutched his hand with both of hers, saying over and over again how lucky it was they had both got out of the house when they did. And such terrible news about Mr. McGarry of course. A real tragedy. Such a nice man.

He nodded. Smiled reassuringly. Said nothing.

Perhaps a week later, when both he and Julio had been discharged from hospital, and after his mom's paranoia had diminished enough to allow him out for a while unattended, he walked past McGarry's house. It was a mess. Most of the upper floor and roof had collapsed down on what lay beneath. It would have to be demolished, his dad said, and as far as Chris was concerned that couldn't happen soon enough.

He couldn't see much charring, though.

He still didn't know what to think about what had happened. It made even less sense the more he thought about it. It was as if he'd… caught a glimpse of something. Something that most people never saw.

Chris was damn sure that he never wanted to see it again.

Without really knowing why, he walked round to the other side of McGarry's property, which faced a road that Chris rarely walked along. The fence at the edge of his front garden had collapsed, probably blown down by the force of the explosion in the basement, or whatever it had been. But then… so too had a wall on the other side of the road. And the wall *beyond* that one.

He stood there for a while, staring at the collapsed walls. He remembered something that he had heard at school yesterday, the first day that he had gone back since the explosion. A group of kids had been talking in the corridor. Chris hadn't really been listening, but had caught the gist of the conversation as he passed; something about glowing lights they'd seen the night before, that had woken a few from their sleep.

They only lived a few blocks away.

Despite the heat of the sun beating down on him, Chris felt cold. He turned, and hurried home.

Still Life with Ferris Wheel

Jenn Cavanaugh

Papa Luis had often told Eva that her smile could open any door. It had, however, proven utterly ineffective against this boarded-up boardwalk, and Eva was easily ten minutes past smiling. She finally had to wedge the corroded padlock into the gap between the massive double doors so she could turn the key with both hands. The right door caught a gust off the ocean and slammed into the wooden fence behind it, throwing up a sharp clatter of splinters. The left door crunched into the uneven gravel at its foot mere inches before it would have bashed her head in. She didn't even flinch. Eva's brother Miguel had gone through a 10-year phase of pretending to backhand her when annoyed; it had conditioned her to stand her ground.

The gate was wedged tight. Eva resolved the temporary impasse by picking her way around it in her outrageously insensible white heels. A caved-in neon sign that had been unceremoniously dragged just inside the gate to further bar the entrance welcomed her to Demitri's Garden of Delights. In all its very former glory. She could see now with her own eyes what her computer guy Jaden had seen on-screen. Ten minutes into his rudimentary title search, he had texted his official take on the property.

Jaden: Too many ghosts to buy and not enough to sell IMHO.

Eva: Zoning???

Jaden: It's got 99 problems, but zoning ain't one. Place has seen it all and been everything.

Jaden: Except successful.

In fact, the defunct amusement pier and adjoining beach seemed to have eluded zoning altogether. It had reverted to public property for tax reasons twenty years ago and languished since. The hardest part about acquiring the site from San Cicaro's beleaguered City Council was convincing them that it was theirs to sell. Visibly elated over an agenda item that might draw new money into the city, they voted on the spot to re-categorize the boardwalk an "attractive nuisance." They even knocked a zero off the back of the appraised value so that GEM Development Partners could start construction on Eva's proposed live/work complex immediately.

They hadn't asked, so she hadn't told them that GEM (Great Expectations Met) Development Partners consisted solely of herself. Well, with the occasional technical assistance of Jaden, whom she paid in alumni-rate Banshee basketball tickets. When necessary, she credited Charles as her unsuspecting CFO. Really, though, he was a fellow alum she let take her to dinner whenever he approved another loan she probably shouldn't have. The council hadn't even suspected that redeeming this scant acre of ruined boardwalk would be her first major project.

The site, she decided, was neither attractive nor a nuisance. Not a bother to anyone, just an inexcusable waste of what should have been prime real estate. She had been here once as a child but little struck her as familiar, and whatever did was several sizes smaller than she remembered. There was something claustrophobic and self-restrained in its hideousness. Something holding itself back, shy of its appearance, self-conscious about not living up to its potential.

Without warning, the oversized gate slammed shut behind her. The impact knocked loose a few volts from some residual power source, causing the neon entryway sign to flicker on in spots.

"Coastal breezes," she murmured, quoting her own four-color prospectus. Though she hadn't felt any wind.

Fully enclosed, the space seemed to telescope another size smaller again. The roller coaster twisted in on itself too tightly. Eva's imagination failed to conjure enough room between the rails to ride. It loomed like so much contorted scrap metal over a joyless alley of arcade games. The white-washed booths along the boardwalk were too sun-bleached to read. Faint gray squiggles suggested the fonts had been groovy. Ubiquitous clown faces decomposed into their constituent triangles and circles.

The chain-link fence surrounding the pier was wrapped in tattered army green plastic that flapped open occasionally onto the Pacific. Eva suspected she could rip the whole thing out with her bare hands. She felt a crazy urge to do so. To air this breathless place out. To gain immediate access to the 360-degree views her prospectus promised.

She mastered the impulse and gave the fence a wide berth in deference to her white pantsuit. Also, tetanus. Her vaccination schedule had not been a priority for the last 15 years.

They'd have to dismantle the rides before they could be sure, but Eva doubted there was much hope of saving the boardwalk and pier. The place seemed strangely overgrown for something built on treated wood sand and sea. Eva hoped Papa Luis had ended up somewhere with a good view of all this. He would be having a good laugh at his *princesa* right now; plowing her half of the proceeds from his tidy little farm in Pitiquito into this rangy mess of vines and creepers. Vegetation spilled out of the arcade booths in heaps. Kudzu? She'd never seen it before, but this was some impressive and destructive stuff. How it found a place to root was a mystery, but the roller coaster made an impressive trellis.

She moved in closer to take pictures, focusing on some of the yellow spots amongst the leaves. All the while chanting under her breath one of the rote prayers of her profession; "Please don't be some exotic fungus that costs extra to remove. Please don't be some exotic fungus that costs…"

The Garden smelled of rust and salt. She always did, and yet she flourished. Masao blew flecks of corroded barbed wire from the bushy heads of the chrysanthemums. A dark-haired woman in white had taken an unusual interest in the pattypan squash. By some trick of the light she struck him as more substantial than the other echoes rattling around in Demi's mind.

Masao found most of the garden's spectral visitors bothersome and ignored them as best he could. He couldn't recall having seen this one before, however. At least not alone. They were rarely alone. He'd stumbled on the occasional couple in the funhouse he used as a shed, sure, and there was the lost child with the balloon, bawling her eyes out.

And Hana, of course.

Mostly the echoes appeared in the heat of the day, rushing from one ride to the next in overlapping crowds, their smiles too full of teeth. Like they were biting down on something in pain. Time muffled their forced shrieks of laughter into distant howls barely distinguishable from the wind whistling through the holes in the fence.

But at this point he'd thought he'd seen all the loners, and the Garden didn't make new memories. He blinked twice and squinted. The Latina woman taking pictures with her smartphone was as alive as he was, he realized, dropping his shears in the soft soil of the shooting gallery.

Unwilling to move any closer, Eva zoomed in on the yellow blotches on the vine. It was that starfish-shaped kind of squash. Impossible. They'd grown it in Pitiquito and that kind didn't sprawl like that, much less take over something the size of a rollercoaster.

The rollercoaster, too, was wrong. Demitri's Garden never had one. It had a Ferris wheel. And a carousel. Right where she was standing there had been a carousel.

There was a sudden crunch of calliope music, like an ice cream truck running over tin pots. Running over her, it was so close and loud. Everything spun. She counter-pivoted, her heel catching on something buried in the dirt beneath her, stumbling until—

She is six years old, righting herself, clutching the outstretched leg of a carousel horse. She has walked out of her sandal. There is gum on it, she remembers. It sticks to the scorching silver floor of the ride and the hot black asphalt around it and she's thoroughly sick of it. She stands on one foot, leaning against the boring stationary sled to work her shoe off the platform. So that's what these stupid things are for, she remembers thinking, proud of her precocious cynicism. "Hey, Miguel!" she calls, but her brother and the neighbor boy, Jerry, have left without her. Suddenly the ride starts again, too soon, with a jerk. There's not even anyone else on it yet. A carousel horse charges her, tail afire, wild-eyed and blistered. She reaches for the sled but there's nothing there

—and nothing was moving and she found her thirty-something self on her hands and knees in the dirt for no apparent reason.

The neon sign buzzed to life for another split second. "Demi___'s GARDEN," she read on the back of her eyelids.

A softer, more organic sound brought her scrambling to her feet. An old Japanese man stood inside the shooting gallery not 40 feet away. They both jumped. His hands flew up. Hers reached instinctively for her purse. Only one of the air rifles remained attached to the counter. He stood just behind it, his arms posed in classic cop-show surrender, his face and gray hair arranged in classic anime shock.

Eva practically collapsed into laughter. Hysterical. The worst kind, but she really couldn't help it. His comically wide eyes followed her gaze to the barrel pointed directly below his navel. He looked back up at her, turned bright red, and closed his mouth into a grin.

"Ya got me," he said.

She hated it, but she giggled. She must have been more stressed out lately than she'd admitted to herself.

"Well, all right, partner," she drawled in her best, and incidentally worst, John Wayne impression. "Come out of there with your hands up and tell me everything you know. Starting with what happened to my carousel."

What did Masao know? He knew it was hard to be a good Buddhist in San Cicaro. Masao's grandfather had insisted that the Buddha was formless, but God's presence here was too palpable in every sun-drenched thing. Being a good Christian was no easier though; the devil seemed to have a lot more clout here than the Japanese Presbyterian church credited him with. Masao had finally given up trying to assign the spirits to either theology at his disposal. He'd decided rather, that they weren't spirits at all. More like echoes bouncing around an ancient mind that had gone a bit senile and tended to live in the past. The place was old, was all, and had serious short-term memory issues. Like many venerable elders, it had taken up landscape painting in its dotage, and it itself was the landscape.

This was everything Masao knew, but he couldn't imagine telling a stranger all that.

What he told her instead was, "My neighbor asked me to walk her dog. As a favor. I mean, she's doing me a favor, reminding me to get out of my apartment every day. So one day I let Tiger off leash on the beach and he finds a hole under the fence…"

"Wait, the dog's name is Tiger?" she asked, stopping Masao cold. If something as simple as the dog's name was going inspire incredulity in this young woman, this was going to be a very difficult conversation.

"Mm, his owner says he's half cat. She's a little odd," he whispered conspiratorially. "So, anyway I walk up to the road and around the fence until I find the gate, and I follow him in."

"You just wandered in through a padlocked gate."

"I, uh, don't think the garden remembered it was locked at the time."

The old guy looked a little frantic, but technically it had been public land until quite recently. Plus, Eva wasn't about to kick this project off with a lawsuit against a harmless coot. She tried an indulgent sigh, but that wasn't her best impression either. It came out more like a huff.

"Listen, as long as you weren't doing anything horribly illegal, I frankly don't care, but I am going to have to ask you not to take advantage of such forgetfulness any more. For your own safety. I've got condos going in here starting tomorrow. This is going to be an active construction site."

Eva appraised his outfit. He had dirt on the knees of his slacks and his brown leather shoes, but they were both brand name and his collared shirt said this was as casual as he got. She switched into sales mode.

"I'm sorry, I should introduce myself. I'm Eva."

"Masao."

"Masao. Well, Masao, if you like this place now, maybe you should consider buying, because wait till you see what I'm making of it. I've got a prospectus right here." She rummaged in her bag. "Sorry it's a bit crumpled, but…"

"I feel I should… ah, thank you." Masao took the trifold brochure with both hands and pretended to study it. He was obviously struggling, but to say something or to not say something, she couldn't tell.

"I'm not sure it will take, is all," he managed. "You might be going to a lot of trouble and expense for nothing."

She perked an eyebrow at this.

He sighed. "I'm afraid she can't remember much that's happened since the first time they closed the amusement park in 1973. You saw what happened to the carousel."

Eva had a standing policy of letting crazy roll on by her, but that piqued her curiosity. "What *did* happen to the carousel?"

"It burned," he answered. "In the second pier fire. Some other developer hauled the wreckage off. In the late eighties, if I remember correctly. But that's not why it's gone. The rollercoaster burned in the first fire and was replaced by a Ferris wheel, but you can see which one stuck. Although…"

He pursed his lips and turned in a little outward-facing circle. "It might be worth jogging her memory about the Ferris wheel. It could be like a revolving nursery of greenhouses. You could plant from seed all winter, spin the wheel when one needed more or less direct sun…"

"Masao," she interrupted, "if I poke around a little more, I'm not going to find *medicinal* herbs in your freaky little grow operation, am I?"

He grimaced seriously. He apparently had no register between serious and giddy. "Let me see. There's Russian sage and hyssop in the ring toss booth, but I'm afraid I don't know much about how to use them medicinally…"

Eva's amused expression finally got her meaning across.

"Oh! Oh no, nothing like that." He paused, eyes sliding sideways as if suspicious. "Although I can't vouch for the back corners of the mini golf course."

Two weeks later Tiger insisted on the beach route and Masao found he could resist no longer. He waited respectfully at the open gate, but Tiger snuffed a beeline for Eva's ankles, entwining himself around them. She air-patted him awkwardly, then shooed him awkwardly, then made her awkward way toward Masao with Tiger circling one leg. Eva didn't strike him as someone accustomed to being awkward.

"I have to admit," he greeted her, "I like what you've done so far. It's not at all what I pictured based on your brochure."

"That's because this," Eva waved her arms in the air, "is not at all what I planned."

She pointed accusingly at a dozen white and pink flowering trees. "As soon as the ground was cleared, we planted these ornamental dwarf cherries." Eva stressed the adjectives. "Most of the landscaping will be done once the building is in, but I like to give the trees as much time to settle in as I can. I hate those new developments surrounded by caged sticks."

"Ah, you probably needn't have worried about that here."

"Needn't have worried? They grew three feet in ten days. They're never supposed to get this tall. At this rate, they were going to grow right through my second-story balconies. So I had them ripped out and these miniaturized orange trees in planters carted in to replace them."

"But aren't those…?"

"The cherry trees, yes. Right back where they were. No worse for wear and in full bloom. Then I come in this morning. The planters are empty, and the orange trees have somehow taken root dead center in the ground cleared for the foundation."

As Eva elaborated in unprompted detail, Masao could just picture Demi good-naturedly observing the so-called improvements by day. Only to putter around undoing most of them by night. Any work done jackhammering up the pavement, prying up boards and planting, however, it seemed the Garden generously honored. Masao smiled as he followed Eva's gestures toward the oceanfront.

"I know the crime rate in San Cicaro is nothing to sneer at, but an *entire* security fence stolen? Twice?"

Masao's brow rose, though he said nothing. He was a little surprised to hear about the level of resistance Demi put up. Especially considering she seemed to have made her peace with the drab-wrapped chain-link eyesore that had been there the better part of a century. Maybe it had been grandfathered in? Maybe she had deemed it a necessary evil for the protection it had provided from the elements. Whatever the case it seemed anything the least bit more solid disappeared overnight.

"I'll have to hire a guard at this rate." Eva scowled, shaking her head.

"Well, I am sorry you're having such a rough time of it. We'd better leave you to it," Masao replied before calling Tiger to him. At this point, though, it was obvious that Demi simply would not have it. The more Eva would try to fence her in, the more open he would find the place the next time he and Tiger made their rounds.

It was simply not the direction Demi wanted to go.

"This place is just hemorrhaging materials," Eva complained by way of good morning when Masao and Tiger came by two weeks later. Their visits had become a daily routine. Masao had started bringing homemade snacks. "Aren't there any other construction sites these people can target for a few days, so we can make some headway?"

"What about the security you hired?" he asked.

"Francine said she was 'wore ragged' after three nights of trying to investigate every odd sound and light. Every morning she shoved her old-school pedometer in my face moaning about the enormity of her step-count that night, but things still went missing. The next guy I posted on the construction trailer steps and told him not to budge. Instead, he moved fifty grand worth of lumber. And the trailer. I sicced the cops on the guy, the lumber, and the trailer, but there's still no sign of any of them."

Masao shuddered. Had Demi forgotten the unfamiliar guard as well the unfamiliar trailer? Where did the things she forgot go? What happened if she forgot a living person?

"What about the one who was here Monday? Ajay?" He looked up to the sky and tried to regulate his breathing. Ajay had a wife and three kids.

"Yeah, him I just took to Urgent Care with a concussion. He cracked his head on something in the wee hours."

"Oh good," he sighed before he could think through how it would sound. Masao suspected Eva forgave his odd responses because she saw him as a potential client. And sure enough, she decided to continue after only a short pause.

"I woke him up easily enough, but he was raving about a Ferris wheel sneaking up on him. Said it had been cropping up in a different part of the park every night but last night it clocked him from behind when it did."

Masao put both hands to his mouth. "I am so sorry. I should never have mentioned the Ferris wheel. It sounds like now she's trying to remember where she put it."

Another pause. Longer this time. Indefinite.

"Well, I should be getting Tiger home," he trailed off lamely.

If Eva had any advantage in the business world, it was that she had accepted early on that business, like every other sphere of life, was full of crazies. It did no good to insist other people be as rational as herself just because this was business. Better to simply identify which brand of crazy she was dealing with and humor it. Masao talked about her project site like Papa Luis had talked about his farm—as if it were alive and willful. The basis of Masao's connection to the boardwalk was more obscure than that of her grandfather's to his farm. Yet she recognized a lonely widower married to the land when she saw one, and she could indulge the type.

Masao had brought what he humbly called chicken-salad sandwiches. Eva could identify a dozen different ingredients and tell there had to be a dozen more. Home-made bread. They sat companionably on the only remaining lumber pile, which they had discovered this morning arranged into the contours of a park bench. Eva wondered if this crazy might be the only thing currently keeping her sane.

"You know," Eva mused, eyes closed as she chewed, "I came here when there was a Ferris wheel, and it was no great shakes."

Masao nodded eagerly. "I couldn't agree more, and besides," he added rather loudly, "the log ride boats would serve just as well as planters."

Eva stared at him, bemused. He tacked on a few more exaggerated nods and a wink, then tilted his head before asking, "Excuse me, but did you say you had come here before?"

"I did. Me and my brother. The well-meaning neighbor lady was trying to get us out of the house, too."

Miguel and Jerry Jenkins had been the same age, but not friends. Mrs. Jenkins herself had always hovered around just this side of mean. She was the one who would yell out her window at Eva and Miguel if they stayed out a minute past nine o'clock on a summer night, "You kids stop yer howlin' or I'll give ya something to howl about!"

Still, Mrs. Jenkins was always polite enough to their mother, who never said no when asked to keep an eye on Jerry while she ran daytime errands. Such favors were never reciprocated. When their mother ran errands, they tagged along. When she worked, they solemnly swore not to burn the house down in exchange for not having to be watched by Mrs. Jenkins. And pinched at every opportunity by Jerry. But the day after Eva's father had come home from the hospital coughing worse than when he'd gone in, Mrs. Jenkins offered to get them out of her mother's hair. And Eva's mother, by then too pregnant to work, had gratefully agreed.

"How about you?" she asked Masao. "You have some history here, too, don't you?"

He stopped chewing and stared at the ocean. She had never seen Masao so still. In fishing for a logical reason for the complicity between this man and this place, she had intruded. But the fly was cast, as it were, so she let the line play out.

"You could say that less well-intentioned neighbors wanted us out of the house." He had coaxed the words into neutrality, but there was a darkness beneath them that unsettled her. She moved on for both their sakes.

"Anyway, if you have any ideas about securing this place, do tell, because I can't afford another incident. The insurance adjuster is already reviewing my rates, and if people are going to get hurt…"

Her curiosity about the past now completely overwhelmed by her concerns for the present, she stood up to pace. "I wouldn't even need security if we could just get the freaking fence raised. I didn't know it was possible to be this far off schedule and over budget this early on."

She would have kicked the bench if she'd had enough money in the bank to replace her shoes. "Charles is going to get the wrong idea if we have dinner twice in one month."

It was Masao's turn to pause, long and hard. "Maybe try bamboo?"

Three mornings later, Masao, Tiger, and Eva arrived at the same time to find the fence completely replaced by a bamboo grove almost a foot thick. The new wood line hemmed the garden around on three sides, breaking only for the gate and the pier which opened to the ocean. Masao wondered that it had stopped at the highway. He suspected that this road, too, might be old and as staunch in its character as the Garden.

The plantings were still haphazard, the structures dilapidated, but the garden was transformed in the bamboo-filtered, green-gold light. Reunited with her older friends, the wind and the waves, Demi had apparently given up the company of the funfair crowds. There wasn't a single echo to be seen.

Eva's industrious site was luminous and content. It reminded her of the women of Pitiquito, mending clothes and grinding corn together in the mornings and evenings. They would sit, illuminated in the odd angles of the sun, carrying on decades-long conversations their mothers had started. Hands always busy, but at a pace they could maintain for the rest of their lives, until their daughters picked up where they left off. Willfulness Eva understood. Against stubbornness she could fight fire with fire, but there seemed to be a deeper power at work here. And she'd been duped into playing right into its hands.

Masao caught the look on Eva's face and raised a palm in farewell rather than risk saying a word.

Jaden took it upon himself to dig up even more ghosts and send them Eva's way. Unable to suspend disbelief long enough to open the second attachment, she called him.

"Ha, ha, Jaden. I know you've decided this project is cursed, but no way was there ever a Japanese internment camp here on the freaking beach. I suppose the other file you sent was about an old Native American burial ground? Maybe a couple of dragon nests?"

"Good morning, Eva," Jaden replied. "You're sounding caffeinated. Actually, it was about how the pier originally housed a small Coast Guard station that had been mothballed six months prior to the internment order. Lighthouse malfunction, tragic accident. I told you all this, and sent you that YouTube link. The rescued crew and the rescuers themselves all swore the lighthouse just plain vanished that night. Did you at least read the pull quotes? That's not even the strangest thing they claimed to see. Not to mention the singing…"

"Yes, Jaden, I've heard all your ghost stories about Gatsby Rock, but an internment camp? Not even the U.S. Government detains people at the beach. Of all the idiotic…" She was about to devolve into some very un-businesslike Spanish, so she stopped and regrouped. "Wouldn't the usual procedure be to round them all up and send them inland to build their own camp rather than gumming up the locals' view?"

Even as she said it, though, it was coming back to her how she knew that. Eleventh grade Social Studies. Damn it, there had been something around here somewhere, not a camp, but something.

"Again, if you had bothered to read the file, you would have read that this was used as more of a reporting station. A temporary assembly and holding site. Families might spend a week or two in the dozen or so buildings there before being hauled off to Manzanita."

"Manzanar," she corrected.

"Oh, you *did* read it!"

"No," she corrected.

"Turns out, the place was ideal for PR purposes. Think of the news reel footage; children playing on the beach, well-dressed parents hanging out under palm trees outside their free government housing. I found a short the City Council had filmed, because hey… a little subtle advertising for the growing town of San Cicaro, too, if you knew how to read between the lines: 'Welcome to Paradise: New Middle-Class Homes Available Daily.'"

Eva hung up. He'd lifted that snide tagline word for word from her precious prospectus.

Masao unclipped Tiger's leash, dug his bare toes into the wet sand, and squatted on his heels. The sun was fairly high in the sky. The pier didn't cast much of a shadow, but he recognized the exact angle of the wedge of shade. He knew in his heart it was right, it was time. He just hoped that the Garden hadn't given up Hana's company as well as that of the fairgoers. Two breaths later—

The little girl steps out of the shadow an inch from his bent knees. As always, she stares down the waves, squares her shoulders and sets out with her intrepid plastic bucket for water. She returns, squats as Masao has, and proceeds to ceremoniously sprinkle fistfuls of sand over the surface of the water. Absorbed in her methodical work, she adds handful after handful of dry sand to the bucket. Displaced water sloshes over the side. She startles, looks around, and finally looks up. The pier is not raised very far off the beach. But she is quite small, and she must hold her hat onto the back of her head, so it doesn't fall off. A little boy in navy blue shorts drops down just behind him. Masao doesn't turn to look at the boy, he just reads his part.

"Haven't you ever built a sand castle before?" he asks, as his wife of 57 years dissolves like a summer fog.

The only evidence of yesterday's installation of the motorized gate was a single three-by-six-foot panel that could barely be seen for all the sunflowers. Eva swore they turned their heads in her direction to see what she was going to do about it. She had no idea. She was lost, and she could not afford to lose. It was the closest she had come to tears since the last time she had stood on what might be this exact spot. She clamped her bleary eyes shut and opened them to see—

herself, six years old, in pedal pushers that had been full-length pants the year before, when her father was last able to work. She has a stupid pale pink balloon tied to her wrist. She hates pink, hates stupid baby balloons, hates that Mrs. Jenkins wouldn't buy her the teal one she wanted, hates Mrs. Jenkins, but mostly she hates that she's lost. Not because the boys left her. She doesn't care at all where those stupid boys went. But she is still lost because her father is dying and her mother is praying for him to live forever or for him to die before the baby comes so she can take them back to someplace in Mexico she never used to talk about. So Eva's blubbering like a baby, which Eva sees now that she was. She wants to comfort this echo of a broken girl, but something stops her, tells her to wait; she's forgetting something.

Little Eva is too ashamed of crying in the middle of the park to feel better for it, so she decides to take Mrs. Jenkins' advice and give herself something to howl about. She pulls the loose end of the bow to rid herself of the wretched balloon and give herself a public pretext for her sobbing. It backfires spectacularly. The balloon doesn't fly away. It bobs around her, like an affectionate pet. It rubs along her cheek, circles her head twice only to bop her nose lightly. The girl is too mesmerized to cry any more. Eva's eyes fill with tears again, too many to blink away, and her echo disappears.

She hadn't remembered the bit about the balloon. At all. Had that even happened? No way that happened and she forgot it. Though to be fair, her father had died the next day; perhaps that memory had simply not made the cut? She couldn't remember anything between her father's death and the move to Pitiquito beyond a sense of loss and flurry. In fact, she barely recognized that broken little girl at all—there had been a significant gap in her photographic record—but she had no doubt that was her.

The lost girl of the San Cicaro Pier.

Or so this place would have her be, trapping her in time. Just as her mother would have trapped her in place by letting Eva's precious U.S. passport expire. Instead, Eva had moved herself back to San Cicaro almost exactly ten years after the flight to Pitiquito. The address she had memorized in kindergarten still sufficed to register herself at Yeats High School. She couch-surfed through her junior and senior years, hoarding her fast-food income towards getting her own place. She got the first real job she interviewed for, then the next one, and the next. She lived on beans and rice and a succession of immaculately maintained consignment-shop pantsuits. Until she'd saved almost enough capital for a down payment on some place that needed her, any place, this place.

Masao had used the word echoes for the memories that bounced around this troubled place. But he had said that the garden hadn't made any new memories since the early seventies. That lost girl was what, 1987? Why was she here? Why had the garden remembered her? Remembered more of her than she had herself and at the weakest she had ever been? Was she supposed to feel honored? She didn't, Eva decided; she sincerely didn't. She pulled a coil of vines off the roller coaster.

"Listen, bruja, I get it. You're haunted by the past. So what? We all are. Doesn't make you special. Doesn't make me broken. Doesn't give you the right to keep me broken in your diseased mind, or to try to break me again, or whatever it is you're doing here. I am not an echo of any past, not even my own."

No, it was this place that was cracked and broken, not her. Eva was sore in spots, with aches that flared up under certain conditions, but she was solid—not a shadow of herself, and not lost. She knew right where she was: locked in a battle of wills with a force of Nature, a battle she literally could not afford to lose.

"They say that's good for the plants, but please Eva, don't encourage her. She already doesn't know when to stop," Masao warned, smiling in greeting.

Eva stopped muttering at the pattypan and looked at him blankly. He, too, seemed an echo of the past. The light resonated off him somehow. As if to prove his corporality, he made to pat one of the yellow stars and it came off in his hand. He offered it to Eva. "You should take some home. The garden will always grow more."

"Mmm, must taste like creosote." She realized Masao never said good morning either. They just fell in together over the gar... over the site.

"See, I was expecting it would have a metallic ring to it, but no. It's exceptional, really. Probably higher in iron than normal, but that's a good thing, right?"

Eva preferred taking offense over playing defense. Opting to let the iron-deficiency remark slide, she ran with the other opening. "I have no interest in harvesting squash. It's not instinctive to la Raza, you know."

"It's no problem. I'll do it. I have gloves. You wouldn't want to get your hands dirty."

She knew he didn't mean anything by this remark either. She hadn't managed to catch him in a single bad intention, nary a blush from him since their first encounter. He sincerely wanted to preserve her manicure. But she was itching for a good, honest fight. "Why are you growing vegetables here anyway? Shouldn't you be tending bonsai and ornamental bridges?"

Here he looked abashed, though she couldn't imagine why, when she was the one misbehaving. "Almost all the plants are volunteers, and she seems to like useful plants. I did a little light weeding, but I always had the impression it was something she just hadn't quite gotten around to it yet herself. Like she was letting me feel useful as well.

"The only things I planted...." He turned and walked toward the shooting gallery where they'd first met. "I suppose it does make this a sort of Japanese garden. Or a shrine."

Eva joined him. "Masao, I suspect you're a better Buddhist than you give yourself credit for."

The chrysanthemums were taller than he was. A bouquet-sized spray jutted out at eye-level from a pale pink tea rose.

"My wife's favorite flower. I met her... very near here. I was five. She was four."

Eva did the math. Masao didn't look 81 to her, but it was possible. He could have reported here with his family in the summer of 1942. "I lost my wife eight months ago. Two weeks later I found the garden. I planted the mums for my grandfather, and the roses for Hana."

Eva touched the stems lightly. There weren't any thorns. She pictured Masao's wife as sweet and correct as Masao and as hardily delicate as this pastel rosebush. Masao pulled on his gloves and magically produced a pair of shears from under an inch of rich topsoil. One snip and the spray of roses came away in Eva's hands. Except now the blooms were a feisty shade of coral. Her favorite color. The fight went out of her in a moment, converted to wonder.

Masao looked only mildly surprised. "A peace offering, perhaps?"

Eva wondered who else in the world even knew her favorite color anymore. Her own mother still sent her turquoise jewelry every year at Christmas.

"If you wanted to come back for some squash after the crew kicks off work at six, no one would ever be the wiser, I suppose."

The next morning Eva wouldn't have been any wiser either, if Masao hadn't offered her a still-warm squash *pupusa* first thing. The vines were still as densely studded with yellow calabaza as they had been yesterday.

"You know, I could make a dozen batches a day and never keep up," Masao said.

"It strikes me as ironic," Eva said, holding the stuffed pocket of dough in both hands, "that this is all I have to show for everything I went through to get here."

He was quiet a moment to match her silence. Finally, he asked "It's yours, isn't it? Why not sell it?"

"The site? Who would buy it?"

"No, the vegetables."

"Now you're suggesting I set up a produce stand on the side of the road." Seriously, maybe the innocent face was just a ploy. This guy probably had a gig at the senior center teaching advanced courses on insulting Latinx.

"Not just a stand. You could set up a whole market with everything that grows here."

"Run a farmer's market? Just because it's trendy doesn't mean it's lucrative. In fact, I can't think of a better way to lose money besides, well…." Here she faltered. "Besides whatever it is I'm doing here already, I guess."

Despite herself, her brain started spinning the numbers. No way was there enough margin in renting stalls to recoup any significant portion of her losses. But then, it wouldn't be a traditional farmer's market model….

He caught her thinking about it. "I don't know if it was my right to do it, but I woke up early one morning about six weeks ago feeling old and restless and useless and just decided to harvest everything I could before noon. I borrowed a neighbor's pickup and took five full loads to the food bank and the soup kitchen. A few days later I could finally walk normally again and well, that's when you showed up. You saw how well the garden had recovered by then. I know she's not opposed to art for art's sake, but I think she has a thing or two in her past she wants to atone for. I think she wants to feed people."

"What do you want, Eva?"

"I want what I've always wanted—to make something out of less than nothing." She had unconsciously quoted her standard cover letter, but that didn't make it any less true.

"And if this place is already doing that itself? Do we need to force it to do so according to our ideas about it?"

Demi just wanted to be a garden and Eva, a developer. Was there really some way they could both come into their own here? Eva didn't know the first thing about markets, but since when had she not done a thing because she had something to learn? What she did know was location, and this place was poised perfectly along the scenic route, yet close to downtown. If it really could produce enough… "I honestly don't know what I have to offer a project like this."

"Resolve," Masao answered. "Resourcefulness, marketing, strategic thinking—all the things it takes to start any new enterprise."

"But… plants. If you only knew how much of my life I've spent actively resisting any knowledge about plants…"

Masao switched to serious mode. "You might need a gardener, but while I've enjoyed fancying myself one lately, I must admit that I don't know the first thing. I go through the motions I learned watching Hana, but mostly I've been coasting on Demi's ability and hospitality."

Then he made his effortless leap back to delight. "Ajay! The security guard! He told me he wanted daytime work, and he seemed to know his way around a garden. He was especially taken with the peppers, said he'd identified five different kinds on three different bushes."

"Masacito, I kind of doubt Ajay would want to come back in any capacity, considering this place landed him in the hospital."

"Oh, but that was a simple misunderstanding. I'm sure they could work things out."

"We can always ask. I guess we owe him one, if it turns out he's interested. But I would be…" No. She would never be lost here, with or without him, but she couldn't imagine trying to negotiate this opinionated site without Masao on her side.

"Any chance I could hire you as some kind of consultant or… garden-whisperer? I don't suppose you're into women's basketball?"

He looked confused, so she asked the question she should have asked instead. "What do you want, Masao?"

"Ah, huh, well, actually… I've made another discovery since Hana's death. Besides the Garden. I find I… I love cooking. Not cooking for one—that's depressing—but for armies. I'm a bad Buddhist and a bad Christian, but for some reason I can meditate in the kitchen."

Eva smiled. "Because it keeps your hands busy."

He nodded slowly. That seemed right.

"So, what do you think?" he asked shyly, shifting his nod toward Eva's left hand. "That's my daughter-in-law's recipe, but I think I've got it just about right. Of course, it's gotten cold."

Eva had to look to see what she was holding. She'd been using the *pupusa* he'd made her as a gesticulating device but hadn't tried it yet. She took a nibble, then started making up for lost time.

"Maybe you could include a prepared food stand?" he hazarded. "I could come by a couple times a week with a few dozen. See how things are going, pull a few weeds. My repertoire is limited for now, but I could mix things up as time goes on. Maybe soups come fall…"

She stuffed the rest in her mouth and said around it, "Mmm, anything you want, any time you want, my friend. Standing invitation."

"I don't mind work, but I have reached a point in life when not working is more difficult and more important. A time to cultivate one's own uselessness."

He paused to let her parse his statement. "It will make more sense in forty years, but basically, I have all I need, and my work is to remember that. What I want most, I suppose, is to dispense with my lifelong addiction to having to feel indispensable."

He brightened again. "The asparagus around the kiddy log ride is excellent and it grows back every third day. That weedy-looking stuff growing down to the beach is daikon. It's basically pickled in sea salt when you harvest it. You could probably sell seventy or eighty dollars' worth daily."

"There's some kind of golden tomato I've never seen before going gangbusters alongside the Twirlygig," Eva continued. "Call them heirloom, and that's probably another two hundred. Tomatoes are about the only food I ever buy fresh."

"I have a feeling that if you planted some more flowers and a little greenery, she'd grow her own arrangements. She is quite the artist."

"Masao, do you even know how much zero-transport bouquets would sell for?"

"Eva, I don't even know what that means," he admitted. "But it does sound expensive."

"Wait, wait, get this. U-pick strawberries for the kids on weekends... and Wednesdays! We'd only need like 30 square feet. Hell, U-pick everything! I have a manicure to maintain here." She wiggled her fingers at him.

"You could put the neon sign back up over the gate, the part of it that works, and vend right out of the arcade booths."

"Retro charm. Repurposed materials." The prospectus was rewriting itself. "Even comes with a name. I suck at naming things."

"Demi would likely welcome repairs, and if you stayed close to the original base colors, I'm sure she'd consent to a coat of paint."

"Uh, yeah. Wouldn't want the dissolving clowns scaring the children."

Eva suddenly felt like they were pitching an outdoor room. Her eyes scanned the garden, looking for the nod, the go-ahead, the high sign, the subconscious tell of assent that her silent partner was in on the deal.

Eva raised her voice a notch. "Demi's Garden could be a real asset to the community, a refuge from the darkness of the city. We might even be in the black by the end of the year." At any rate, factoring in sunk cost and low overhead, she shouldn't need another dinner with Charles until the balloon payment came due in the spring.

"And who knows, maybe there's another site nearby that would be more amenable, I mean, *suitable* for the original project," she added. "I'm thinking that development in San Cicaro might require a more... specialized kind of groundwork." The more she thought about it, the more reasonable it seemed to treat the land itself like any other opinionated or eccentric stakeholder.

"You know that bluff just down the road where the apartment complex burned down last year?" Masao asked.

"Uh-huh." She was distracted by a flutter of green and pink behind him.

"It might be desperate for some company by now."

"I'll have Jaden look into it. Make sure the ghosts are friendly. A market here would about double its Walk Score, so that could be a win-win. Um, was that there when we started this conversation?" Eva pointed over Masao's shoulder to a single, perfect strawberry plant bearing a single, perfect strawberry that seemed to be deepening in color before their eyes.

Masao turned back to her, dimples dancing. "I suspect you know your market better than you give yourself credit for. She has a real soft spot for children."

The Saucier

Eric Stoveken

At the end of a feast which could have fed twelve, the three guests at table seven requested the presence of Martin Hartley, the saucier. Such requests were generally targeted at the Head Chef and the specificity of the demand sent a ripple of curiosity through the kitchen.

Martin made his way out to the floor of the restaurant, bristling at being taken from his work. One of the things he loved about his job was the anonymity that saved him from having to hobnob with customers. Still, he understood that such a small table racking up such a large bill received certain entitlements.

He was among the best in the world at his trade, having turned down many offers to become a Sous Chef and beyond. Still, he had no need for the self-promotion and showmanship of the modern celebrity chef and, fleeting interest in the other kitchen stations. Sauce and sauté were his media. Let others master the grilling of meat, the preparation of vegetables and the wooing of patrons. Martin Hartley was a saucier and had dedicated himself entirely to that art.

Table seven was a secluded corner booth for secret lovers and discreet celebrities. Martin noted that the table was darker than usual. The lights emitted only a faint glow, as if frozen in the dimming moment after they had popped. The center patron of the trio was masked in complete shadow. Martin attempted to adjust to the darkness; but the shadows kept shifting, erasing any image before it could arise from the murk.

The companions flanking him were nearly as inscrutable, almost featureless. Their flawless skin and facial symmetry subliminally disturbed any careful observer. The shellacked precision of their identical haircuts looked as though it were fashioned not from a collection of individual hairs but from a single lump of blonde clay. They looked airbrushed, more like the concept of well-groomed yuppies than actual ones.

"You are the Saucier?" asked the unseen questioner, his voice a smoky baritone softened around the edges by a vaguely aristocratic accent.

"Yes. Martin Hart—"

"No names. If all goes well, I shall call you 'Saucier' when speaking to you directly and 'The Saucier' when referencing you to others. I called you out here because your preparations were far and away the star of the evening's meal. All else was a backdrop." While the speaker remained unseen, his companions smiled and nodded encouragingly as if prompting Martin to give thanks.

Martin did not take the bait. "Bullshit."

"Excuse me?" came the faceless voice.

"If it were true it would be an insult and if I took it otherwise, I'd be an asshole. Then again, if you're as serious as you're acting, you already know all that."

"An excellent response."

This served as a cue for one of the speaker's companions to hand Martin a written invitation. The motion was fleeting yet flourished, seemingly casual though undeniably ceremonial. The fine piece of hand embossed card stock was being *presented*, about that there could be no doubt.

The Saucier would later recall that the hand in question was gnarled by age in stark contrast to the bland youth of its owner's face. The fingernails appeared to be fashioned from highly polished oak, the teeth of the assistant's smile gleamed fleetingly opalescent. These observations would only be made in retrospect however, since he was focused on the invitation.

The Saucier was no stranger to the world of underground dining. He had supped in the employee-run backrooms of Seattle's finest establishments, and in return, hosted exotic and clandestine feasts. He had attended banquets at private clubs where membership was strictly hereditary and heard tales of consensual cannibalism at a million dollars a plate. Quiet whispers in afterhours havens were the usual medium for such invitations. So such a brazen show as this suggested either an amateur or a player of dangerous games. The invitation's simplicity stood in stark contrast to its elaborate script:

Saucier
The Meal – San Cicaro, CA
500k per annum
50 hours a week

"Half a million a year… for a saucier? I'm good, but nobody is that good."

"I would expect no less a reaction," came the reply, triggering the other companion to slide a conspicuously thick envelope across the table. "Truth to tell, no one is that good yet. You will be. The offer's size is to secure your commitment to becoming worthy of it."

The Saucier glanced down at the envelope, choosing not to pick it up for fear of silently accepting the offer. "What's that?"

"Twenty-five thousand dollars for relocation expenses."

A glance inside the envelope ruled out the possibility of a prank. The Saucier pocketed it.

"We will expect your arrival in one week. Until then ponder this, you are what you eat. What does one eat if he wishes to be a god?"

The Saucier arrived in San Cicaro a few days later eager to procure an apartment before his first day at The Meal. Although he had not shared his travel plans with his new employer, a car and sprightly chauffeuse awaited him at the baggage claim.

The Saucier assumed that he was going to be taken to his new place of employment. Instead, he was surprised when the chauffeuse asked, "Where to?"

"I was going to try and get myself an apartment."

The chauffeuse gave an affirmative nod, suggesting that the Saucier had somehow managed to give her all the information she needed.

They soon arrived in a neighborhood which somehow seemed to be surfing simultaneous waves of gentrification and decline. The street appeared older than a lot of the other areas that he had been driven through. It had the mature look of an established city, as opposed to the odd, movie set polish some regarded as the hallmark of west coast metropolises. Businesses that looked like they had tenaciously clung to life for decades rubbed up against a-little-too-hip startups. However, a fair share of empty storefronts served as a warning to both.

The car parked in front of the Livingston, a grand old apartment building whose design perfectly blended gothic and art deco aesthetics. Its timeless permanence grounded the neighborhood, assuring that while San Cicaro's fortunes might wax and wane, the blocks around the Livingston would always have something to offer.

"I hear this place has a few units available."

It all felt so fluid. More specifically it felt choreographed, as though some great magnet was pulling the Saucier through this unlikely series of events. It was a sensation which, as the Saucier peered out the tinted windows, started to feel wrong. It was too easy.

The Saucier thought about the twenty-four thousand dollars remaining in his pocket. He appeared to be in the unique position of being able to set himself up with a whole new life. He could walk away should things get too strange, he surmised.

In the few moments it took Martin to evaluate his situation, the chauffeuse grew impatient. She tapped her pearly nails on the steering wheel and peered in the rear-view mirror with gold flecked eyes. The Saucier became uncomfortable, and was left with little choice but to take the suggestion.

The surly leasing agent was oddly offended by Martin's arrival. There was a territoriality about the man that made little sense considering his job. However, the moment the chaffeuse popped in to see if the Saucier would be needing anything else, he became rather accommodating.

After an all too expedient lease signing which only intensified Martin's concerns, he found himself sitting in the middle of his fully furnished apartment. He pondered just what kind of monster he was working for.

Martin decided he needed to hit the streets. He had always been a city dweller: New York, Chicago, Los Angeles, Seattle. He went wherever he heard the scene was starting to heat up, and his information was always solid.

His arrival in a new city would always begin with the hunt for a gig. It was how he got to know his new environment. He would hop from bar to restaurant to late night hang. Always feeling his way around the culinary scene that would underlay a town just as invisibly and vitally as the power grid or subway system.

This new course felt wrong, as though he were abandoning his instincts. Even if a whole new life had been handed to him, Martin needed to explore.

As he cruised through San Cicaro's arts district, he was reminded of the rumors he had heard about the town from time to time. It had a chance to break big a while back. Reading the crowds at the bars and coffee shops he could see why. San Cicaro hummed with an energy that comes from rubbing money and talent together. Sipping a Negroni in a bustling cocktail bar, engulfed by the smell of venture capitalists on the make, Martin wondered why San Cicaro wasn't on more people's radar.

An hour later, he stood in front of a new age shop. Some of the molecular gastronomists he knew had opened a restaurant at the site a few years earlier. At the time, they had described San Cicaro as the next Silicon Valley. Now, the restaurateurs in question hadn't been heard from in a year. Their venture had been erased to make room for an emporium of incense and disturbingly detailed voodoo dolls.

Those guys had been a couple of real golden boys and they crashed and burned in sudden and almost complete obscurity. Martin wondered if he might be the next to have a disappointing tale of failed relocation.

Then again, he thought, *those guys weren't walking away from a guaranteed half mil a year.*

That was a simultaneous source of comfort and anxiety. He need only hang around for a few months to earn himself a degree of security and freedom he had never known. At the same time, he had to wonder what would be required of him to earn that pay.

His first day on the line brought little in the way of clarity. The menu was quite limited as The Meal took the "do a few things exceptionally well" approach to menu planning. The Saucier was essentially responsible for a sauce Béarnaise, two different wine reductions, and steady stream of sautéed sea bass and green beans.

The work was brisk enough for a Tuesday night, and the staff was obviously a group of professionals. Yet there was nothing about the gig that struck him as worthy of the salary he had been promised. He had worked far harder as a Waffle House line cook when he was working his way through college. If anything, the mechanical precision of the kitchen's operation seemed like clockwork compared to the more organic workflow of his previous gigs.

The Legumier mentioned that the Head Chef was rarely on site. The owner, Marcel Radnitzky, kept the Chef constantly traveling in search of new ingredients and ideas. His influence over the kitchen was almost exclusively through letters handwritten on parchment. These missives typically accompanied shipments of mysterious herbs or exotic produce. Occasionally these included a recipe, but often there were guidelines allowing the staff to prepare and present the ingredients as the Chef thought best.

The result was that the Sous Chef was the functional head of the kitchen. And Martin had to admit that the Sous Chef was the best he had ever seen. He still insisted on finishing every plate himself. His garnishes were precise and intricate, and he constantly seemed to be handling four or five plates simultaneously.

The Saucier did not have much time to observe him work, but whenever he could, Martin found himself disoriented by the Sous Chef's motions. The swift were often referred to as "blurs," but there was something literal about this description of the Sous Chef. In fact, sitting at home after his first night on the line, Martin realized he had no idea what the Sous Chef looked like. Even though he had spent hours standing across the room from him.

After a week in San Cicaro, Martin was starting to settle into a routine. The eccentricities of his employer aside, his day-to-day life was reaching a comfortable baseline of sorts. He made time in his routine to walk along the beachfront, and sample some of the local produce at the farmer's market there. The strawberries there were divine, and he longed to produce a compote with them for The Meal. The Legumier warned him off.

"The strawberries won't keep. They'd be sour and brown before they got here," she said.

"Chill them and they would. The beach isn't that far away."

But the Legumier would not hear it. "Trust me, they won't."

The Saucier accepted that reluctantly. That wouldn't stop him going every day to sample the luscious fruits himself of course.

The thing about routines is that they can be tracked, and someone was keeping a very close eye on Martin's comings and goings.

Dr. Phineas Edwards made a point of keeping tabs on notable arrivals in San Cicaro. Moguls, celebrities, and occultists tended to be the most prominent parties to capture his attention. However, people in the employ of Marcel Ratnitzky were often of higher interest to the doctor.

Experience and family tradition had taught Phineas the value of patience. He waited to make sure that Martin had enough time to settle in but wanted to move swiftly before he became unreachable.

On Martin's eighth day in San Cicaro, Phineas approached him at the eccentric little tea house that had satisfied his daily Yerba Matte fix.

"I've seen you around," the doctor began, wagging his finger as though trying to remember where we had encountered his subject.

"Probably. I'm in here almost every day."

"No. No. Do you work over at The Meal?"

"Yeah. I work in the kitchen."

"Man, that's gotta be weird."

Phineas could tell he had caught Martin off guard. He was interested to see how he would respond. "I'm sorry. I didn't catch your name. I'm Martin Hartley."

Martin extended his hand, which was enthusiastically grasped. "Dr. Phineas Edwards. I'm the co-chair of surgery over at Lucia Bella."

"Now that sounds like an interesting job."

"It has its moments. Mind if I join you?"

Martin gestured at the chair across from him and Phineas took a seat. "So why do you think it's got to be weird working at The Meal?"

"I just hear a lot of odd stories about the owner. Marcel doesn't exactly sport your typical resume. I mean, the guy spends years in the construction game, opens a donut shop out of nowhere and parlays that into a Michelin starred fine dining restaurant? Wild."

"I'll be honest, I didn't research much beyond his check clearing, but that's quite the rags to riches story."

Phineas shook his head. "Oh, there were no rags involved. His is one of the older families in San Cicaro. If you believe some of the rumors, they may still own a good portion of it. During the last couple tech booms, the Radnitzky Group designed and built most of Silicon Row. Of course, the documentation as to who owns the properties is such an arcane nesting doll of shell companies and anonymous benefactors that it's difficult to say what's going on. Heck, maybe I own half the town and don't even know it," Phineas chuckled.

Martin nodded politely. "So real estate is the family's legacy?"

"Legacy...?" Phineas repeated as he considered the question, rolling the word on his tongue as if pondering its particular nuances. "It is what the family has long been best known for. His grandfather designed Lucia Bella Hospital."

Martin had marveled at the grand edifice on his exploratory strolls, and nodded in what might have been admiration. "That's one hell of a building you've got over there."

The doctor laughed a little too long at the comment before replying. "You have no idea. I suppose a kind of genius runs in their family. A kind of eccentricity as well."

"The hell are you talking about?"

"Don't get me wrong. I'm not talking about full tilt crazy. It's not like they're running around on street corners with sauce pans on their heads screaming about the government conspiracy to replace God with a large block of cheese. It comes across in the little things, the way they staff their businesses, the quirks of their approach to architecture and design. You ever take a look at the floor in your kitchen?"

"The tiles?"

"When you go in tonight, take a closer look. It'll help if you have a familiarity with Enochian script, runes, or Pictish writing as elements of all three are incorporated into part of the restaurant that customers were never meant to see."

Martin looked at Phineas skeptically, and the doctor feared he had overplayed his hand. Deciding he may as well swing for the fences, he added, "Of course, my colleague says the markings on the floor have a lot to do with the Sous Chef. Though that seems kind of far-fetched to me."

The saucier's distrusting brow softened. Phineas could tell that something about the Sous Chef bothered the younger man. Such instincts could prove useful in the future.

"Anyway, I need to get going. It's been nice meeting you, Martin." With that, Dr. Phineas Edwards got up and headed out into the golden afternoon.

Martin wondered what his conversation with the eccentric doctor meant. Calling out the Sous Chef, in particular, seemed to carry some inexplicable weight.

A week in, and he still could not describe what the Sous Chef looked like. He couldn't even remember hearing his voice, the same voice that gave orders and instructions in a never-ending stream of patter. He couldn't tell you if the Sous Chef had an accent, or if it was high or deep. It was as if the sound completely left Martin's head when he departed The Meal.

The Sous Chef remained the one thing that Martin had not come to accept in his brief time working at The Meal. And Phineas' reference was just enough to pique his interest.

That afternoon when he came in for dinner prep, the Saucier immediately looked at the kitchen floor. As Dr. Edwards had suggested, the tile was odd, its pattern intricate, but not ornate. In fact, the pattern seemed designed to avoid ornamentation. But if the goal was to avoid any embellishments, why have triangles within squares within circles?

The shapes were clearly there, mostly defined in the grout, as the tiles themselves did not vary in color or texture. They were all the same slate gray that had become popular in recent years.

Or were they? Certainly, the gray was uniform enough from one tile to the other, but within each tile there were slight variations. On most, these differences took the form of natural mottling. In others—those that sat on the perimeter or in the center of the subtle shapes—there seemed to be symbols or patterns. The doctor's mention of Enochian script and runes seemed a little less crazy.

The Saucier's perusal of the floor was cut short by the sight of a pair of enormous feet. They belonged to the Sous Chef, though the Saucier did not remember hearing or seeing him enter.

"Menu change, people!" the Sous Chef bellowed. Three crates were brought in through the back door, filled to overflowing with fragrant green tendrils.

"Garlic scapes, bitches!" the Legumier called out. A cheer rose from the kitchen staff. The Saucier appreciated the flavorful greens of the garlic plant as much as the next foodie, but was startled by the staff's synchronized enthusiasm.

The Sous Chef approached. "Saucier! We will be serving rabbit and need a garlic scape chimichurri sauce to go with it."

"Yes, Chef," the Saucier said as he set to work, yet he watched his supervisor from the corner of his eye. The Sous Chef selected the longest, slenderest garlic scapes and knotted them, presumably for some sort of garnish. His fingers were a blur, and the results remarkably intricate, pushing the flexibility of the stems to their very limits. Yet they maintained their shape through the tension of five graceful arcs pushing and pulling against one another.

Once he had a couple dozen of the knotted scapes set up in a bowl, the Sous Chef called over the Legumier. "Simmer each of these individually in a cup of clean water with Baltic sea salt and a pinch of galangal. Bring me the first cup for tasting before proceeding."

The Legumier eyed up the knotted scapes with a darkly amused smile. She glanced at the Saucier as if trying to gauge his reaction to the recipe. He had none.

"Yes, Chef," she answered.

The Saucier continued his work, stealing glances at the floor as he chopped. The doctor's words echoed in his head a little louder as he realized that most of the odd tilework seemed confined to the Sous Chef's station. There were still some of the inscribed tiles along the perimeter of the kitchen work area. Yet there was nothing like what the Saucier had observed on the other side of the prep station.

My colleague says the markings have a lot to do with the Sous Chef...

What colleague? Phineas Edwards was the head of surgery at the hospital. Why would his fellow surgeons be discussing esoteric markings on the floor a restaurant kitchen? Why would something as expensive and integral to the building's construction as custom tile be linked to any particular member of staff? And how did the doctor know about it in the first place? The Saucier resolved to follow up on these questions the next time he saw him.

Just then, the Sous Chef called him over. "Yes, Chef?"

"Here. Drink this." He extended a cup of the scape and galangal infusion that the Legumier had brought over.

The Legumier interjected, softening the brusque order. "You seem a bit distracted. This should perk you up. Help you focus."

The Legumier, the Saucier knew her by no other name, had a charming gravitas about her. Just the statement that the broth would "perk him up" carried the weight of a prescription.

The Saucier drank it down.

The effect was as the Legumier had promised. He found his focus increased dramatically, no longer distracted by… whatever was on his mind beforehand. With the newfound concentration, the Saucier never missed a beat. For the first time since he started at The Meal, he felt like he was completely and utterly in sync with the rest of the line. Anticipating needs, avoiding timing mistakes, and operating with the clockwork precision that had struck him as almost too ritualistic when he had first joined the staff.

On perfect point.

It was a good night, and the Sous Chef was particularly pleased. The Saucier went home with a warm feeling of accomplishment at having done right by the restaurant.

He slept soundly and dreamed of a cider-infused beurre blanc.

Upon waking the next day, Martin the Saucier felt a little bit agitated. He couldn't quite identify the source of his anxiety. It wasn't the kind that demands to be wrapped in blankets and kept from the world. Rather it was like having a strong, strange puppy tied to his wrist, an edginess that demanded action.

Instead of his usual scrambled eggs and avocado, he went with a variation on Eggs Benedict topped with a freshly made hollandaise. He accompanied it with a quickly thrown together tomato vinaigrette as well.

Well fed, but still feeling the tug of that antsy puppy, Martin the Saucier decided to go to the restaurant and get a jump on his prep work. He was so determined to get started, he almost walked right past his coffee shop.

Almost.

As it was, Dr. Phineas Edwards was enjoying his cappuccino at one of the shop's charming outdoor tables. If asked, he would claim he was simply grabbing some fresh air. The truth of the matter was that he was running surveillance on the Livingston.

When he saw Martin, he perked up. There was something different in the saucier's body language, a determined rigidity that put the doctor on edge. His informants had mentioned that something was up with one of the building's tenants of interest, but couldn't or wouldn't elaborate further. Seeing Martin's mechanized gait, the doctor was quite certain that he was the subject of his informants' concern.

"Martin!" he called from his seat, trying to remain casual while still drawing the subject in. "No Yerba Matte today?"

Martin paused. "You know, you're right. A little jolt will get me moving. Let me really get on top of things, you know? I've got a few ideas for this one fragrant herb that was sent to us from sort of monastery in the Pyrenees and I want to try some of that in a quail egg and goat butter hollandaise. Sort of a next level béarnaise, if you know what I mean, though I'm thinking a Buddha hand lemon might provide a more harmonious accompaniment to the slight earthiness of the goat butter. So yeah, a little caffeine and anti-oxidants might be just what the doctor ordered no pun intended."

Halfway into the saucier's reply, Phineas had pulled out his phone and frantically texted the barista with his analysis of Martin's situation. As such, when Martin went in to order his usual, he was told that they were out of Yerba Matte.

Phineas had followed him inside to return his cup and order a black coffee to go. "Have you tried their chai? Very good stuff. They blend the tea and spices in house."

"Fair enough. I'll give that a try. Come to think of it, the profile of chai could make an interesting addition to a pan gravy for game birds. Pheasant comes to mind. Or whatever that swan-like creature was that we served the other night."

Phineas nodded at the barista, who quickly set about preparing the beverage as she spoke. "Why don't you guys go ahead and grab a seat. I'll bring your chai over as soon as it's ready."

The two sat down at a nearby table, where Phineas spent a few moments quietly observing Martin's distracted restlessness before pursuing his line of questioning. "So did you ever get a chance to check out those funky floor tiles I mentioned?"

Martin snapped his attention back towards Phineas. "What?"

"The floor tiles in the kitchen. Did you get a chance to look at them?"

"Oh. Yeah, yeah. They're cool. Very precise. A kind of testament to the way the place is run, you know. Hidden, enriching complexity couched in apparent simplicity. Fuckin' genius, man…"

As he spoke, Phineas looked anxiously towards the counter. The barista was quick about getting Martin's chai.

"Here you go," she said as she approached. "Let me know how you like it."

Martin took a sip of the chai, initially recoiling. "Whoa! That's intense. A bit more bitter than I'm used to." He took another sip. "Though I have to say, there's a lot of interesting stuff going on. It's exotic, but kind of homey."

With each sip Martin took, Phineas could see the tension melting away. Finally, Martin seemed to have come down from his earlier kinetic state. "Is it really only eleven? Yikes."

"You seemed really intent on getting to work early for some reason."

"Yeah. I was rearing to go. Weird. Don't get me wrong, I like my gig, but I'm not even sure what the hell I was actually going in for…" Martin shook his head, suddenly looking a little worn down.

"Were you given anything to eat or drink last night?"

"Some garlic scape broth."

"Garlic scape?"

"It's the plant that grows out of garlic bulbs. A long, slender stalk with a kind of tight bud at the top."

Phineas pondered the concept for a few moments. A slender stalk could be used for any number of esoteric applications. Determining one that might account for Martin's was the trick. Finally, he pulled a pen from his breast pocket and grabbed a napkin, drawing a looping knot-like design.

"Does this look at all familiar to you?"

Martin only had to consider the drawing for a moment. "Yeah. It looks a lot like the knot that the Sous Chef tied each of the garlic scapes into."

"Each of them? How many did he tie?"

"A couple dozen, easy. Why?"

"Do you have any idea who was dining at The Meal last night?"

"No."

"Is there any way you could get us a copy of the reservation list from last night?"

"*What?* No. I mean, maybe. But it would be weird. Why would you—"

"Would you believe me if I told you that you were acting so strange because you were under a spell?"

"Come again?"

"What if I were to tell you that you were so focused on getting to work and being the best employee you could possibly be, because you had been given a potion that was essentially a spell in liquid form?"

"I—"

"Specifically, a spell meant to bind you to the will of the caster. In this case, the Sous Chef."

Martin looked at the doctor with more than a little skepticism. "I'd say you sound like a fucking nut."

"That's fair. You probably also would think I sound crazy if I told you that our esteemed barista, Julie, is one of the finest kitchen witches on the entire west coast."

"I would say that is an oddly specific accolade. Then I would ask you what the hell a kitchen witch is."

Julie came out from behind the counter, a cup of tea in hand. "We actually prefer the term 'folk mages.'"

Phineas gave her a confused look. "No, you don't."

"Not me, personally, but there are definitely people in the guild who think the term kitchen witch is belittling."

"The guild?" Martin asked with the exasperated tone of a man who was thought he was being played.

"It's really more informal than it sounds. These days it's pretty much an online chat group with periodic regional meetups in ice cream joints."

"Of course it is," Martin replied.

Phineas could feel the conversation getting away from its original point, and tried to steer things back to the revelations he was trying to impart. "Martin, the important thing I want you to realize is that you have been brought in to something considerably bigger than a gig at a renowned restaurant. We're not sure what's at play here, but members of the Radnitzky family has been pursuing something more ambitious than terrestrial wealth for generations. Signals point to Marcel closing in on some sort of epiphany. The Meal is part of that. Every member of staff has been selected to facilitate this plan."

Martin nodded, but seemed not to be processing the full implication.

Julie clarified, "That means that *you* were chosen to play some role in whatever is coming down the line."

This snapped Martin out of his bemused revelry. "Me? What? Is Marcel Radnitzky planning to drown his enemies in a fearsome sea of béchamel? Does he want the streets to run red with bordelaise? This is ridiculous."

Julie's casual explanatory tone snapped to something far more defensive. "Everything has power if you know how to access it. The five fundamental elements of magic are Earth, Air, Fire, Water, and—for want of a more definitive word—Spark. All are present when one is cooking. Add to that the fact that the restaurant itself was built from the ground up as a conduit for magical energies, and beyond that, was strategically placed in this city. A city whose very design was influenced by and lives in synergy with the natural forces that were present in the land before humanity ever dragged itself out of the muck, and you have something disturbingly powerful."

Phineas leaned in closely, as much to bring down the volume of the conversation as to convey his seriousness. He whispered, "San Cicaro is a source of tremendous power. People have a hard time truly harnessing it. That is why prosperity here sort of comes and goes the way it does. Sometimes San Cicaro destroys your dreams, sometimes it will grow you a garden. I think your employer may be attempting to tap in a lot more directly than mortals should, to tip the scales in his favor."

Martin sighed with exhaustion. "Here's a wild idea for you guys. Proof. Give me some reason to believe this absolute insanity. Because right now all you've given me is a funny story to tell about the couple of yahoos—"

"No! You must tell no one."

"Give me some evidence."

Phineas and Julie had a conversation entirely in a series of exchanged looks and shrugs. Finally, Phineas turned to Martin and asked, "Would you like to meet my informant?"

"If your informant is the host of whatever hidden camera prank show I'm on, sure."

Julie went behind the counter to grab something.

"Oh, she's better than that." As Phineas spoke, Julie returned with a tiny tea cup that appeared to contain a drop of honey. "*Penelope?* I think you'll agree that the time has come to reveal yourself."

Martin winced as something zipped past his head. He instinctively swatted at it, but missed completely. Julie pointed a stern finger at him. "None of that, now. It would not end well for you."

The creature landed next to the tiny tea cup and Martin's brow shot up. It was a faerie. A tiny female body with iridescent wings. The whole bit. In that moment, Martin face went slack with the look a man whose entire concept of reality had just shifted beneath him.

"This is crazy." Martin leaned in close to the creature. He was obviously fascinated, but Phineas could tell he sought to unveil an increasingly elaborate ruse.

The faerie looked at him and spoke. Phineas smiled at Penelope's humorous rhetorical question, but he knew that to the untrained ear of the saucier, her voice sounded like a high pitch whine. As if an old TV was on somewhere in the next room.

"This is your informant?" Martin asked incredulously. "So what, she follows me around? Spies on me?"

"She doesn't need to follow you around, she's your neighbor."

"Of course she is. Now, what exactly is she saying?"

Phineas took it upon himself to translate. "She's telling us not to dawdle. Apparently, a couple of Radnitzky's offling fanatics have rolled into town, which could mean big things are afoot. Look, we need to know who was given that binding broth. Can you get us the reservation list or not?"

Martin rolled his jaw, and Phineas couldn't guess what the young man was thinking. He looked at Penelope, the existence of something as absurd as fairies clearly playing into his calculation. "If I can do it without letting on why, I will. I don't want people to think I'm cra—"

"It's more important than appearances!" Phineas half-shouted, before reining in his volume. "Anyone at that restaurant can be a willing part of this thing. You absolutely have to play it as though nothing is amiss."

Julie perked up in realization. "Come to think of it…"

Phineas shook his head. "Damn it. The binding spell."

"What about it? You seemed to have broken it."

"That's the problem. The Sous Chef will smell that from a mile away. Suspicions will be raised."

"Maybe he'll think it just wore off?"

Phineas and Julie considered the possibility for a moment.

"It's possible…" Phineas began.

"But if you were able to shake a binding spell like that in less than 24 hours, that would draw a great deal of attention," Julie continued.

"However, if they suspect that Martin has serious innate mojo, it could expedite his induction into the inner circle."

"If they plan on looping him in at all. Don't forget, we have no idea how the work is constructed. If he's just a potion mixer, he doesn't necessarily need to provide the intent. Especially if our suspicions about the Sous Chef are correct."

As the doctor and barista continued to discuss his situation, Martin started to bristle. His gaze went to each participant as they spoke, but the consternation on his face only deepened.

"Even so, if they think he's got the juice to shake off the binding spell, they might decide to bring him fully on board."

Penelope let out another high-pitched whine, an argument that made perfect sense to the more well-trained ears at the table. Julie and Phineas both nodded in agreement.

"Having a man deep inside *would* make things easier. Especially since Marcel has taken such comprehensive precautions against fae surveillance."

Penelope responded with a sustained barrage of high frequency noise. From the way she paced around the table and the back and forth of her gesticulations, it was clear that she was verbally working through some particularly thorny tactical question, though only Phineas and Julie were privy to these thoughts. However, even a casual observer could tell that the stakes were rising with each hypothetical being considered.

Martin finally burst. "Look! I don't know what the hell is going on here, but I will need to get my ass to work sooner than later. I would really prefer if I was not stabbed with a ceremonial knife or whatever the hell you're afraid might happen as soon as I walk in the door. Now is someone going to tell me how to play this, or do I have to go tell my sous chef what I've seen and heard here today?"

No sooner had the threat escaped Martin's lips than Penelope shot up off the table at his chest, knocking him and his chair to the ground. The fairy leaped onto the tip of his nose and started yelling at him loudly.

"Penelope!" Phineas shouted, "I'm sure he didn't mean that. He is understandably frustrated. We've rattled his entire understanding of the world, and we've implied that his life might be in danger. I think his demand for a course of action is perfectly reasonable. Why don't you let him up? We'll figure this out."

The faerie nodded and returned to her spot on the table. Her suspicious eyes still fell on Martin, but it was a good deal better than her holding the saucier to the floor with her otherworldly strength.

In the end, it was decided that he would play dumb. He would show up for work free of the binding spell as if nothing had happened.

"Maybe mention having a weird dream of having to hack your way out of a jungle overrun with vines. That's the kind of thing your subconscious might throw at you while un-working the spell," suggested Julie.

"If you can get last night's reservation list without anyone knowing, please do. But not under any other circumstances." Phineas instructed. "Don't worry if it's suspicious or not. Anything you do will be under heavy scrutiny once they think you can shake off a binding spell with a good night's sleep."

Martin nodded. And Phineas could only pray their desperate plan would work.

When he arrived in the kitchen around his usual time, the Saucier was taken aback at the frantic energy of the place. People were in overdrive. As he approached his station one of the dishwashers scurried up to him.

"The Head Chef is in the building!" he breathlessly whispered, before returning to his position.

No sooner had the Saucier strapped on his apron than the door burst open and in walked a man who could only be the Head Chef. He bore a sharp, drawn face with a beak-like nose and high cheekbones. The face stood in gaunt contrast to the rest of his body, which looked rugged and strong for his presumed age. The Saucier reminded himself that the Chef had been traveling the world for years. It only made sense that he looked like he could climb the Himalayas in search of a possibly extinct species of cumin.

The Head Chef surveyed the kitchen with a quick and dismissive eye. Everything was as it should be, and therefore drew no special interest. That was until his gaze fell upon the Saucier. At that moment, he turned to the Sous Chef—who Martin could swear had not been standing there a moment before—and raised an eyebrow.

The Sous Chef nodded in response to an unasked question, and the Head Chef inquisitively approached the Saucier.

"You are settling in well?" he asked, his accent a mystery.

"Yes, Chef."

"Do you find San Cicaro to your liking?"

"It's a quirky city, but I'm enjoying it so far."

The Head Chef nodded in such a way that it was clear he was already bored with the small talk. He sniffed at the Saucier for a moment. "Open your mouth. Wide."

Though confused, the Saucier complied. The Head Chef promptly inserted three fingers into his mouth, swabbing his cheeks and tongue before smelling and tasting his fingers. "Chai, a little heavy on the cardamom for my taste, with hints of wormwood and stinging nettle. Fascinating recipe. Did you make it yourself?"

"Um. No."

"Please tell me you didn't get it from that rancid little hole in the wall near your apartment building?"

"Yeah, but how do you know where—"

"Look out for those weird bastards. They'll spout all sorts of nonsense. Half of it probably inspired by their intake of wormwood and other psychotropics. You're lucky you're not hallucinating. Well, rest assured, the Sous Chef is *not* a demonic demigod invoked from an infernal alternate dimension."

The Saucier laughed, as he thought was expected of him. "I certainly hope not, securing his work visa would be an unimaginable pain in the ass."

As the Head Chef laughed and clapped him on the back, all Martin could think was how neither Phineas, Julie, nor Penelope, to the best of his knowledge, had said anything about the Sous Chef being a pan-dimensional being. He began mincing shallots, while out of the corner of his eye, he could swear he caught a glimpse of the Sous Chef's face morphing in its skin.

The Saucier's hands trembled.

He saw now that everything Phineas had said and hinted at was true. He stole another glance at the Sous Chef. There was something wrong. The creature that was finishing the plates was constantly shifting form, ever changing. This was why Martin could never conjure him in his mind's eye.

Still, he kept mincing his shallots and preparing his *au jus*. He smiled sardonically to himself, *I guess the price of my soul is a half mil per year. That sounds fair.*

Perhaps he was in over his head. Maybe he was going to somehow bring about the end of the world. Whatever the case, he was well paid to make good food.

He had no real intention of even *trying* to get his hands on the reservation list. His goal now was to keep his head down, do his work, and try to have as uneventful a night as possible.

Martin may not have been entirely comfortable with the situation, but there was nothing more that the Saucier could ask for.

Proof of Magic

Leora Spitzer

Like many used bookstores, Nephilim Books was larger on the inside than one might expect from the narrow storefront. There was no immediately discernible system to the organization of the shelves. And the arrangement of the aisles seemed labyrinthian from a glimpse through the shop's window.

Tamar inhaled deeply as she entered, releasing a tension in her shoulders along with the breath. While the flickering lights and overstuffed bookshelves might be the opening to someone else's horror story, the presence of so many books always relaxed Tamar Gold. Although her excitement also tended to make her fingers twitch. She stepped further into the shop, unzipping her jacket as she walked.

San Cicaro had not been her intended destination. For that matter, she was not planning on staying more than a couple days. Her plan, such as it was, involved driving along the Californian coast with her sketchbook. She hoped that travel would rejuvenate the creativity she'd always prided herself on. San Cicaro, with its eclectic architecture and gorgeous coastal views, had seemed like as good a place as any to stop. She smirked and then sighed at the thought of how Sandra would respond to her cavalier approach to the highest-crime city in the state.

"Can I help you find anything?" someone asked.

Tamar jolted slightly. Turning away from her perusal of what might have been fantasy set in Victorian England, she saw the proprietor of the shop for the first time.

The bookseller wore a deep green vest with an opal bolo tie and had a neat grey haircut. Tamar immediately categorized it as Lesbian Haircut #3 before second-guessing herself. It could, after all, simply be a variety of Generic Older Man Haircut.

"Is there something you're looking for?" they repeated, arching an eyebrow at Tamar's failure to respond. Or perhaps at her staring.

"No, thank you," Tamar stuttered belatedly. She gestured at the shelf behind her. "I'm just browsing."

"Hm." This time it was the shopkeeper's turn to survey the guest. From her teal-fringed undercut (Queer Millennial Haircut #7, Sandra's voice helpfully supplied) to her red hoodie with the grease spots, to her ragged fingernails, to her polished Doc Martens. "Well. My name is Cedar. Just call for me if you need anything."

As Cedar turned away, a beam of sunlight caught the bolo tie, and the colors on the opal shifted and shimmered.

"Do you believe in magic?" Tamar blurted, then blushed. Cedar turned back to her. Tamar muttered, "Never mind. It's just… I thought I saw…"

Cedar laughed. Tamar had read laughter described as a "burbling brook" before but had always dismissed it as poetic hyperbole. Yet the sound of Cedar's mirth instantly conjured a memory of splashing in the stream when she was eight.

"You're in a bookstore, child," Cedar said, still chuckling. "What more proof of magic do you want?"

Later, unpacking her new books in her room at the San Cicaro Sunset Hotel, Tamar reflected on Cedar's comment. There *was* something particularly magical about being able to transfer images, stories and ideas via an organization of shapes printed on pulped dead tree. She could even know the thoughts of people long dead. Still, that hadn't been what she was been asking. Tamar had the well-honed skepticism of a bibliophile consistently disappointed by the failure of adventure to appear or magical spells to work.

Accordingly, she had dismissed the rumors of strange happenings in San Cicaro as the product of overactive imaginations. She glanced at one of her purchases. *The Truth of Gatsby Rock: My Story* by Manny Cargille. Another lurid tell-all. Such books were a guilty pleasure of hers—fantasy with the veneer of plausibility. Perhaps these stories were just an unusual strategy from the San Cicaro tourism department, trying to distract visitors from the exceptionally high crime rate. Or maybe it was just men like Manny, trying to make themselves relevant in a world which didn't care anymore?

It was harder to come up with an explanation for the scene she'd glimpsed walking down the block that morning. Maybe it was just evidence of those crime rates, but Tamar couldn't shake the feeling that there had been something more. She had skirted around the scene, avoiding the pack of cop cars and the swarms of officers talking seriously into radios. All staying well away from the plethora of police tape surrounding an ominous sheet.

An oddly localized gust of wind had blown the sheet down the road while barely rustling Tamar's fringe. It was then that she'd seen the corpse, splayed out like in one of those trashy crime shows Sandra enjoyed. Maybe something was weird with the angle, or the flashing lights confused her eyes, or she was just shaken by her first sight of an actual dead person.

But it damn well looked like the body was *hovering*.

And it was minor compared to a murder, but as long as she was doubting her memory or eyesight… she could've sworn that the concierge's red dragon tattoo had been on his right arm when she first checked in. Yet it had definitely been on his left arm when she returned from the bookstore.

"You're imagining things again," she told herself sternly. Tamar needed to keep herself grounded and practice the basics like Sandra had always said to do. She pulled out the sketchbook and began a still-life of the bedside table.

Tamar had little idea how long it had been when she put down her pencil. She flexed her fingers, rubbing the palm of her writing hand with her thumb to ease away the ache. Then she looked at her sketch and blinked. "Huh."

The glass of water was clear, and the telephone looked realistic enough. But instead of the lamp, she had drawn a pixie trapped in a conical cage, its face snarling in outrage and its hair piled atop its head. She could see, looking at the lamp now, where the curve of the stand had suggested a body. The pixie's hairdo was distinctly light bulb-shaped. "Huh. Well. So much for staying grounded."

"I'm terribly sorry," Tamar said to the concierge, tugging at her teal fringe. "I must've bumped into it in my sleep, though I really can't imagine how I slept through the crash."

The concierge looked from the shattered lamp on the floor to the young woman and back to the mess on the floor.

"I'll pay for the damages, of course," Tamar continued.

"Not to worry, ma'am," he said smoothly, belied by a wrinkle on his forehead. "This shouldn't have happened, but I'll get it all cleaned up for you. Why don't you explore for a while and come back in an hour or so? Or longer, if you're enjoying yourself. I can recommend some excellent destinations."

As he ushered her out the door, Tamar saw the dragon tattoo again. It *was* on his left arm—she must've been tired and gotten it wrong that first time. But she hadn't seen the dragon's face before, inked in a fierce, angry, snarl.

The concierge had not, in fact, given her any useful recommendations. Disinterested in visiting the seafront wharf, and without any better ideas, Tamar returned to Nephilim Books. Despite her several purchases the previous day (or perhaps because of them), Cedar appeared unsurprised to see her back. Today they wore a purple button-down with a pattern of feathers and the same opal bolo tie.

"Can I help you find anything?" they asked.

"Actually, yes," Tamar said, the idea occurring to her as she spoke. "Do you have any books of magical creatures? Like a Zoology 101 textbook but for dragons and unicorns and things?"

She envisioned a whole series of magical creatures in mundane locations to accompany her pixie-lamp. Like a werewolf in a dog park or a unicorn pulling one of those quaint tourist carriages she'd seen on her walk over. It would be helpful to have inspiration for other animals.

"Hmm," Cedar said, eyeing her thoughtfully. "Yes, I do have something like that. Come."

Tamar followed Cedar to the back of the shop. Ducking their head, Cedar walked down a set of stairs Tamar hadn't even suspected of being there. They entered another maze of bookcases. The proprietor didn't hesitate, following an unknown path before stopping abruptly. Close behind, Tamar bumped into their back, bouncing off without upsetting Cedar's balance in the slightest. Cedar, humming tunelessly under their breath, ran a finger along the shelf.

Angling her neck to read titles along with them, Tamar spotted illustrated volumes of botany and zoology. A few, like the *"Potioneer's Guide to Foraging,"* were clearly fictional. But others would not have been out of place in a high school science classroom. Just as Tamar began reflecting again on Cedar's nonsensical organization, the bookseller gave a triumphant "Ha!" and slid a large book off the shelf.

"Decryptifying Cryptozoology: A Sourcebook for Information and Facts Describing Animals and Beings Long Considered Myth and Legend."

"Perfect!" Tamar reached up to take the book from Cedar eagerly and began flipping through it. Each page featured a detailed drawing of a different fantastical creature. The image was followed by information about its habitat, its weight, its magical element, and a few sentences describing general behavior. She grinned at the notation that a bigfoot's big feet averaged between two and two and a half feet long. And she ran a finger along the intricate linework of the scales on the image of the basilisk. As she glimpsed the next page, she gasped and fumbled. The heavy volume would have dropped had Cedar not steadied both her and the book with remarkable speed.

"Are you alright?" Cedar asked, leading her to a convenient small table and guiding her into a seat. Tamar, preoccupied with her thoughts, barely noted the beautifully carved oak table. She set the book down, exhaling in time with its solid *thunk*. Hands suddenly clammy, she flipped awkwardly back to the entry that had startled her. She and Cedar read together:

Bright-Headed Pixie

The bright-headed Pixie is a winged hominid native to the coasts of North America. Adult bright-headed pixies typically weigh between 5 and 7 lb. (2 and 3 kg), making them among the heaviest members of the fae family, and reach approximately 8.5 inches (25.6 cm) in height. The bright-headed pixie is known for the distinctive glowing hair from which it derives its name, thought to have developed as part of its elaborate mating rituals. It is unknown how many live in the wild, but the species is classified as Endangered due to hunting in the early twentieth century as an alternate light source far more pleasant than kerosene or whale oil. However, hunting has died out as alchemic experimentation failed to find a means of preserving the pixie's bioluminescence post-mortem. Bright-headed pixies are social creatures and generally can be found in families of between six and eight.

Next to the text was a drawing of the pixie, from its tiny pointed ears and luxurious mane of hair to its three-toed feet, all covered in a soft layer of fur. Wordlessly, Tamar pulled her sketchbook out of her satchel and opened it next to the sourcebook. Aside from their hairdos and the expressions on their faces, hers furious and the other faintly bored, the two pixies were nearly identical.

"I swear I've never even heard of a bright-headed pixie before." Tamar was conscious of Cedar's mild curiosity sharpening into a tight focus beside her.

"You drew this," the bookseller stated, tapping a gentle finger against Tamar's sketchbook. "At the hotel last night?"

Tamar nodded.

"Which hotel?" Cedar spoke calmly, but with a gravitas that had been missing earlier. Tamar had the sudden impression that the bookseller was twice as large as the space they actually occupied.

"San Cicaro Sunset Hotel," she replied. "You know, it's kinda funny. The lamp I used as the model for this broke overnight."

"Broke?" There was a hint of restrained fury in Cedar's voice. Later it would occur to Tamar that she, who had always shrunk away from anyone's anger, had not been frightened at all.

"Well, I broke it, or I must've. I don't mean to avoid responsibility, I'm just not sure what happened. But it was on the table when I went to sleep, and on the floor in pieces when I woke up. The concierge wasn't too thrilled with me. That's why I came here, actually—he wanted me out of the room while he cleaned up."

The bookseller's lips whitened as they stared at the drawing of the caged pixie. "Did you leave anything in the hotel room?"

"I mean, my books. Clothes, toiletrie—" Tamar stopped in response to Cedar's sharp head shake.

"Anything *irreplaceable*?" the bookseller clarified. Tamar thought of the velvet-lined wooden box Sandra had given her and nodded silently.

"Naturally," Cedar sighed. In response to her confused look, Cedar continued "It would've simplified things if you could've just abandoned everything. But that would've been too easy, I suppose."

"Abandoned my things?" Tamar asked incredulously. She chuckled nervously. "It's just a broken lamp. You're not taking this seriously, are you? It's just a weird coincidence."

The bookseller gave her a look painfully reminiscent of ones she'd gotten from her mother her whole life. A look that said *I know you're smarter than this so why are you persisting with this ridiculous delusion.* Tamar received it whenever she had tried to make a coincidence into something more, something magical.

But though the look and the tone were the same, the sentiment Cedar expressed was the polar opposite of her mother. "Tamar, you're a reader and an artist. Yesterday you asked me about magic. Are you really going to stick to the *weird coincidence* line?"

"Okay," Tamar said, standing up.

"Okay." They replied evenly.

She ran her fingers along the bookshelf, closing her eyes, as if drawing strength from their spines. She had always been frustrated with characters who refused to see the evidence of magic before their eyes. The first possible explanation was that bright-headed pixies were real and she had drawn one. The second possibility was that she had somehow unconsciously reproduced an identical image of a totally made-up creature. If she set aside her ideas about reality, the first option seemed much more plausible. Besides, there was Pascal's Wager to consider—who would it hurt if she proceeded as if it was real and it turned out to be a strange, elaborate hoax? Well, it would hurt her. Half her childhood had been bitter disappointments when magic failed to materialize. Yet, what if it *were* real, but she refused to believe, and continued to stay in an evil hotel of pixie-torturers...? "Okay. Okay, what now?"

The bookseller awarded her with a faint smile. "What do you want?"

Tamar blurted, "I want to make good art. I want to discover something magical. I want my girlfriend back. I want my mom to stop trying to set me up with her friends' sons. I want to live in a library. I want an ice cream sundae with a ridiculous amount of whipped cream. I want cuddles I want to be happy I want a tattoo I want—"

"Enough," Cedar said, halting her uncontrolled speech.

A blush rose to her cheeks as she realized everything she had just revealed. The bookseller seemed to recognize this, their eyes softening.

"My apologies." They paused, looking at her thoughtfully, "Well then. Let's go."

"Erm. Where?" Tamar asked hesitantly, nervous she'd let another torrent of words slip out.

Cedar laughed, and Tamar once again saw that stream in the woods behind her childhood home. "To get ice cream, of course!"

Just down the block from Cedar's store was a bustling commercial area, a street trying to hold onto its own economic successes as the city crumbled around it. Cedar guided her past various stores and restaurants, dodging around diners taking advantage of the weather to eat outside. And soon they reached a small ice cream store nestled between a thrift shop and a Mexican restaurant.

Bells jingled cheerfully as Cedar pushed open the door. Inside, the temperature was cool and the decor was warm. Looking around, Tamar thought that this would be a fun place to paint.

"Cedar!" called the woman behind the cash register, her long blue-green locks (Mermaid Hair #2) swinging over the arms of her wheelchair. "Haven't seen you around in a while."

She rolled towards the display case, closer to where Tamar and Cedar stood. Cedar grinned. "Sorry, Rae, I just get so caught up in my books."

"I'm shocked," Rae said dryly. "Your usual?"

Cedar nodded in anticipation.

Tamar took a step closer to examine the ice cream options. Apparently, this shop's shtick was to name its flavors after emotions, with a smaller subheading describing their actual contents. A pale pink was labeled *Joy (Cherries and Cream)* while others included *Nostalgia (Vanilla Plus), Comfort (Chocolate Brownie Chunk)* and *Energy (Coffee)*. Rae leaned over the case to get two large scoops of *Hope (Apple Pie)* and plopped them into a waffle cone for Cedar.

"And what'll it be for you?" she asked Tamar, handing the ice cream cone to Cedar. "You can have whipped cream on the house, for getting this one out of their hermitage." She jerked her head to indicate Cedar.

"I want to say I'm not that bad, but I can't lie," Cedar admitted. "This is Tamar. She's an excellent customer and expressed a deep need for ice cream, among other things. It seemed like the obvious next step to come here."

Rae eyed her friend as though she knew they had not told the whole story but let it slide for the moment. "Well, what can I get for you, madam book-and-ice-cream lover? With everything going as it is, Cedar hasn't asked for anything but *Hope* in the last several years, but maybe you want something less subtle?"

"Hope is the thing with feathers," Tamar quoted absently, surveying the ice cream case.

"Very appropriate, then," Cedar remarked. "You want to make good art. Perhaps consider *Creativity*?"

Tamar looked at the description and shook her head. *Creativity* apparently contained some of everything—chocolate and vanilla swirl with chocolate chips, caramel, pretzels, waffle cone, cookie dough, brownie chunks, peanut butter cups, and more.

"Nah, I don't like things in my ice cream," she said offhandedly.

"What does 'vanilla plus,' mean?" she asked.

"It's hard to describe," Rae said, smiling without showing her teeth. "Everyone has a different experience."

"Could I try a taste of that?"

Rae grabbed a mini spoon and sighed. The *Nostalgia* container was out of easy reach. She lifted herself out of the wheelchair, retrieved the small bite of ice cream, handed the spoon to Tamar. She then slipped back into her chair with a small sigh of relief. She narrowed her eyes at Tamar's look of surprise.

"I'm just excited to try this ice cream," Tamar said. While she had been momentarily startled to see the other woman stand, it was something else, something she couldn't quite place about Rae's movement, that had made her stare. But either way, it was rude. It certainly was not her job to police anyone else's disability. There were plenty of reasons for someone to use a wheelchair aside from total inability to stand.

Putting action to her claim, Tamar took a bite of the ice cream on her spoon and promptly forgot anything else.

"Plus cinnamon?" she asked, licking the spoon clean. "It reminds me of my bubbie's rugelach. This is delicious."

Rae said, a little smugly, "I made it myself, with local products. The cherries in *Joy* were picked fresh this morning, right on the seafront."

Tamar blinked. She had never heard of produce being grown so close to the ocean, and thought to check that seafront market out later. "Well, it's phenomenal. I'd like a scoop of *Nostalgia* and, let's see, a scoop of the *Relaxation*, too."

"Cup or cone?"

"Cup."

Rae scooped out the ice cream and added the promised whipped cream. She rolled over to the cash register, where Cedar awaited with exact change, a half-finished cone, and a small smile.

After paying, Tamar and Cedar sat down to enjoy their ice cream. As there was no sign of any other customers, Rae wheeled around the counter to join them at the little table. Suppressing a squeal of excitement, Tamar took a bite. The smooth caramel of the *Relaxation* flavor soothed her throat, and a little tension went out of her shoulders. She closed her eyes to savor the next bite.

"My mom used to say that even though ice cream can't solve most problems, there are very few situations it doesn't improve," she said around another spoonful of the *Nostalgia*.

"Oh, I do like this one," Rae said to Cedar. "I told you I got into the right business. No matter how bad things get, people will still want ice cream."

Cedar laughed. "Oh, I know it. And one day, people will realize how much they need books. Things can't keep getting bad forever."

Rae shrugged. "That's never stopped things before."

"Have you heard anything of Florence recently?"

"Not seen her. I hardly see any of the old crowd now."

"What's really bothering you?" Cedar asked, looking at their friend intently.

"Oh, just the general crumbling of my city, the ineptitude of the SCPD, and I haven't had—" Rae snapped her mouth shut and glared at her friend. "I told you not to do that anymore."

Cedar shifted uncomfortably. "Sorry. I just worry."

The bookseller licked the last traces of ice cream from their cone. "Things really are rough right now, but remember how it used to be? I believe this city can be great again, Rae."

She snorted. "That's just the ice cream talking, hun."

"Doesn't mean it's not true. Ice cream, books—these are things that bring brightness and joy and *purpose* to a life. The healthy kind of magic. We are making a difference, Rae, you know it."

Tamar listened vaguely to the two friends chatting and smiled. She thought about how pleasant this was, how restful after the nonstop stress of the last few years. It took her a moment to notice when Cedar tensed, and another minute to place what had triggered them. In the distance, something wailed. At first, Tamar thought it sounded like a desperate cat or crying baby before realizing it was police sirens.

"I need to get back," Cedar said. "I shouldn't have left the store so long. Without me there, there's nothing preventing people… I mean, aside from their better natures, but…"

"Go," Rae urged. "If your instincts say to go, go."

Cedar nodded distractedly to Tamar. "Take care. I'm sure everything will be fine for you and you will make incredible art like you dream of, but you might want to check out of that hotel soon."

With that, the bookseller left the shop in a hurry.

Rae looked at Tamar, who was finishing her ice cream despite being deserted by the only guide she had in this city.

"Yes, they're always like that," the shop owner said. "I don't know how someone that honest still exists in this town, but they are a treasure. And it's amazing that you even got them out of that shop in the first place. *Hope* is about the only thing that draws them out."

Tamar said, "I only met them yesterday and they've been so helpful already. They don't owe me any more help."

She licked her spoon and looked regretfully at the empty ice cream cup. "This really was some of the best ice cream I've ever had Rae. I feel so much better I can't even tell you."

Rae grinned. "That's what I like to hear."

Tamar gathered up her trash and Cedar's abandoned napkins to throw away. "Really, thanks. This made my day much brighter."

"You're welcome. Take care of yourself." Rae frowned suddenly. "Seriously, just be careful and take care of yourself. Cedar is rarely wrong and never lies, but they might not have gotten the whole truth, especially after two scoops of *Hope*. It does tend to paint a rosy sort of picture."

Tamar laughed. "There are worse things than some hope. I'm sure I'll be fine. But thank you."

Tamar slipped back into her hotel room and dumped her satchel and jacket on the newly-made bed. After checking the power meter, she plugged her phone in to charge on the bedside table beside a new lamp, nearly identical to the previous one. With the flowered bedspread and neatly arranged abundance of pillows, especially those annoying cylindrical kind hotels used as decorations, the room looked so mundane, so ordinary. So much like any other hotel room in America. It was hard to hold on to her own misgivings, or Cedar's ominous worries.

Nevertheless, Tamar began repacking, trying to fit her new books into the bag without damaging the spines or edges. The precious paints in their wooden box were still nestled among her clothes for padding, but Tamar unwrapped them just to be sure they were alright.

She lifted one delicate bottle from its niche and raised it to the light, trying to decide which paints would best capture the pixie's uniquely glowing hair. Sandra had given her these paints several months ago. She had hoped to inspire more of the vibrant, colorful portraits that Tamar had been crafting when they first met.

Three years ago, an art professor had invited Sandra to give a guest lecture; the students of her portraiture class were endeavoring to get hairstyles and textures right. By the end of the week, Sandra had given Tamar her first undercut in exchange for a portrait. The two women bonded over their shared love of color, art, novels, and pizza. For a while, Sandra's preponderance to regularly change hair colors provided inspiration for Tamar's palettes, but her art couldn't pay the bills. And the long hours at her retail job drained both energy and motivation for painting. That was when Sandra had started encouraging her—nagging her, if she was being less generous—to sketch regularly before bed. To keep those muscles sharp and not let creativity stagnate. It had been hard not to resent Sandra for her creative fulfillment, and that had put such a strain on their relationship…

A chirp from her phone startled Tamar out of her reverie. Hastily, she placed the bottle back in its spot and went to check for messages.

It was a guilt-tripping text from her mom (*it's been a while since we talked and i just wanted to check in. i miss you!!!*) but the phone battery was nearly dead. It plainly had not been charging. Tamar groaned and fidgeted with the cable, but the red battery icon stubbornly refused to change. The lamp, plugged into the same outlet, shone brightly. Tamar, irritated, yanked the lamp cord out to see if that plug would work any better for her dying phone.

The lamp stayed on.

Tamar blinked down at the cord in her hand, following it up to confirm that it did, indeed, belong to the still-lit lamp.

"Oh, I'm sorry," she said faintly. Tamar glanced at her satchel, which still held her newest book.

"Are you also a bright-headed pixie?" she asked the lamp, feeling a little ridiculous. "You must be lonely... I'm sorry, little pixie. You deserve better."

There was a bright, blinding flash. Tamar heard a flutter and felt something soft brush against her hands. When her vision returned, rainbow starbursts still dancing in her eyes, she realized she held shattered porcelain fragments of a second broken lamp.

"Fuck," Tamar breathed, shaking with the sudden rush of adrenaline. At least, she thought it must be adrenaline, maybe it was a panic attack. She hurried to shove the last few things into her suitcase. She grabbed the toiletries from the bathroom sink and unplugged that useless phone charger.

It's real it's real it's real played on a loop in her head, echoed each time by *I'm screwed I'm screwed I'm screwed*. She struggled to get out the door, terrified of facing whomever believed it was morally acceptable to imprison magical beings away from their families.

And giddy. Excited at the notion that the magic she had been searching for since she first began to read was real.

The concierge met her in the hallway.

"Leaving so soon?" he asked mildly, eyeing her suitcase. Mutely, Tamar nodded. "Let me just inspect the room and we'll get your paperwork all finalized before we check you out."

He swiped the master key and entered the bedroom. For a split second, Tamar considered bolting, but before she could the concierge was back. His dragon tattoo had wings and claws extended as though it was about to swoop down on a slow-moving deer.

"The manager will want to speak with you," he said, ushering her into the elevator.

The manager's office looked like a set designer's default of what a manager's office should look like. It had a large desk, file cabinets, a wheeled leather armchair, and a generic painting of a mountain range over the desk. The manager himself was a white man of average height wearing a navy business suit. He was writing in a notebook with a fountain pen, using a deep maroon ink.

"You must be the lamp-breaker from room 305," he chuckled as they walked in, setting down his pen. "You do understand that there will be an additional price to pay for this damage, yes?"

Tamar nodded.

"Excellent," he said, gesturing to the concierge, who went over to the file cabinets and retrieved a form. "Would you mind signing here please? This just acknowledges your responsibility for the property damage."

Tamar hesitated, but she could see no alternative. After all, in one way or another, she *had* been responsible for two broken lamps, even if they had been of evil design. An extra fee didn't seem like too much to pay for the freedom of two endangered pixies.

The manager watched her closely. "Perhaps you think you know better than professionals? Perhaps you feel we are being unfair?"

"She did seem genuinely confused about the first lamp, though I can't imagine how it was accidental. But the second one was definitely deliberate," the concierge offered.

"To break one lamp, Ms. Gold, could be carelessness. To lose two looks like maliciousness," the manager drawled.

He laughed at her surprised expression. "Oh, yes, I see you also read Oscar Wilde. I'm an educated man Ms. Gold, and you are guilty. Now sign." As he tapped the signature line impatiently, Tamar saw a scorpion tattoo curled over his knuckles in the same red ink as the concierge's dragon.

She signed.

The manager inspected the document carefully. "Contrary to what you may think, Ms. Gold, we are not cruel people. We simply have a business to run, and we cannot countenance troublemakers upsetting our regular clientele. So please, consider this a warning."

Deliberately, he splattered some of the pen's strange maroon ink over Tamar's signature. As he did, he muttered a few words in what Tamar was fairly confident was Biblical Hebrew.

Something shifted.

At first, Tamar thought a cloud over the sun had cast a shadow over her vision. The ink splotches on the paper now appeared a dark grey, nearly black. A moment later, she realized that the light was the same—it was the colors that had changed. The standard pale brown file folder was now an off-white. As Tamar lifted her eyes, she saw the whole room had shifted to shades of black and white. She looked down at her own hands, now alarmingly clammy. They too were now grey.

The manager smiled at her pleasantly. "Would you like directions to the nearest highway? I am sure the concierge can provide you with a map. There are many other lovely places to visit far from here."

He tapped her paperwork almost absently with a single long finger. The sudden thought struck Tamar that her face would likely be white with fear even without this strange absence of color bleaching her features. A panicked giggle caught in her throat. Seizing her suitcase, she nodded to the manager and the concierge and hurried out of the office and then the hotel.

Outside, San Cicaro's narrow streets, tall buildings, and cracked sidewalks were all in shades of grey. Even the glimpse of the ocean through the trees and fences was leached of its vibrant interplays of blues and greens. The whole world looked like she had stepped through a television screen into an old movie.

Tamar fled. But as far as she drove, hunched over her steering wheel with only her own gasping breaths as company, the colors never returned.

One year later, excerpt from The New England Artist:

This past Sunday, I had the opportunity to sit down for a chat with one of America's Up and Coming Artists, Tamar Gold. Gold's stunning pen and ink series "Secrets of San Cicaro," features images of fantasy creatures melded seamlessly into modern daily life. These drawings are surreal, gorgeous, and often haunting— an angel in a vest reading a novel, a golem vacuuming an office building, a pixie imprisoned in a lampshade, a naga sitting in a wheelchair eating an ice cream cone. And many, many more.

I meet Gold for lunch at a charming cafe with a patio overlooking the Boston Harbor. She arrives with a satchel slung over her shoulder and audibly sighs with relief as she sets it down.

"My sketchbook," she responds to my questioning gaze, and laughs, adding, "and a novel or four."

We make our introductions. Gold is plainly nervous, fidgeting with her menu, but relaxes slightly as I tell her how excited I am for this conversation.

Gold is a modern punk nerd, with her dyed pure white undercut and her bag full of books. She calls herself a typical millennial and cites Frida Kahlo as one of her role models. "Frida was always honest and stunning in her art," Gold explains, apparently on first-name terms with the famous artist. "Even when her art is surreal, she's telling a deeper kind of truth than the raw facts. Frida Kahlo faced painful truths head-on in a way most people avoid." Gold hesitates when I ask if there are any painful truths she's been avoiding.

"I think the artist's job is to tell the truth in one way or another," she says finally. "And that's what I try to do in my art."

One of Gold's most famous pieces, "Unicorn Rides," shows an exhausted unicorn pulling a carriage full of tourists. Many critics have suggested that this piece is a critique of the treatment of real-life horses by tourist companies. I ask if this is an example of the kind of truth she's talking about, and she nods.

"I won't say exactly what I was thinking when I created it. But I do think that it's interesting and problematic that people barely give overtired horses a second glance. But suddenly make it a unicorn and everyone's like 'oh that poor thing.' It really says something about our society's values when we empathize more with beings that, as far as we know, don't exist. More so than with the actual people and animals we interact with every day."

I ask her where the inspiration for her art comes from, and she cites a long history of loving fantasy novels.

"I read constantly as a kid, especially fantasy and fairytales," she says. "I read and reread all the Tamora Pierce books. Oh, and Enchanted Forest Chronicles, those are great. And I just really wanted for all that magic to be real, you know? I kept trying to cast spells or create potions or hunt for leprechauns, or whatever the magic system was in my most recent book. My mom thought it was so silly, but I just wanted to find something special, something inexplicable. So, in part, this series came from trying to find that magical in the mundane. And it was very much inspired by all my reading."

She shrugs after a moment and admits, "Sometimes I feel like an imposter. I didn't really invent the beings in my art or anything. In many ways, I just draw what I see."

"Then you must see a much more interesting world than the rest of us!" I say. She doesn't smile. I try again, pointing out the various rewards and accolades she's received to honor her talent. She shrugs and concedes the point ("I'm glad my art has moved so many people, and I am very grateful that I have been able to make a living doing what I love") but she doesn't seem convinced.

Early in her career, Gold regularly used a far more psychedelic palette in her paintings. Her recent series, done entirely in black ink, is so different from her previous style that it almost seems as if they were created by different people. When I ask if she has any plans to return to her colorful roots, Gold responds characteristically, with a tangent about a book.

"There's this section in Carpe Jugulum, by Terry Pratchett, where they're talking about the nature of sin, and one character discusses nuance and shades of grey. Then the other character says that there's no such thing as shades of grey, there's only white that's got grubby. I think about that a lot, when I walk through the world and with my art. Lots of times, nuance really does matter, but sometimes we get so obsessed with balance that we lose sight of basic ethics. People think they can just do what they want because they have the money and the power. There aren't shades of grey to that, just white that's got really grubby."

There is a hint of darkness in her eyes, perhaps the source of the tension that makes her artwork so compelling. I ask if there's something in particular that she's thinking of. She stares out behind me for a moment, blinking rapidly. I turn to follow her gaze to the sunlight shimmering on the waves, fiery golds and yellows mingling with the cool greens and oranges of the water. "Let's leave that vague."

Something tells me not to press the issue.

Instead, I ask about the choice of San Cicaro as the location for her drawings.

"It has beautiful and unique architecture that was fun and challenging to draw. And, well, everyone knows San Cicaro is weird. It seemed the obvious choice."

I have a sense that this is not the full truth, so I press further. She confirms that she visited San Cicaro the summer before beginning this project but declines to say more about that visit and its influence on her.

I ask if she has any plans to return to the city.

She looks out at the ocean again.

"No," she says. "I found what I was looking for in San Cicaro, and lost more than I knew I had there."

She lays out a neat stack of bills that constitutes a generous tip and tucks it under the water glass to ensure it won't blow away. She stands up and picks up her satchel while saying, "It was lovely speaking with you."

As she begins to walk away, I can't resist calling out, "What were you looking for?"

Tamar looks back over her shoulder and responds with three words: "Magic, of course!"

As she hurries off, I am left reflecting on her answer. Like much of her art, it raises more questions than it answers, but it is also very typically Tamar Gold—this white-haired nerdy artist who creates more vibrant and haunting scenes with her "shades of white" than many do with a full color palette.

Having heard about her early quests for magic, it does seem obvious that that is what she went searching for while trying to revitalize her artistic career... and, looking at her art, I can almost believe—almost—that she did, as she laughingly claimed, find magic in San Cicaro.

Through the Eyes of Others

JC Hemphill

Most people don't know you can purchase access to other people's webcams. We all know the government can do such a thing. They can even deactivate the little light that lets you know the webcam is on, leaving users unaware that they're being watched by some pimply intel specialist in Virginia. It's all very Orwellian.

But like any crime, enterprising entrepreneurs figured out how to monetize this voyeuristic hack.

So here we are.

For a price, you too can play the part of pimply intel specialist. Pick a target, wire some bitcoin, then bingo-bango, you're in. Watch as that barista you've had a crush on for the last year changes clothes in her bedroom. Hit record as that a-hole boss who calls you "bucko" scours the net for the vilest porn available, then blackmail him for a corporate fast-track to the job of your dreams. Check up on your ex-wife and see if that prick with a full head of hair she's been dating has rounded third base yet. Choose the roulette option and watch as a randomly selected family in Wisconsin pays their bills, does their homework, bickers, laughs, prays, and just goes about their lives. Your private little reality show.

Or there are always celebrities to check-up on.

It's real. Just ask Skip. One of those enterprising entrepreneurs. He knows all about it.

Mostly Skip doesn't ask why his clients want access to other people's webcams. Or the earpieces on their smartphones, Google Homes, laptops, what have you. (Yeah, Skip offers that service as well.) But some people like to talk. Even when they're doing something illegal. Or, perhaps, *especially* when they're doing something illegal. A lot of clients aren't used to breaking the law. These are people who consider themselves fine, upstanding citizens. (Besides, simply watching somebody isn't *really* wrong, is it?) This is a first for them. An exciting taboo. So they get nervous. And nervous people, sometimes they won't shut up. Even when you tell them to.

God how Skip wishes they'd shut up.

A new message had been posted to Skip's PM board:

> She's wicked hot. Like...... I can't even describ how hot. Bitch could b a modal. When... I guess I shouldn't use his real name shuld I? When my freind suggested u I couldn't even beleive it Thank u so much for doing this its the most amazing thing ever!!
>
> Did u get my other message?? Is that every thing u need to find her?? How long until I can start watching?? What if her cpu isnt turned on??
>
> Thanks again
>
> —R.G.

Skip shook his head. It cracked him up that these people always tried being sneaky in their messages. As if Skip couldn't figure out their real identities. Really, it'd be easier to unmask R.G., whose email was TheDude420HellYeah@ yahoo.com, than it would be to ride the elevator down to the first floor of his apartment building. In fact, Skip had dug up R.G.'s real name over his morning coffee. Just in case R.G.—Ryan Grouper, a mechanic from San Cicaro, California who spent half his day on Tinder with zero success—decided to threaten Skip with calling the cops. Not that the police could do much to find Skip, but still, it was his policy to always—*always*—CYA.

And if it was one of the many governmental cybercrime agencies his clients thought they were protecting themselves from, well then Skip had some news for them: If the feds had access to Skip's private message server, then the client was already boned. Big time.

Not Skip, though. Skip CYAed. Hard. He was nothing more than a ghost in the machine. Unmasking him would be like trying to catch a dragon with a butterfly net. More than impossible, straight-up absurd.

Skip typed his reply:

Yes, I received your previous message.

Yes, that's all I need.

Tonight sometime.

If it's a desktop or an open laptop with battery power, it doesn't matter, I can still activate the cam.

Do NOT contact me again until you hear from me.

Skip closed the message board and got to work. After thirty or forty of these webcam hacks, it was pretty mindless going. In this case, it was some chick named Sadie Slight, also of San Cicaro.

The name rang a bell.

Idly, Skip had looked it up. On the mainstream sites, San Cicaro was just another city, smaller than San Francisco. So far, so meh. However, there had been a plane crash over San Cicaro Bay a few months ago. A private plane coming in from Seattle. That's why he knew the place.

But when Skip put "San Cicaro" into YouTube, he got weirder results than he was expecting. Loads of conspiracy theories and found footage; purple lights, UFOs in the sky, that sort of thing. There were half-seen phantoms in the park, the comment section at war over whether the creeping figure between the trees was a sasquatch or a wendigo. The vid with the highest view count was shaky-cam footage of the plane crash itself, taken at night from the shore by some screaming Mexican lady and her Asian buddy. Footage which showed a plane colliding with *something*, mid-air, in a cascade of vivid red fire. Something with huge, spindly wings, which roared as it died...

It all looked like low-rez bullshit to Skip. There was no excuse for video this shitty in the age of smartphones. The channel P.H.a.N.T.o.M Investigations had the best production values, but also looked the fakest. Skip chided himself. He was getting distracted. None of this helped him access Sadie's system. Fortunately, he had his own methods of doing just that.

Like most people, Sadie's idea of net security was a long password. Don't forget to make it a mix of letters and numbers! Throw in a hashtag to really throw those dirty hackers off! All of it culminating in the oh-so-clever "red1152VELVET#"

That'll protect my computer! It's so clever that I'm going to use it for my Amex login, too! And my Wells Fargo account!

Sigh. A simple dictionary attack combined with various iterations of digits that would be easy for her to remember (in this case, the last four of her social—thank you DMV backdoor!), and Skip was in. So easy it's like the girl *wanted* to be hacked.

Several hours, two cups of coffee and a Monster energy drink later, and Skip was in Sadie Slight's apartment.

Apparently, she kept her desktop on the counter, facing toward her kitchen. No Sadie, but he saw the top of a wooden stool just beyond the keyboard and imagined her sitting there checking Facebook. From the mini-fridge and single cooktop plugged into the wall, he guessed this was a studio apartment. Dirty dishes were piled in the sink. He could almost smell the lump of green mold growing inside the clear Tupperware that had been left out.

"I don't care how hot this girl is," Skip muttered, "she's *nasty*."

He was ready to send the video feed on to R.G. and be done with this job. All he needed to do was activate the computer's mic so R.G. would be able to see *and* hear. It also meant that if Sadie decided to slap a post-it note over her webcam, as so many people had since Snowden, R.G. would at least have audio.

The job was complete a few minutes later. Well before the promised ETA of "tonight sometime." He knew this because his own computer speakers woke up with the sound of a woman's voice. Sadie Slight, no doubt.

"…care what the lineup is, it's all the same to me," the voice said in the overloud tone of someone speaking on the phone. "Just get *somebody*. Seriously, if you bother me again with this crap, I'm canceling the whole thing."

Skip clicked over to the video feed out of curiosity—after all, "bitch could b a modal," right?

But, alas, she wasn't in the kitchen. Just heaps of dirty dishes and a Tupperware full of green fuzz. He guessed she'd ended the call because she'd stopped talking, but it had sounded like she'd been standing pretty close to the computer. Maybe she'd make an appearance soon…

After waiting a couple of minutes without seeing or hearing from her, Skip gave up. He returned to his message board and typed:

Done. Transfer the rest of the coin and I'll activate the link. It'll work for seven days, then the link deactivates. You know the deal. If you want more, you pay more. Every Saturday.

What his clients didn't know was that after a week, the price would go up by thirty percent. Nine times out of ten, they paid it. Another thing they didn't know was that voyeurism was ravishingly addictive. Up there with heroin and crack. They'd spend hours watching. Then entire days. Entire days would quickly become entire days and nights. They'd hardly sleep. But they wouldn't mind. Sleeping might mean they'd miss something. They'd call into work sick. Suddenly they'd have some exotic flu that kept them home for two weeks straight. Just staring. Their skin growing pale. Dark rings popping up around their eyes. Wild mood swings. Teeth grinding.

Just like a junkie.

So, after their second week of mainlining the online version of a peephole in the wall of the girl's restroom, Skip *doubled* the original price. And they'd pay. Even if that meant selling their TV or their blood or whatever. They'd get that money.

That was the beauty of Skip's gig. He never felt bad about extorting more and more money from these people. In a way, they deserved it.

"Well hello," the voice of Sadie Slight said.

He'd forgotten to turn off the feed and for a second thought about switching over to the video to see if she'd made an appearance. But the way she'd said hello, he guessed she was greeting someone at the front door. Which meant she wasn't in the kitchen. And since he had no desire to see her moldy Tupperware again, he didn't bother. So he let her go on talking as a second female voice joined Sadie's. They were *soooo* happy to see each other, daaahling.

Sadie was one of those girls. The kind who called people darling and said it with an H instead of an R.

Whatever, it was time to package the feed for R.G. and establish the hyperlink. Let the daaahlings yammer on about their favorite purses or whatever. If he knew his clients, R.G. was obsessively checking the board for new messages from Skip. Which meant the payment would arrive any minute. Any second. And…

Ding!

The auto-notification he'd set-up to let him know when a deposit had been made. A quick check confirmed that R.G. had paid in full.

Already Skip was dreaming of ways to spend the money. The new *Planet of the Apes* movie was out on Blu-ray. Which was *easily* the most kickass movie franchise ever. Maybe it was time to upgrade to 4K Ultra. That would mean he'd need a new 4K-Ultra-compatible Blu-ray player. And a new 4K-Ultra-compatible TV. Might as well upgrade from his current fifty inch to a seventy. R.G.'s payment wouldn't cover all that, but his next one would. So hell, he might as well go ahead and buy new Bose surround speakers while he's out. R.G. was the obsessive type. Skip could feel it.

"Are you sure it's okay for me to stay with you?" the new voice said from somewhere inside Sadie's apartment.

"Absolutely, don't even worry about it," Sadie replied. "The massive dick your boyfriend turned out to be… stay as long as you need. *Mi casa* and all that."

"Okay, Sadie," Skip said to his monitor, "it was nice getting to know you, but I'm not interested in your soap-opera life."

If CYA was his number one rule, his number two was *don't get high on your own supply.* The last thing he needed was to waste his days watching strangers yakking on about their tiny little problems, doing their tiny little chores, living their tiny little lives. Maybe his clients got their rocks off that way, but to him it sounded indistinguishable from hell.

A couple of clicks later and he was ready to sever the connection to Sadie Slight forever. He had his finger over the mouse button to do it and everything. Until he heard...

"So how are we going to do it?" the chick with the dick boyfriend asked in hushed tones.

And here was the clincher, the sentences that really prevented Skip from clicking:

Sadie said, "Very slowly. Very *painfully*."

Skip cocked his head to the side and leaned closer to his computer speaker, unsure he'd heard correctly.

Were these chicks talking about getting revenge on the dick boyfriend?

He switched over to the video feed. Moldy Tupperware. Heaps of dirty dishes. No Sadie. No scorned girlfriend.

"Good," was the other chick's response. And again, "Good. He deserves it."

"Oh honey," Sadie said, and here Skip imagined her taking her friend's hand and holding it warmly, maybe even patting it. "*Of course* he does. You just let me handle it, okay? Nobody does that to my BFF. Nobody."

Skip couldn't help himself. "What the hell did he do?" he said to the computer. "I bet he cheated. Nothing sets a chick off like a cheater."

A little voice in the back of his head reminded him that he wouldn't really know what set chicks off. Ha! that voice said. One two-month-long relationship in high school almost nine years ago doesn't qualify you to know crap about chicks, Skip. You don't even have a sister, Skip. Heck, you barely have a *mom*, Skip.

Those thoughts vanished as the conversation in some studio apartment in San Cicaro continued.

"What did you have in mind?" the other chick asked.

"How about a drink, first?" Sadie's voice changed in a way that told Skip she was on the move. Moving closer to the computer. And then there she was, walking into the kitchen. And. Holy. Balls. Was. She. Hot.

Bitch could b a modal.

Skip's mouth dropped open. Literally. Just popped right open like some bug-eyed, heart-beating-out-of-his-chest cartoon character.

Blue-black hair the color of a raven's wing. Skin like milk. Sharp, pixie-like facial features topping a smooth, curving body. Her bare right shoulder covered in colorful tattoos that disappeared beneath the back of her tank top, the left shoulder a contrasting blank slate that said "POW! My body and my tattoos are both works of art."

Not short, but not taller than Skip, either.

In other words, if he were to *Weird-Science* up his ideal woman, her name would be Sadie Slight. And her hips would sashay exactly like the woman bending over to open her mini-fridge in front of him.

A single word came to his lips: "Jesus."

He watched as Sadie retrieved a pair of beer bottles and spun around on the ball of her foot, facing the webcam full on. Skip's heart pretty much stopped beating. Then the sight of her exposed navel jump-started it. Her looks had killed, then resurrected him. She used her hip to bump the fridge shut and glided back off camera.

Okay, so maybe Skip didn't respect what guys like R.G. spent their time doing, but he sure as hell respected R.G.'s taste in women. He wouldn't be surprised if this chick had five or six stalkers trying to hack her webcam. And seven or eight crowding the tree branches right outside her bedroom window.

"So," Sadie said, accompanied by a couple of *fthsss* sounds as she twisted the beer bottles open. Skip imagined her handing one over to her friend. Then he wondered if the friend was half as hot as Sadie. Maybe so. Hot chicks flocked together like birds. "I'm thinking something biblical. Nothing says wrath like the testaments."

"I'll toast to that," the friend said, followed by a clink of beer bottles.

"Stoned to death?" Sadie suggested.

"Too easy."

"Boils?"

"No, not painful enough."

"Crucifixion?"

Damn this is getting dark, Skip thought.

"Meh, getting better," the friend replied.

"Okay, how about blood seeping out of his every pore? Not enough to kill him, but enough to make him pass out so he can wake up and have it happen all over again. Death would come eventually. But not until he spent a couple of days suffering."

A pause. And then, from the friend, "Now *that's* more like it. Let's do that."

Yeah, sure, they were joking around. Two angry women fantasizing about doing some damage to a pig boyfriend wasn't crazy—he guessed lots of broken-hearted women had similar conversations—but at the same time, these two didn't sound like they were spitting hyperbole. Their tone... so deadpan... it gave Skip a chill. As if they were one-hundred-percent convinced they could make the guy bleed from every pore. Not a game, but a real, tangible option.

Skip chuckled uneasily.

It was strange, but Sadie's macabre bent sort of made her hotter. This girl wasn't as stuck-up as her daaahling suggested. No, not stuck-up at all. Edgy. Dangerous. And those two things meant she was probably also a little kinky.

"When?" the friend asked.

When? Skip thought, his unease about their seriousness jumping another notch.

"These things take time," Sadie said. "And preparation. You don't want to know what happens if we rush this. Girl I knew from way back, she tried something in high school, blew up her whole life. So, I want you to be sure about this Natalie, and be patient."

Finally, Skip thought, a name.

"Okay. Fine. Sure," Natalie replied, sounding excited. "What do we need to do?"

"Do you have anything of his? Something with his DNA on it?"

Natalie *tsked*. "No. I had a little going-away bonfire while he was at work. His clothes, his bathroom stuff, even that World's Worst Boss mug that he thinks is so damned funny. Well, *that* didn't burn, but any DNA on it probably did."

"Can you get the ashes?"

"Hmm… I think so. He usually gets home about ten past six." Skip's eyes jumped to the clock in the corner of his screen. It was 3:33 p.m. his time, 4:33 p.m. in San Cicaro. "It's only a fifteen-minute drive from here. If I leave now, I should be able to get in and out before he gets home."

"That's up to you," Sadie said, her voice moving again. She appeared on camera just long enough to set her empty beer bottle on the counter beside the full sink. Chick could drink. Which seemed to confirm Skip's assumptions of kinkiness. But trying to collate the incredible perfection of this woman with the filthiness of her apartment made his brain overload. Obviously she could afford the flaw, he decided, resigning himself to the mess and the fuzzy Tupperware growth.

Natalie sounded like a woman who'd reached a decision. "All right, I'm doing it."

"Good for you!" Sadie said, once again off camera. "I'll get everything ready while you're gone."

"Thanks, love."

Skip heard some rustling, like maybe they were hugging. Then he heard the door open and shut. A deadbolt clicked into place. Feet shuffled as Sadie walked through her apartment. She either had linoleum or tile. Not carpet. And listening to those feet shuffle, Skip realized he was tensed up. Waiting for her next appearance, like his next breath depended on seeing her again.

Skip was a lucky boy because those feet shuffled straight into the kitchen. She passed so close to the computer that he got a perfect shot of her midriff. Her skin was so white it shone. Like it was preserved in wax.

She stopped halfway between the computer and the mini-fridge, framing her squarely in the camera's lens, from the back of her knees to the top of her head. She was looking around at the cabinets as if trying to remember the location of something. Skip leaned closer to his monitor and stared as she put one hand on the counter and used it to steady herself while she stood on tiptoes to reach a top shelf. The act stretched her already tight tank top, exposing even more midriff.

He watched as she turned into profile, a small wooden bowl in her hands. He leaned even closer as she set that bowl on the counter between the

Tupperware and the computer. This gave Skip a good view as she opened a silverware drawer.

She produced a paring knife and removed the cardboard sleeve covering the blade. She looked the blade over before touching her thumb to the sharp edge. She looked at this connection of blade and flesh curiously, as if she wasn't sure how to proceed. Then she ran her thumb down the entire length of the blade. At first, Skip thought she was just grazing it enough to see if it was sharp. The blood running down the inside of her palm, then her forearm, told him otherwise.

She added the knife to the pile of dishes in the sink and used her other hand to pinch the sides of her sliced thumb. She squeezed. The wound blossomed like a plastic coin purse. She held it over the wooden bowl and let the blood drip in. Collecting. Skip's eyes flicked between this and her face. No signs of pain. Not even the slightest discomfort. Unlike Skip. Skip, who wanted to crawl backward out of his office chair, run into the bathroom, and slam the door shut. Escape the image. The dark blood.

But he didn't.

He watched.

And when she was done, when the dripping from her thumb ebbed and the small wooden bowl was half-full, she bent her knees until her eyes were level with the Tupperware. The one with the mold in it. Fuzzy, green and so gross Skip still thought he could smell it. Like it was right there on his desk. Its fungal spores spreading. Drifting through the air, up his nose, into his lungs.

He watched as she used a fingernail to tap on the lid.

That fuzzy green growth… it twitched.

And because he was watching so closely, Skip screamed.

He looked over his shoulders at his own apartment, knowing there was no one around to witness his girly outburst but checking anyway. By the time he looked back at the screen, Sadie Slight was gone. The wooden bowl and the Tupperware were still on the counter, however.

"What *is* that?" he whispered, as if he worried Sadie or the fuzz in her Tupperware might overhear.

He squinted at the screen. The thing in the plastic container wasn't moving. He enlarged the image as much as he could without distorting the live feed beyond recognition, focusing on the lump of mold—or, what he'd *thought* was a lump of mold—but it basically looked the same: like a baked potato that'd been left out for months to grow a thick, green coat. He could enhance the image with higher resolution if he had it on his video editing software, but it wasn't.

Skip smacked his palm against his forehead. "Dummy!"

He wasn't recording this. If he was, he could transfer it and get a better look. And all he had to do to record it was…

Click

The little red circle in the bottom left corner. A timer appeared, letting him know that a recording was being made. The whole thing was going to his external hard drive.

That was when Sadie showed back up, her thumb bandaged. Her step was still light. No cares weighed her down. Which blew Skip's mind. How could she be so nonchalant? Just thinking about all that blood gave him shivers. But this chick acted like it was another day at the office, like slicing your thumb open and squeezing three tablespoons of blood out was just fine and spiffy and wonderful, daaahling.

She walked over to the counter and stood in front of the bowl and the Tupperware. She lifted the bowl, wafted it below her nostrils like a fine wine, then pried the lid of the Tupperware open with her other hand. The lump of mold moved. It slowly pushed itself against the inside of the Tupperware. A hesitant, gelatinous movement, like it meant to hide but was realizing it was too late.

Sadie reached inside with her index finger extended.

"What are you doing?" Skip yelled, as if this were a horror movie and she a sex-crazed teen opening the closet door where the masked killer hid.

She used her finger to stroke the mold—the creature? the thing?—and said something too quietly for Skip to hear. Something soothing, from the tone. *It's okay, I'm not going to hurt you,* his mind filled in. And then the lump seemed to relax, spread back out into the container. A hole opened near one end and it took Skip a second to realize that hole was a mouth and before he knew it she was pouring the blood from the bowl into the Tupperware, right into that hole, that mouth. The lump was drinking as much as it could and what it couldn't was splashing everywhere, staining its clean, green coat, beading on the inside of the Tupperware. Skip heard the splashing, the hungry lapping, and couldn't understand any of it.

He closed his eyes, squeezed them tight, too freaked out to do anything else. And then Sadie was speaking softly to it again, praising it, and Skip's brain started *screaming, shrieking* in an effort to block out her voice and damn it how was any of this *possible* and what the actual *fuck* and *Jesus* he would never sleep again, would he?

Everything went silent.

Skip waited a few beats before cracking an eye. At first, he was too afraid to look at the monitor, seeing only his keyboard. He opened the other eye and looked up. Not slowly, but fast, like ripping off a Band-Aid.

The Tupperware, the bowl, and Sadie were all gone.

He realized he'd been holding his breath and let it out.

His first instinct was to rationalize. He hadn't seen what he thought he'd seen. It was a gerbil or something... that someone had dyed green... that drank human blood... That was a thing, right?

Hell no. And even if it was, why would somebody keep one as a pet?

Skip reached for the mouse, intending to quickly end the video feed before anymore bat-shit crazy happened. But he couldn't do it, his hand wouldn't work right. He clicked and clicked while waving the little arrow around the screen and nothing was happening because he couldn't hit that tiny close button at the top. So he gave up trying, leaned over the side of his office chair, and turned the entire computer off. Then he turned the monitor off, too, just to be safe.

He slumped back in his chair and didn't blink for a good minute after.

Skip refused to reboot his computer. Which kind of made him feel like a giant pussy, but so what? He was home alone, nobody around to see how freaked out he was, so why not be freaked out?

No reason that he could tell. Bravery was a construct. Something that only existed when other people were looking. Mostly women. If not for them, every man would be holed up at home, trying to impress exactly no one with his "bravery."

Still. Looking across his apartment at the blank screen of his computer made him more ashamed than he felt comfortable with, so he turned the TV on. He watched reruns of *Family Guy*, but he knew the episodes too well. His mind wandered. Instead of paying attention to the show, his brain threw up images of that mold. Its little mouth opening… blood pouring… the thirsty sound of it drinking…

He jumped up from his couch and grabbed the controller for his PlayStation. Shooting some zombie Nazis should do the trick.

Problem there was all the blood. Whether he was winning or losing, there was blood everywhere. Which hadn't been a problem before. But now, he couldn't help comparing the fake video game blood to the real deal. That thumb, being squeezed like a pimple, dripping into a wooden bowl that seemed reserved for that exact thing. Was that how she always fed that… *whatever* in the Tupperware? Did it also eat beef jerky or dog food or something? Or was this a daily ritual to keep it alive? How many times had Sadie Slight sliced herself open for it?

Skip turned the game off. Thought about going out. But where? It's not like he had anywhere to go. His entire world was right here in his 927-square-foot apartment. All his friends were on the net. Digital. Not only did he not go over to their houses, he didn't even know where they lived. Most were in other states.

The store occurred to him. Time to upgrade to 4K Ultra, right? But that dragged his thoughts over to his bank account and R.G.'s recent bitcoin deposit. Skip had never sent him the link.

"Shit!"

He checked the clock on his phone. 10:02 p.m. He suddenly realized it was dark outside. Had been for a while. And it was an hour later in San Cicaro. R.G. was probably going apeshit, thinking he'd been scammed.

"Shit! *Shit!*"

Skip was a lot of things, but he wasn't a thief. Everyone has their lines in the sand and his was there. He believed people should work for what they earned. Had said so in many comment sections on news articles about taxes and welfare and entitled millennials. Maybe that was old fashioned of him, but oh well. He had no intentions of being a hypocrite.

He went to his desk, sat down, and hesitantly turned the power on to his computer and monitor. Once both were booted, he went straight to his PM board where he found a slew of increasingly agitated messages from R.G.

9:16 P.M. — Hello??

9:17 P.M. — U there or what

9:31 P.M. — Did u send alredy??

9:44 P.M. — Dude if your riping me off Im gonna kill u

Skip chuckled at this one. The internet, unlike the real world, was full of tough guys.

9:50 P.M. — seriously MFer u better come thru soon I know people u arent the only hacker POS holler back b4 shit gets real AND SHIT WILL GET REAL BELEVE ME MFER

From there the messages came every minute or two, each longer and more raged-out than the last. The threats and capitalized letters culminated sixty-one minutes after the initial message had been sent with

U DED BITCH

Skip went ahead and assumed "DED" meant "DEAD."

He considered his response for a second. R.G. was hot. Explaining the delay was going to be nearly impossible. If years of trolling had taught him anything, it was that emotions like rage and hate translated into ones and zeros with ease, while things like reason and understanding failed to translate at all. The internet spoke fluent angst. But using the same medium to placate the angsty was like tossing a glass of water at a drowning man.

R.G., I apologize. Sincerely. Something strange happened and I got sidetracked. 100% my fault. Please don't think I intend to scam you. No Nigerian princes here, believe me. I'll even give you a full refund.

He thought about adding more, but decided it was best not to force too much all at once. First he'd let R.G. digest that they were communicating again. Then he could get into the other stuff. Like mold.

Skip couldn't decide if it was surprising or totally expected, but R.G. responded instantly.

U dead

The fact that he'd spelled "dead" correctly was a good sign. He'd calmed down. Not much—it was, after all, still a threat on his life—but at least he wasn't so whipped up that he was misspelling basic words.

I completely understand. It's a lot of money. Like I said, I'll give you a full refund. In fact, I'm sending it now...

Skip did as promised, transferring the bitcoin in less time than it took R.G. to respond.

And the link?? U sending that to??

Okay, so maybe he wasn't ever going to spell *every* basic word correctly, no matter how calm, but at least they were making progress.

That's tougher. Honestly, I don't think you'd want it. She's

Skip paused there. How did he explain that the chick this stalker was obsessed with was... what? A masochist with a pet alien? Was that even the right thing to call her? What exactly did you call someone who fed their blood to a baked-potato-sized mold-creature?

He deleted "She's" and sent the message.

R.G.'s response was quicker than any other.

keep the money i wantthat lunk

You don't understand. That Sadie Slight is into some weird stuff. Like, really, really, REALLY weird stuff. Gross stuff.

BS you want her for uself SHES MINE AHOLE

No dude. Look. She was talking to some other girl about getting revenge on the other girl's boyfriend. They wanted to mess him up and I don't think they were joking. Then I watched her cut herself. It was all kinds of nasty. Demented stuff. If this is someone you know IRL, I'd keep far away from her. Seriously.

R.G.'s next response took much longer. So long that Skip started to think he'd lost him. But no.

Was the other girls name Natalie??

That made the top of Skip's spine tingle. He typed in a flourish.

Yes. It was. Do you know her?

Natalie is my girlfreind She hasnt been home today

Skip did a mental double take. During his research on R.G. earlier that morning, he'd seen that Ryan Grouper spent a lot of time on Tinder looking for a hookup. And even though he swiped right on plenty of chicks, nobody swiped right back. Skip had developed an image of an ugly, lonely boy. Certainly no girlfriend.

It occurred to him that if Natalie *was* his girlfriend, that meant he probably knew Sadie through her.

No wonder she torched his stuff.

Okay, look. I don't know what's up, but it's not good. I think they might try to hurt you.

How??

No idea. I don't know about your girl, but Sadie is psycho. She has a thing for blood. Hers, yours, anybody's I'm guessing.

Several seconds passed without a response. And then:

Send link i want to see

Skip thought this over. He'd found himself in the middle of something here. No telling where it would go. Maybe R.G. would do something stupid. Like a preemptive strike on his ex. For all Skip knew, he was the abusive type. There was also the possibility that the girls really didn't plan to do anything and had been speaking hyperbolically.

Though after what he'd witnessed, he found that unlikely. No, somehow he knew they were the real deal. How they would make him bleed from every pore, Skip didn't know. But maybe that was euphemistic; maybe they intended to stab him a lot or something? And if that was the case, then R.G. deserved a heads up.

So he sent the link. No explanations, no mentions of bloodthirsty mold, no promises it would help.

That was the last time he exchanged messages with R.G.

It was almost midnight and Skip was afflicted with the itch of curiosity. He'd never left his desk, was just clicking around the usual websites, half-heartedly trying to ignore his stubborn urge.

On a more primal level he wanted to embrace the itch—he wanted to *scratch*.

Partially because of the unanswered questions bugging him. Partially for another glimpse of the mold. But mostly it was the intrigue. The way all the players were intertwined, a personal drama between lovers and demons, complete with revenge, violence, sex appeal and sinister villainesses. Nothing on TV or in the movies would ever be so real, so visceral, so emotionally connecting. No matter how good the acting. No matter how masterfully crafted the CG. This was an experience cut straight from real life. Something he could tell his digital friends about.

Something to get those Likes.

Something tangible that would make him feel interesting and desired and alive.

Really, this was the rarest of chances, afforded by his mad hacking skills and the happenstance of being in the right place at the right time. Only *he* could possibly stand witness. If not for the timid voice whispering in the back of his mind. *Nightmare fuel*, it warned him over and over, *PTSD, you fool*. But he'd already be watching the feed of Sadie Slight's apartment.

Skip closed his web browser. He rearranged the action figures on his desk, straightened some, moved others. He picked at the dirt beneath his fingernails. He adjusted the contrast on his monitor, checked the time and cleaned the dust off his keyboard. He pretended that he hadn't already made his decision to scratch that itch so hard it made his leg thump.

The video feed filled his computer screen a moment later.

It was dark in her apartment. Only the green glow of the digital clock on a microwave hanging in midair offered any illumination of the kitchen. It shouldn't have been surprising considering the time of night, yet it was. He'd been expecting more. What exactly he wasn't sure, but not this. Not a void of lights. Activity. Intrigue.

Then his ears began to detect what his eyes couldn't. He heard movement. A kind of shuffling. Like two pieces of felt rubbing together. And tapping. A fingernail on the countertop. No. Countertop wasn't right. A fingernail tapping on something wooden. Something hollow. Like a bowl. A fingernail tapping on a wooden bowl.

Staring into the darkness dominating his screen, listening to those ominous sounds, Skip realized he felt cold. Mostly in his feet. He thought about going for some socks, but doing that would mean looking away from his monitor. Who knew what he might miss? Maybe something good.

He ran his fingers through his beard. He cleared his throat. Adding his own sounds to those coming through his computer speakers comforted him. A reminder that he was hundreds of miles away and not right there in Sadie's kitchen. Which was exactly how it felt. As if he'd been transported there and was standing in the dark, desperately trying to piece together what was going on around him.

A hiss interrupted the intermittent sounds of rubbing and tapping. Not the hiss of a snake, but of air escaping. Gas leaking. A tire deflating.

Someone spoke. Whispered, pained, their voice escaping like air. "*Please.*" A man's voice.

The fingernail tapping continued. As did the slow felt-on-felt rubbing. All of it emanating from the dark. Secrets only Skip could hear.

In that darkness he imagined the mold moving. Sliding against a piece of fabric. A shirt or a tablecloth. Sadie sitting on the floor cross-legged, alone but for the man with the escaping voice, tapping away on the edge of her bloodstained bowl. A hypnotizing beat for her pet. The flute to a dancing cobra, the bell to Pavlov's dogs.

Skip wasn't thinking of running for the bathroom or turning his computer off. Not this time. He had to know. Had to see. Despite the cold spreading up from his feet, the anxiety prickling his mind, the mad thudding in his chest, he *needed* to see. Was R.G. the man with the escaping voice? Of course he was. Skip knew as much. That wasn't even the question. Not really. R.G. had undoubtedly raced over to Sadie's apartment after discovering his ex was shacked up with the woman of his intense desire. No, the question was, could they make R.G. bleed from every pore? Hyperbole or reality? And if the latter, could Skip endure witnessing it?

That itch, it needed scratching, and Skip was prepared to scrape it raw.

A voice floated out of the dark. Not the man's voice, but Sadie's. Light, melodic, the voice of a woman reciting a prayer as she closed her eyes at bedtime; a familiar verse meant to lull herself to sleep.

"With others, you bear no respect. Yet for yourself, you possess infinite respect. With others, nothing is sacred. With yourself, everything is sacred."

She paused, allowing the vacuum of noise to be filled by the soft rubbing and the steady tapping and Skip knew, somehow *knew*, that R.G. was nearby, unmoving but in great pain as he bled from every orifice, every pore. As the thing from the Tupperware moved over his body, sipping his blood as it squeezed through the tiny pores in his skin, taking its time in the knowledge that its source of food would produce for a long time to come. No hurry, no rush, free to take pleasure in its feast.

It was funny that Skip didn't seem to care if this was true or not. Perhaps R.G. was in agony, dying, or perhaps it was all an invention of Skip's mind. Or perhaps it wasn't funny at all? He wasn't sure. Skip only knew that the cold spreading up from his feet was now in his chest and in his arms and reaching up his neck and into his head and that it wouldn't let him move or look away or care. He would watch. Not because he wanted to or because he needed to, but because he was *forced* to by some power emanating through his speakers.

"You know no others," the soft voice of Sadie Slight resumed. "You know only yourself. You know not the pain you transmit, only the joy you absorb. You, the watcher..."

She petered off, as if she'd forgotten the next line in her prayer. The sounds continued, the green clock hovering in the dark changed by a minute, the slow agony of escaping air slithered through the background. That sound traveled through the speakers, up Skip's arm, up his neck and into his ear, where it burrowed and nested and made him want to scream. But he couldn't, because the cold had reached every part of him. It held him and made him hers. And he realized with a new kind of coldness in his heart that she wasn't speaking to R.G. as he'd assumed. Those whispered words... they weren't for a cheating boyfriend. No, those words, traveling from Sadie's lips across hundreds of miles into Skip's brain, those words were for him.

She had brought him here.

"You, the watcher, will forever be aware of others," she said to Skip, so clear now, right there with him, originating in his own apartment, not so distant at all. "No longer will you think of yourself. When you watch, you will watch through the eyes of empathy. Your vision will be their vision. Their pain will be your pain. In this way, you will forever be changed."

A tear rolled down Skip's cheek as he stared into the darkness of his computer monitor. He wished he could look away. Things were shifting in there now. Shadows of shadows. Briefly blocking the green clock light. Raising more sounds. Feet slapping tile or linoleum or whatever Sadie's floor was made of. A flurry of too many feet. Far too many. Dozens of people crammed into that tiny kitchen. Swarming in front of the green light. Whispering half-secrets to one another. Taunting Skip. Pushing through his monitor now, bending the glass outward, into his apartment, shadows of shadows, a horde of them, reaching out to Skip, feeling him. Invading him.

Sadie's voice rose above the others, repeating a single phrase over and over, until it was the only thing Skip could hear.

You will forever see.

You will forever see.

You

Will

Forever

See

Skip went a month and six days without turning his computer on after that night. Nor did he leave his apartment. And even though he subsisted off the many restaurants that delivered to him, he lost twenty-one pounds.

He mostly spent his time watching TV. Nothing too heavy. Cartoons mostly. *Family Guy, Rick and Morty, Adventure Time*. Nothing with real people.

Stuff with real people was too hard to watch. Too emotional. The few times he did watch shows with real people in them—particularly dramas—he found himself overcome with emotion. Any pathetic situation, any pain a character suffered, it triggered him in ways he couldn't understand.

As if they were transmitting their pain to him.

It didn't matter that it was acted, scripted, unreal. An episode of *Law and Order* where a single mother found her young daughter smothered to death (by her own estranged father, it turned out) hit Skip so hard that he spent two whole days curled up in bed, sobbing, moaning and thinking about how unfair it was for that single mother to have everything stripped from her like that. And that little girl—so young, so much of her life still to live—it was the most tragic thing this dismal life had to offer.

It was, almost, as if that exact situation had happened to Skip. As if his own daughter had been murdered and he'd been powerless to prevent it, and now he had nothing but sorrow to see him through the rest of his life.

After that, it was all cartoons all the time. Something about animated people just didn't have the same effect. He made the mistake of watching something with a cartoon dragon in it, and that just made him think of the plane crash over San Cicaro. The shrieking of the woman chilled his blood, and the thought of so many people's lives snuffed out in an instant turned his stomach. The more he remembered it, the less fake it seemed. If Sadie's power was real, was it all real?

Skip tried not to think about that night in Sadie Slight's apartment. Not that it did much good. All the questions he was left with—so, *so* many questions— kept popping up, an itch demanding to be scratched. An itch that he couldn't reach, no matter how badly he wanted to.

One month and seven days after that night, Skip decided it was time to turn his computer back on. Mostly because rent was due in a week and he wasn't sure how long his bank account could support him if he didn't start earning money soon. He briefly considered leaving the apartment to find a traditional job, but that felt infinitely scarier than booting up his desktop. He knew on some level that he wouldn't be able to handle face-to-face interactions. If he couldn't even watch TV without experiencing emotional overloads, how could he possibly stand to be around real people with real problems?

So, he sat in his old, familiar office chair and he pushed the buttons to turn the machines on, and he held his breath while it all whirred to life. He must've sat staring at the icons on his desktop for a good ten minutes before finding the courage to open his PM board. The one he'd used to talk to R.G., in what felt like a decade past.

Several new messages from potential clients awaited him. Most were too old to consider responding to, but one was from the last few days. Even though he suspected opening it would be a mistake, some sort of trick that would transport him to Sadie Slight's apartment, or her to his, he clicked on it anyway.

Hello,

I hope you don't mind me contacting you. A friend referred me, said you did good work. I, uh, feel kind of funny doing this, but I'm not sure what else to do. I guess you could say I'm desperate.

I think my wife might be cheating on me. I've come home from work a couple of times to find brown hairs on our bed. Since I'm bald and what little hair I do have is gray, and since my wife is blonde… it's difficult not to be suspicious. I suppose those hairs could be floating in from somewhere else, but still, some confirmation would do my heart good. Or bad, depending on the outcome. She keeps a laptop on a desk in our bedroom, and I would just set it to record while I'm gone, but I worry she'll discover my plan. She'll call me paranoid. And I guess I am.

Anyway, I'm told you can help. Can you?

Just this man's story made Skip's heart wither and die, then swell back up with so much impotent rage that he couldn't help but cry a little. He hated what was happening to him. This wasn't who he was. But at the same time, he didn't seem to have any power over it either. It was, he knew, a curse straight from San Cicaro. One that he probably deserved.

Skip pulled himself together enough to message this man back, saying he would take the job. They communicated over the next day, agreed on a price, and soon Skip was hacking into a laptop that sat in the bedroom of one Mr. and Mrs. Franklin Baum.

Skip, looking at the live feed of a neatly-made bed in an empty bedroom that was the size of his entire apartment, decided to do things a little differently.

He watched.

For hours he sat in front of his monitor, staring at that empty room. Mrs. Baum came and went a couple of times, but mostly nothing happened. Then he did the same thing again the next day. Only this time when Mrs. Baum appeared shortly before noon, she was accompanied by another man. Someone young. He wore a canary yellow polo and powder blue shorts and was undoubtedly in a fraternity. Skip watched until they began to undress each other and then shut the feed off.

After a good long cry in honor of Mr. Baum, he packaged the video and audio, and posted the link to the message board, giving Mrs. Baum and her lover just enough time to finish and leave.

Then he re-accessed that bedroom laptop. Only this time he didn't go to the video and instead hacked her email account. He sent her an email from a fictional account that he invented for just this purpose.

In that email was a plea. Skip, taking on the emotional persona of Franklin Baum, explained that he knew all about what she was doing behind her husband's back. He didn't explain how he knew, only that he did. He told her in the kindest way possible that her actions hurt people. That he wasn't going to make her stop, this wasn't blackmail, but that she should take a long hard look at herself and her soul and ask herself if she could live with what she was doing. To her husband, to herself, even to the young man she was bringing into her marital bed.

In essence, he tried using a mix of sentiment and reason to convince her to choose to change before she did irreparable harm. He even suggested confessing and asking forgiveness.

No threats, no promises, just an appeal for decency.

It might not change anything, Skip knew. It might just compel her to do a better job of hiding her affairs. But if so, that would be on her.

It'd make her think. That was his reasoning. Empathy. Even if it was only for a split second, she would see things through her husband's eyes. Maybe it would even make her remorseful.

This act didn't lessen what Skip was going through—not one bit—but he thought maybe he finally understood why Sadie Slight had given him this curse to begin with.

Turning the computer off, letting silence seep back into his apartment, Skip looked around at the walls of his cramped home and wondered if he'd ever have the strength to go outside. If he'd ever be able to watch a movie or a TV show again without spinning into a deep depression.

It was bad, but this was better than what he assumed R.G. had suffered. Bleeding from every pore for days on end, whilst a lump of mold drank from him.

Surely this was better?

Surely.

In the Overmorrow, The Offling

Larry Kay

Xiomara drove through San Cicaro with the windows down to let the fragrant wind, and the Tijuana murder ballads of Rico Bene Hana, detonate the specters from her conscience. She slapped the steering wheel to tragic lyrics over dense rhythms as she glided by bodegas and hookers and hookah bars.

Her thoughts sailed past the flotsam and the Nephilim just trying to chisel an angle or cheat an angel in what passed for life here. She smelled their sin and forgave them all, because she had a date tonight. It had been too long since she had just been a young woman hoping for a young man to buy her an amaretto sour and claim that he saw stars in her eyes.

The rendezvous for the evening was the Golgonooza, a dive bar for locals that used to be a newspaper processing plant. The Golgo had too much space TBH, but it allowed folks to spread out and shadows to conveniently spill and sulk for those that might need to embrace mother night. There were already a few in that night; shuffling, hooded figures, hobbling around on pillaged, mismatched legs.

Xiomara was a known commodity at the Golgo; a paladin to some, harridan to others. She would always listen to your story. That was known. She could be plied with drink. She could be bargained with, and cheated, and lied to. But no one pushed her too hard because she bore the mark, and she had ultimate judgment squatting behind her eyes.

She parked in the lot behind the Golgo and checked her smoky mascara. She pocketed a vial of pepper spray laced with iron filings, turmeric, and holy water blessed by a defrocked transgender priest. She ignored the couple making out against the beat-up Ford F-150 despite their pungent auras. His was pent up violence and lust, and hers was Mammon's top-ten-must-haves-delivered-same-day-from-Amazon-Prime. Let them have each other's tongue. She did not have to harmonize every off-tune chord.

She slapped flesh with the bouncer Inek, a hairy bare-chested Ukrainian man that would offer folks a chance to shave his back for a discount entry. The inside was quiet, but it was early yet. A few regulars and lost tourists sat at their respective tables and eyeballed each other for either redemption or entertainment.

She nodded at a musician with fringed ears and an extra finger, who tipped his hat at her while he fondled his mandolin. Anyone else would have thought his appearance just makeup and body mods, like other millennials who altered themselves to look half-animal or elven.

And never realizing the truth. Even as he played *Going to California* for them on eight strings.

Offling, Xiomara mentally dubbed him. One of San Cicaro's new half-breeds: off-kilter, tainted with the Other, made for the near future that was in the offing. She didn't know where the term started, surmising it a mix of halfling and offering. Yet nobody could know what the city would belch up next, or demand as payment.

Except maybe Ostrander. That was the moniker the barkeep answered to and he joked that he was a retired Sumo wrestler. He didn't look Japanese but that did not mean as much anymore. He was one of only three beings in the entire city who could disguise his aura from Xiomara.

It was quite possible he was divine. *He certainly could play Dionysus*, she thought, as he smiled and slid a shot glass of fragrant amber liquid down the polished spruce bar top. Xiomara threw it down her gullet with a practiced hand and tossed the empty to the floor with a crash. She eyeballed the tourists, smirked at Ostrander, and found a booth with a view of the door. It felt good to shake things up. She knew Ostrander would hand her a broom later.

The ancient whiskey settled her nerves. The man coming to meet her wanted an interview. He wanted to ask her about her recent fight with a full offling caught on YouTube. Xiomara was "YouTube Famous" now and she hated it most of the time. The coming newshound wanted to ask about the secrets of the city, and her own past. She would probably lie to him. Xiomara wanted a date, not an inquisition. Hence, he had his work cut out for him.

She checked her phone. It was overfilled with responses to reports of her earlier exorcism. She didn't like the e-word, but language was just not up to the job of describing life in San Cicaro. The spirit wrangling had been a private affair that had turned loud and public, and thus filmed and dissected online. Happy grannies, angry firefighters, curious newsies, and trembling priests all got their quotes and Snaps and Chats.

Xiomara required her interviewer, sorry, her *date*, to buy her a pair of whiskeys and a trio of mahi-mahi tacos just to begin digesting her day.

She was halfway through an apricot sake some deluded tourist had sent her when her date, the News Man, entered the bar. He wore the hungry coyote appearance she had begun to associate with wanna-be truth seekers: lanky frame, searching gaze, pale skin and dark leather laptop bag. She rubbed at the mark on her chest; it seemed cold and quiet. Good.

She watched Ostrander point him her way. She ignored him as he approached the table, but her third eye widened, reading his aura, his need for answers, his own mysteries, his pain.

No one ever approached her without pain these days.

"Excuse, me. Are you Xiomara Chivara?"

Without looking up, Xiomara said, "I am today," and downed the sake. He had pronounced her name correctly too: "sho-mara." She had spoken with a world-weariness she felt most days but amplified for him to seem cool and interesting. She waved at the opposite seat when he hesitated. He did not so much sit, as he inserted his angles into the booth, pushing his bag in front of him. It was what a werewolf would do having forgotten how human legs operate. He rummaged through his bag. He seemed nervous, but he smelled nice, woodsy even. He slid a card across the table.

She read it as he continued to dither: Brezh Badac, News Finder. The rest of the card was filled with social media handles and an image of a chess bishop. His name sounded fake to her. She made up a name for him on the spot: Bishop Badass. It made her smile because she knew he was neither.

He caught the smile and took it for encouragement. "Thank you for meeting me. I was surprised you agreed to an interview honestly."

She nodded, observing his preparations, his long fingers, his artful stubble. She hated disappointing folk's expectations. And they had so many. Xiomara was no savior, no guru, no savant. She was just a girl in a world where foul things, things that folks had no language for and so called them demons, popped up and either clawed your face off, or ran for office. But when had it been any different? Only now they showed their horns and dared you to call them out.

He fiddled with his phone, and said, "I'd like to b—"

"Rules," Xiomara announced, raising a hand with a little too much liquor-induced intensity. He shut up instantly. Points for him.

She said, softer this time, "Rules. No pics, no video. Audio only. First, you buy me tacos. The barkeep knows what I like."

He nodded. Good, he was trainable.

"Second. When I say we're done, we're done. If I say pass, move on. Savvy?" He narrowed his eyes at that one. Well. News Dude did not like being told his bi'ness. Tough luck. "Third, I get to ask you questions too. Okay, Brevvy Badac?"

His jaw and eyebrow worked to indicate his patience was ending. She could have that effect on men, and she grinned. She said, "I have more rules, but I'll keep 'em to myself unless you overstep."

Badac, stonier now, said, "It's pronounced Brezh BA-dach." He uncurled from the booth to place her order, but asked, "You like guac?"

"Oooh. Big spender. Hells yeah, I do."

Avocados were mega-expensive now. Why couldn't the new weird gods that played with the city work on that? Even drooling tentacle beasts must like guacamole. She'd have to convince Demi, that old romantic, to grow her up a batch. Xiomara was just pondering how exactly she'd go about bribing a garden, when Badac returned.

He came with the tacos, some ahi tuna version for himself, and small beers. They munched and kept their talk trivial. It felt like a date and Xiomara warmed to the evening. "Call me Xio."

She noticed he wore no ring and did not like his hands getting sticky. The tail of a serpent tattoo peeked out from behind his ear. That would be a story. Maybe if they had a second date. Fueled by the liquor, her imagination skipped to the third date where she would be licking that tattoo and watching him shiver underneath her.

As they ate, she called him Brezhy, and Brezhnev, and Bishop. She needled him about his height and his clothes like she always did on a date when she hoped for banter and snark, and maybe they would end up hating the same things, which was close enough to romance for her.

"Do you know about Golgonooza?" he asked.

"Of course. This is like my second office."

"No, I mean the name."

Xiomara shrugged. She just liked the sound, like "Golgotha," and "gulag," and "lollapalooza" rolled together. A festival, a prison, and a place where messiahs die. In other words, a demon party. It fit just right.

"It's from a William Blake poem," said Badac. His eyes twinkled when he explained stuff, she noticed. "He was this eighteenth century visionary artist that wrote epic poetry and freaked people out. I almost got ink of one of his fallen angels."

Xiomara ran her finger around the bowl of guac and nodded. "I'm glad the owner was on his game then. San Cicaro is probably a big draw for visionary poets that freak people out."

Badac wiped his mouth and placed his phone formally between them. "Speaking of people freaking out."

Xiomara pouted. Aww. The date was over.

His eyes entreated her to accept the interview. She felt warm and appreciated. She even sort of smiled. "I am fortified with your kindly offered cervezas and munchables. You may begin."

He bowed his head. "Ms. Chivara."

"Call me Xio."

He smirked. "The YouTube clip showing you fighting a demon has been seen by over a million people."

Xiomara avoided his question, stared at the tourists clandestinely pointing at her. She sighed and turned her gaze to the stained floor.

"Many viewers claim it was a stunt, a gimmick to make you famous, like with the P.H.a.N.T.o.M. Investigations controversies last year." Badac waited, his face a little too eager.

"I have no desire to be famous. And I don't like the D-word." She said, shaking her head. "It was a mistake."

"A mistake?"

"An abortion. Of the spiritual sort. It needed to wail and lash, and I was there to tend to it in its dying hour."

"As I recall you choked it to death with its own tentacles."

"To-may-to, to-mah-to."

Badac almost smiled but that would not have been professional. "At the end, it appears that the creature spoke to you?"

"That's private."

"People want to know—"

She narrowed her gaze. "Next."

He nodded. "And are you the same person who grabbed a haunted... thing... from the river, shoved it in a Foster's beer can, and then let it loose in the town hall? Several news agencies named you as the perpetrator. Politicians denounced you as an eco-terrorist."

She turned her most charming smile on Badac. "How long have you lived in the city?"

"Six years." He scratched his chest. "It's been rep—"

"Do you have any siblings?" she asked.

"I'm an only. About the river ghost... how do you get something so big in a can? It took them weeks to clean out the building."

Xiomara's lips pursed in frustration. "It was a forty ounce can."

He waited. She grunted.

She drew interlocking circles in the condensation on the table. "River spirits are particular. What was withdrawn from the water was anger. Anger at the phosphate leaks from Radnitzky's chemical plant outside the city. Anger made manifest in a rambunctious form that insisted on speaking to those in charge. This spirit wanted to go to city hall."

"So, you're admitting it was you?"

Xiomara fiddled with her glass. Reflections of ghosts circling the rafters appeared to swim in the glass. She said, "The person fingered for such an act would be open to many lawsuits, I'm thinking. I simply have an unhealthy interest in river spirits."

He nodded and did not pursue it. "That brings me to my real question."

Here it comes, she thought.

"Do you know why the city is… disturbed? The sightings, events. Ms. Chivara, when will it all stop?"

She nodded slowly. It was the question he was being paid to ask, but not his true need. She thought of dismissing him, of teasing him, maybe reaching over and kissing him. Apparently, she paused too long because now his tone was taut, expectant.

"Ms. Chivara, the citizens of San Cicaro demand an explanation. An ivy plant was reported to snake from one building to another and grab a cat. A group of women claimed to see a child with no face riding a tricycle up the walls of the Ensmuth building. A recent video suggested that lightning struck the same spot in the harbor for twenty minutes. Do you know what is going on?"

She grimaced. "God really hated a few fish."

He frowned.

She said, "The short answer is no."

"And the long answer?"

She caught Ostrander's eye across the bar, but no magic emerged from him to allow her to avoid the conversation. She finally spoke. "Nothing draws a crowd… like a crowd."

He opened his hands as if she would drop answers into them. "Meaning?"

"Something happened. Doors opened." She shrugged. "I don't know. Forget it."

"That's not good enough, Ms. Chivara. People are scared. They need an answer."

"I'm no Yoda."

"You seem to know more than most."

She banged her palms on the table edge. "I don't know what's plaguing San Cicaro! 'It' may not even have happened yet. What we're seeing may just be scalpers selling tickets to the show."

"I don't understand." He had leaned away from her outburst, but he'd held her gaze.

"I—look—it's hard to explain. I've had some personal difficulties with… time. I think something might be leaking from our future and things are showing up to… case the joint." She paused but Badac said nothing. "First, it's a stain on a wall that looks like the Madonna. Then a shrine appears. People watch. A crowd grows. Someone claims to be healed. Folks take sides, claim it for their cause. Lovers embrace beneath it. Then a killer smears the blood of a dog across it. Is the stain good? Is it evil? Is it being perverted by our attention? What if Baby Superman was found by meth heads?"

"I'm sorry?"

"I said it was hard to explain."

She stared at her empty glass and willed more beer to appear. She had not yet been granted that power. She rubbed at the brand on her chest. It felt warmer.

Badac's tone changed, became conversational again. "How did you first get involved with… the madness? You said you had a difficulty with time?"

Xiomara's face twisted as memories of her family assaulted her. She blinked and swallowed. "Look. I'll tell you how I was dragged into this life, if you ask me the question you've been hiding."

"What?" Badac pushed back against the wood behind him as if she had grown antlers.

Xiomara just stared at him and waited. She knew when she thought of her mark, the burn on her chest, and stared at folks, they became uncomfortable. Badac's mouth worked but he said nothing. He glanced at the door, and at Ostrander. She kept her gaze on him, watched him chew his need and his ache. Finally, he turned off the recorder on his phone.

"You first," he said, rubbing at his own chest as if he had heartburn. She knew he didn't.

The no-longer-hidden pain was so writ on his face, she didn't mind sharing. He had not earned the whole story, but she would give him something.

Xiomara gazed at the ceiling. Spirits circled lazily and smelled like sunshine. They were probably drunk again. "I was a weird girl into weird shit. I performed a ritual in my house. Saint's candles and charms and faerie recipes and angel writing. Everything and a bag of chips."

Badac did not react, but listened intently, his face shadowed, his soul hungry. She continued.

"I did it all the time. School was crap and freaky magic was like therapy. Until that night. That night it wasn't 'wasting time to make myself feel good.' Something was called."

Xiomara observed his face: not judgy, not just professionally interested, but genuinely curious, grateful even. Without looking, she knew Ostrander was glancing at them. The mark on her chest itched. She felt the vile memories unburying themselves and tromping across her psyche…

Young Xiomara sat cross-legged in an octogram, because pentagrams were so last century. She had just finished the words when a rush of wind, seemingly from the floor, lifted her hair and broke her concentration. The candle lights spurted like they were trick birthday sparklers.

When she recovered her wits, she realized every chalk line was still in place, and every candle was still lit, but something was off.

Then the shadows moved. No. *Something* moved from the shadows. *Somethings.* Three of them. Humanoid.

Xiomara thought of Timelords and Cenobites, but the three newcomers were dressed like characters from *Casablanca*: a detective, a flapper, and a man in a red, striped suit that might have been a woman. They had skin so black it was blue. They were exquisite, but they had lamprey suckers for eyes and blood leaked out of their mouths when they laughed.

And they laughed at her.

The Dancer reached past Xiomara's wards, smiling as if she was a mischievous baby, and stroked her face and neck. Then she ripped the girl's shirt open. Xiomara's flesh froze while her soul screamed. The Dancer cut her bra off with a sharp fingernail. Then she licked her claw and traced a design on her breastbone. Xiomara gasped as the stranger's finger burned her skin.

Giggling, the Dancer stepped away with a flourish and a spin. The Detective was next. He leaned down and examined her as if she was guilty of every sin humanity had committed. He sneered at her as if her bare chest was her own fault, like she was dirty, before he slid his finger across the burn the Dancer had made and drew his own mark.

Young Xiomara whimpered and shuddered, trying not to think about the smell of her own roasting skin. The Detective stepped away and the Androgyne sauntered forward, as if Xiomara was an unfinished sculpture and she the artist. She smiled and ran her burning finger under Xiomara's left breast, linking her brand to the others. Tears streamed from Xiomara's eyes, but she could not scream or move.

Finally, the three intruders left her and without a word, slowly walked upstairs. Xiomara knew she should warn her family, but she curled into a ball, sobbing and writhing on the floor.

With clenched fists and gritted teeth, Xiomara sat in the booth, visibly steaming, staring off into space, breathing raggedly. Her mark illuminated her face as if she was possessed. She squeezed the table's edge and the white parts of her fingernails turned red.

Badac, eyes wide in alarm, said, "Xiomara…"

The slamming door snapped her from her past, and Xiomara glanced around the room. The tourists had fled, but her Bishop Badass was still there. Ostrander gave her a lingering glance and then waved at the musician. The upbeat tune he pulled from the guitar banished the tension.

Xiomara collapsed into herself, and the glow faded from her breast. Badac held out a hand. She didn't take it, but she smiled at him.

"When everything settled, my family was trapped inside, and I was exiled outside," she said as if that explained everything.

A plate of fried doughnuts in the shape of koalas showed up. Xiomara waved at Ostrander for his offering. Food is love.

Badac frowned and asked, "Could you elaborate?"

"No." Xiomara tried to banish the memories and concentrate on fried dough.

Badac nodded and changed the subject. They talked about sports teams they didn't care about and celebrities until the emotional miasma had lifted.

Finally, Brezh Badac straightened and Xiomara knew he was ready to unburden himself. She calmed her mind and responded to his tone, because that's what she was now; a professional weird-people-fixer.

"I had a dream where I had a third nipple," he said. She gave him a ghost of a grin for the novel strangeness. He continued. "Faerie things flew in my window and suckled... on me. When I woke up I was wonderfully drunk and I... I drew a nipple on my chest with a purple sharpie."

"Did you go to bed drunk?" Xiomara wanted to make a joke, but he was suffering, and he needed her to be serious.

"Nope." He glanced down, and now Xiomara stared at his chest. He said, "And now they come for real. When I sleep, these... pixies come, always on the fifteenth, and... *feed* from me."

His voice was so indignant, but part of her wanted to be sarcastic. If Badac had been a woman, child-bearing or no, the conversation would have been different.

Badac grew angry at her silence. "You don't believe me?"

When she said nothing, he started grimly unbuttoning his shirt.

She stopped him. "I believe you."

"It hurts." He raised a hand as if to gingerly touch a wound. "I'm sore, but I have... visions."

"Of what?"

He shook his head, baffled. "Faerie places I guess. It's a rocky, desolate landscape, but the sea is close. Not San Cicaro."

Not yet, Xiomara thought. She asked, "Are you there too? Can you see yourself?"

"I'm not sure." He ran his hand down his forearm. "I'm thinner now too. And I... uh... crave weird stuff."

Uh oh, she thought. An idea hit her hard. "Like what?"

"I bought all the oranges this one store had and ate them till my tongue burned. Once, I had this urge to go out at dawn and climb trees and hang upside-down. When I see a crescent moon, I want to sing but when I try, all I do is scream until I'm hoarse."

She rubbed a knuckle on her chin as she considered his plight. Maybe he was cursed. It didn't feel like possession. Her helpful brain conjured an image of herself sucking on his nipple.

He said, "I don't recognize my own smell anymore. I feel off inside."

"Maybe you're pregnant?" It was only half a joke.

His grin was painful. "I've thought of that. I actually bought a pregnancy test and then threw it away. What would I do if it said I was?"

He definitely needed help. She glanced at her phone.

"Do you need to go?" The plea and hurt in his voice was surgical.

"No. I was checking the date. It's the twelfth."

"I know."

"So, we have three days to get ready."

"You'll help me?"

"It's what I do, Brezhy BA-dach. It's what I do."

Badac's place, set amongst a slew of industrialized warehouses, was going to be a renovated office until an enterprising soul had sold it as a shabby chic apartment. His only nod to decoration was a dozen black-and-white photos that depicted oddities from around the city: the suspicious ivy plant, a school bus filled with pearly slime, and several close-ups of people's faces as they had been telling their stories. It felt a little like being watched by them, judged even. The apartment felt spartan and lacking in joy, but his fridge was covered in colorful photos of a big family having fun wherever they went. A younger, chunkier Badac on display.

Xiomara had spread her tech out over his only table and she felt like she had taken over his place. She had her typical exorcism kit, plus a bicycle pump, a deflated basketball, a thick collection of Seurat art, and a few knives. Each knife had designs carved in the blade and handle. She wore a lab coat covered with hand-drawn stick figures of her own exploits and broken up with a few stitched-on Tibetan mandalas.

It had taken her forty-eight hours of straight experimental thaumaturgy to get everything together. Some of the tech was untested against real beasties but Xiomara felt very confident. She was also this close to tasting colors and she should have taken a nap, but this was the hand and she would play it. Crap cards though they might be.

"Brezy, get out here already!" She shook her hands and jumped in place like she used to do before a game.

Badac emerged from his room wearing a robe she had forced on him. The white robe was completely blank, but she had washed it many times in her own patented faerie-repellant and it stank like seaweed.

"I feel stupid," he said.

"If it's any comfort, you smell bad and you look weird, so it's a trifecta."

"You're not helping."

"I know. Come sit down."

Badac, all hairy arms and long legs, folded into a chair and examined her arcane bric-a-brac. "Uh, all this seems like a grab bag of every religion. Some I've not heard of."

"Broad but not deep was my upbringing. The key here is to find a recipe which excites just the right neurons and chakras and whatsits, so you get a demonstrable effect. Preferably the same effect each time."

"And do you?"

"Seventy percent of the time, it works sixty percent of the time."

"So, less than half?" He pulled at the robe, accidentally revealing his chest.

"Abuelas swear by me." Xiomara tried not to eyeball his hairy chest, or his tight calves, or his butt. He was naked underneath at her insistence, for important magical reasons. She tapped at an open book. "I need you to draw hexes on the basketball just like the ones on this page."

"This is your magic cure for me…?"

"I know it seems like a potluck approach, but the key thing is focused willpower plus clear intent equals power. The recipe just gets you there."

He nodded. "I'm not an artist."

"You're not being graded. The art being in your hand is important though. It's like you posting a sign saying 'No Demon Parking.'"

"Should I use the same purple sharpie I used… on me?"

"Oooh, that's a good idea."

Badac grabbed the marker from a junk drawer and did his best with the hexes while Xiomara rechecked her supplies, and her weapons.

"I think there's a joke here about Harold and the Purple Crayon, but I can't quite make it work," said Xiomara.

Badac smiled, then turned serious. "Xiomara."

She turned to him. She knew he was nervous, but he had been fine so far. *No backsies*, she thought. Tonight was the fifteenth.

He asked, "Can I see your mark?"

That took her by surprise. Few people asked. It was like asking a nun to peruse your browser history.

Xiomara fiddled with her shirt's fabric. She wanted Badac to think she was pretty, and her demon-scar was anything but. She pursed her lips and measured his need versus her hazy boundaries. "Sometimes… it destroys people."

Badac grunted and twitched but seemed determined. She went on.

"It doesn't react to all evil, so don't worry about parking tickets, but if you have any serious vile history, or you've had sex with a demon, this will burn your face off." She tried to grin encouragingly. "I did have one offling say it was like bathing in peppermint sunshine though."

Badac stayed serious. "I'd like to see."

She knew what he was thinking. Because he might die tonight. "Okay."

She unbuttoned her top button and could not help but give him a trace of a saucy grin. The mark responded to her thoughts and Badac's need with a soft golden glow. Xiomara never knew for certain if someone would be turned to ash. Demons, yes. Time jumping a-holes, probably. Offlings, maybe. Regular folk, rarely. Badac should be fine.

The light against his face as she undid the second button was like a pressure on them both. It moved his hair, and his eyes widened as he felt the force of it. She had to brace herself slightly.

She undid the third button and pulled the fabric back to reveal a ghastly scar that wove from a mass on her breastbone and then under the curve of her left breast. Bras were expensive, so she had removed it earlier just in case she had to perform some Super Girl-esque shirt-rip-off-demon-blasting magic.

Badac was mesmerized by the light, his face soft and curious, and she toyed with the idea of taking off her shirt and seeing what happened. *Bad Xiomara*, she thought. *Down girl. Stay focused.*

She traced the edge of the three overlapping scars, one for each dieselpunk demon that had scoured her flesh. Sometimes it felt like the scars moved. It was not a symbol she recognized, despite her research.

Her faithful newshound did not turn to ash. Xiomara buttoned her shirt. She realized, with a trace of disappointment, that she had wanted some sort of reaction.

Badac blinked, swallowed, stretched his neck, and rearranged his robe. "I guess… I guess I was wrong."

"About…?" Xiomara felt clearer now, calmer, ready to get to work.

"My ex. I guess she wasn't really a demon after all."

Xiomara grinned, and played along. "Maybe a quarter-demon? I'm still fine-tuning it."

Badac rubbed at his chest, and his swollen, fake nipple. "What if all this magic stuff doesn't work?"

"I also have a gun."

"Really?"

She reached under her lab coat and withdrew it from the holster, revealing a revolver with painted runes along the barrel. "Smith & Wesson & Shadrach & Chivara."

"Works on faeries?"

"Probably not. But it makes me feel good."

It was almost one in the morning. Badac lay in a trance on his faded leather couch, and had been for over an hour. Xiomara knew the faeries, or whatever they really were, visited between midnight and three.

Xiomara had already dozed off once so had dutifully set her phone to ping every ten minutes. She couldn't afford any errors here. The magic of the basketball, filled with air from his lungs and his place, and covered in hexes by his hand, would keep bad actors out. It should also keep sound from escaping. She didn't need cops or nosy nellies knocking on the door until they were done. Of course, if mosquito demons showed up, then no one would hear their screams for help either.

Xiomara arose to raid the fridge again when she heard the plink at the window. She crossed herself, checked her pepper spray (which *would* work on faeries) and peered around the corner. Sure enough, a little glowing feyshitheel with butterfly wings was knocking on the glass. It had a scrunched-up bat face, and a ratty tail. Not a pretty sight at all.

Then there were two, then five, then eight. They started punching the glass. Really, they were striking the ward, and crystalline fractures formed immediately. The front row would get tired and rotate in the swarm behind them. *Damn*, she thought, as the shield continued to fail. Plan A was a total bust.

She opened the Seurat art book and activated the enchantment. She hoped the colorful dots would tantalize the pixie scum, draw them away from Badac, maybe even allow her to capture a few.

Xiomara buttoned the lab coat, turned up the collar and took out a surgical mask and a pair of goggles. So armored, she waited. When they faeries finally bashed a hole the size of a grapefruit, they crawled in and cascaded about Badac, rubbing their hands together and gnashing their teeth.

Well, so much for Seurat, she thought. On to Plan C. Fortunately, none of them even noticed her behind her ensorcelled getup, so that had worked at least. The hard part of Plan C was that she had to figure out exactly what they were doing and why, and how to counter them while they were draining poor Badac.

The first faerie, selected after an intense, tinny screaming match, dove down and landed on his chest. It sucked at Badac's fake, purple nipple, pulling on the sore flesh with both tiny hands. Xiomara winced as she heard the slurping and then the moans and chanting of the others.

While each bat-faced faerie took a turn, the sated ones sat on the couch, or on his legs and chest, and fondled their distended bellies. They crooned as if drunk on Thanksgiving.

By the fifteenth feeding, Badac's skin had darkened, his breathing grew shallow, his lips blue. Xiomara observed and read auras and calculated how best to attack. Should she try to kill them? Should she try to capture one and scatter the rest? She could just let them finish and then run tests on Badac.

When the last one was done, every muscle in his body was rigid, his back arching off the couch. His face was a rictus of tension. His manhood was fully erect and free of the robe. For once, Xiomara was not distracted. She needed to act now while the rat-tailed ickies were all dopey and lounging about.

Xiomara pulled out her pepper spray, and a half-empty pickle jar. She could tell from their auras they were transforming their stolen fluid, using their own nature to perform personalized alchemy. If she could capture one in this state, then analyze the fluid, that would be of much help. It was time to act.

As she crept forward, hoping she remained invisible to them, they started to recover from their stupor. She froze, waiting. A faerie crawled over Badac's belly and vomited its measure of amber liquid into his belly button, which absorbed it immediately. Xiomara, fascinated and revolted, caught a whiff of whiskey and cat pee.

A second, then a third, repeated the disgorgement, and Badac's belly began to bloom. *Damn*, she thought. What would happen to Brezhy if she halted this? She knew so little. Better she acts now, than wait too long and witness him pop.

Xiomara rushed forward and sprayed a mass of faeries with her spray. They all screamed and fled to the ceiling. She grabbed the one who had just finished puking luminescent bile into Badac and stuffed it in a pickle jar. The remaining fat-bellied pack of pixies squealed at her and tried to hide.

She shook the pickle jar. "Now's let's see what makes you tick."

Xiomara was in a victorious mid-snarl at her captive when the front door exploded off its hinges.

A bald priest with pale blue skin, pointed ears and fangs stepped inside. He had his hands in a prayer and grinned. "Time to bless the coming of the Mara Riganis."

Xiomara let out a short scream before she regained her self-control. "Stay where you are, or I smash this faerie."

She assumed they were together. She needed time to think. This intruder had knocked down her ward like it was wax, and she had not even heard him approach.

The stranger stepped into the room slowly, observed Badac with interest, then bent down with a groan and grabbed the door. He propped it back into place and gave it a little shimmy. "Sorry about the door. I love a showy entrance. And you are?"

"Fed up with this faerie bullshit. What's a Mary Riganis? What do you want?" She needed the bald baddie to keep talking until she figured out if she should reach for her gun or try something freaky. Maybe *he* would like the Seurat book.

"In the overmorrow the offling shall inherit the earth. And our loathly lady will rule them all. The seed of the Mara Riganis germinates within him. His visions and desires and flesh will feed our death queen."

Xiomara scowled. "Well, that clears up everything. What the fuck does 'overmorrow' mean?"

"You need a tutor, someone to show you your devoirs."

She snarled at him. He smiled in reply.

"It means the day after tomorrow. Now, you must decide, Xiomara. Would you be handmaiden or meal, my dear?" He had not moved away from the door, and his every gesture was slow, his voice comforting.

She sensed he was coiling, waiting, watchful. She said, "I'm neither. I'm the gatekeeper. And you can tell your pixie buds to leave."

"The huldu are finished."

Xiomara glanced back at Badac. Indeed, all the bat-faeries were slumped over him, or the couch, or prone on the floor. None of them moved. Even the one in her pickle jar floated like a dead fish. Shit, things were moving too fast.

Badac had relaxed and regained some color. His poor penis had shrunk, but his belly was distended and bruised, something coiling within him like an evil eel. Xiomara grimaced. Fuck it. She had tried to be clever and that had failed. Now it was time to be violent.

She pulled the revolver and aimed at the fey priest's head. "This wouldn't work on the little guys, but I bet it'll blow you all to hell."

He shrugged. "But if I bleed my last on the linoleum floor then you'll never learn why. And I have such answers. I can taste your delicious need to know."

She rotated her shoulders. "Fine. Talk. I've an ear for bullshit and I've half a mind to shoot a kneecap. You'll still be able to speak."

"So fierce."

She fake-smiled at him.

He raised his hands as if leading a congregation in prayer. "The bars are being lifted. San Cicaro will be the first liberated city."

"Liberated from what?"

"Reality."

Xiomara grunted in disdain. "A New World Order?"

"An Old World Order. And you could be a Valkyrie. You could claim you were there at the birth of the Dread Mother. First among many. Xiomara Chivara, you would be raised above—praised, adored, loved."

"Being popular always sounded like a lot of work to me. I prefer to lurk and snark."

"Your trapped and tragic family then. We could save them." He tried to adopt a kind, loving face, but it looked all the more sinister to Xiomara.

He continued to woo her. Even his gestures conveyed openness. "I know the face in the window that scared your young brother. That scares him still."

Xiomara's eyes hardened. This blue-skinned bastard from the other side wasn't the first to offer to save her family or explain her misery. She knew a politician's promise when she heard it. Even though her mind knew this, her heart stretched and ripped at the thought.

"Tell me."

He smiled but not unkindly. "*Your* face."

Xiomara whimpered. "No."

The priest gestured, and Xiomara's memories ransacked through her being…

Young Xiomara bolted upright when she heard her brother scream. Her chest felt like it was on fire, but she managed to struggle to her feet on trembling legs and drag herself upstairs.

The house smelled like fireworks had been set off in every room. Red smoke clung to the walls and moved of its own accord, around chairs and plants and microwaves. She spotted no sign of the three demons.

When her brother screamed again, she limped into the hall that led to his bedroom and halted. Her parents were already there but trapped. The hallway had become a strobing nightmare of rabid time. At her end were her parents, frozen in place, concerned and frightened, caught as they rushed to help.

At the other end they were corpses on the floor, rotting and still. In between, they aged and died before they could even realize their horrible fate, caught in a demon's slipstream of amok time.

Xiomara watched her brother curl on the floor, hiding from the gruesome horrors around him. Had he seen his parents die like plants in a time-lapse video in bio class? She had to protect him, hug away his fears. She knew she could not reach him through the hall and ran outside.

And then she realized her mistake. The house was now an unknowable Schrodinger's horror show. She could no longer go back in, exiled from her family's torture. Her brother was trapped in life and fear, as her parents were trapped in concern and death.

Xiomara rocked back on her heels as if she had been struck. As if her own nightmares were not bad enough, this fey bastard had to whip her with her failures.

As the images faded, she remembered her vow to save her family. She would build the tools she needed to pop the bubble of demon-time and save them.

The priest, closer now, examining but not touching her, said, "Years from now, you will grow cold and jaded with constant failure, and you will barter with demons to go back in time to undo it all. But you will only be able to stare into your brother's bedroom, terrify him, and begin the whole sorry chain of events that lead you here. To me and my offer."

Xiomara's breathing grew ragged with his doom-saying. This fey shit-stain had forced her back into her own abyss. He had to pay for that.

Tears stained her cheeks as she pulled the trigger.

Shocked, the offling priest collapsed to the ground clutching his chest. Even so, his voice stayed patient, paternal even. "You can't stop it. The babe is coming e'en now. You could still be its mother, Xiomara. Save yourself... from the deluge of pain that's coming."

"No." She shot the pointy-eared priest four more times.

She had one bullet left. Badac's defiled flesh lay waiting for her judgement. Xiomara was not going to let some bloody bat-elf messiah into the world.

Badac pushed himself up on his elbow. He touched his bruised and bloody stomach. It hurt, and the bandage stank like antiseptic and pickle juice, but his extra nipple was gone. "So, it's over?"

"Do you really want to know?" Xiomara dried her hands on a towel and sat down heavily. Her cheeks were sunken, while the dark skin under her eyes matched the abyss of sludge she had dealt with.

"Yes, but not right now." He lay back down. "I'm just glad my life will return to normal."

Xiomara didn't say that she doubted he would be normal again. He had hosted an eldritch thing. He had been made holy by the oldest forces. They would not likely give him up easily. And some demons might consider him extra-tasty now. Offlings might even worship him. But Brezh Badac did not need to know any of that right now.

Badac shifted and grunted in pain. "Did you... tear something out of me?"

"After I shot you, yes."

He shuddered at the very idea and stared at her in disbelief. "You shot me?"

"Yes. I aimed at the bad parts."

He considered the bloody stains near his door. "Who else got shot?"

"A big faerie."

He sighed deeply. "It's not really over is it?"

Xiomara sagged in sympathetic fatigue. How could she explain the last three hours...?

... tongue between her teeth in total concentration, Xiomara used a knife of blessed reindeer antler to carve runes into a special bullet.

She slowly aimed and shot into Badac's distended, horrifying belly. The sacred abomination within wailed as it thrashed and died.

She grimaced as she drained the glowing pink pus from his abdomen into a Tupperware container used to dealing with peas or noodles. Her lame first aid, bandages and Bactine, would have to be enough for now.

She tossed the horrible, dead creature into the tub. It slid along the smooth ceramic and left gritty stains. Then she dragged the priest, lighter than he should be for his size, into the bathtub.

Xiomara enchanted a jug of Drano into an acid strong enough to dissolve dragon bones. She poured it over the two figures and crossed herself for protection against the horrid fumes.

She cleaned herself and Badac with a towel soaked in warm water and a vial of virgin's tears. She upended the whole vial on Badac's bullets wounds and prayed it would be enough.

Xiomara blinked away her recent memories and smiled knowingly at Badac. "This is for you," She held out an ugly fragment of metal.

"What is it?"

"The bullet. Keep it with you. A charm against evil. Also, you will need a new couch."

He accepted that fact without comment.

"Do you have someone who can come over and watch you? My sutures are good, but it pays to be cautious."

"I'll call my cousin." He touched her lightly. "You can stay if you like."

She liked the concern and the interest, even if she could do nothing about it right now. Nor could he, truly.

Xiomara laid a hand on his shoulder and pretended she had not seen or done what she had this evening. "I would like that, but I'm about to sleep for three days, so I would be no good to you, and less to myself."

His sad grin was acknowledgement of the truth. Badac sipped from the water she had left him.

"But, I will have to check on you repeatedly. Say eight o'clock next Saturday? You pick me up. I like 80's hip hop and I'm feeling like some Samoan fritters."

"I might be on crutches, I think."

"No excuses. Don't be late."

She grabbed her kit and sundries and left without looking back. The early morning sun felt like a mother's touch on her forehead. Maybe the old gods did not love her, but *someone* did. She did not have the energy to smile but she drove away hopeful. She didn't know if she had an ally or a friend in Brezh Badac, or a second date, but she would let thumping music and sweet fried food do their best.

Xiomara considered visiting the neighborhood church and lighting a candle for her family. Who really knew how far a little faith would go these days in San Cicaro?

Sentimental Pines

Ian Ableson

Once upon a time San Cicaro's tourist business had been a healthy supplement to the city's already-booming economy.

The rooftop ice rink was a popular first choice. The Center for Alliance in Energy, with its bizarrely spiky architecture that looked like the Sydney Opera House had gone through a goth phase, was another top contender. And the Tesla Museum, which hosted the largest Tesla Coil in the world and held awe-inspiring physics demonstrations on the weekends, was the Mecca of many a science enthusiast.

But even before the incidents began, before unexplained disappearances, bad press, and sensationalist media began scaring the tourists away, almost nobody visited San Cicaro for the parks.

Which, in the opinion of Senior Park Naturalist Hugo Debois, was a little unfair. Four large nature parks, each with its own visitor center and extensive trail system. Nine well-groomed sports parks with soccer fields, tennis courts, and even one velodrome. All this and other amenities were just a slice of greenery to break up the urban landscape's monotony. You could surround yourself with pine trees in the nature parks, close your eyes, and pretend that you'd left the city behind.

The parks commissions manuscripts listed a myriad of benefits to having parks nestled in the busy city; prominent among them was "relief from urban closeness." Hugo wasn't very good at government-speak, but there was a much simpler term: peace. He could see the serenity in the eyes of the business types who walked a lap around one of the parks during their lunch hours, clearing the stress of their mornings from their minds. He spotted it in the joggers who began their days with music, exercise, and a vista of trees. Most of all he noticed it in children, some of whom might not get to enjoy nature any other way in their lives.

Hugo absentmindedly cleaned his glasses as he gazed at the trees through the window, seated at his desk at the Sentimental Pines Nature Center. Apart from a two-year stint at Glacier National Park in his late twenties, he'd lived in San Cicaro for his entire, 35-year long career. By now he was as deeply rooted into the city's parks as their eldest oak. The park staff regularly joked that Hugo would never retire—he would just fall over dead on the trail one day and crumble into the detritus.

At this point, Hugo just hoped he would get the chance to stick around even to retirement age. With all the disappearances and murders, the city had siphoned most of San Cicaro Parks and Recreation's money into emergency services. Hugo had to admit that trail maintenance wasn't as important when pieces of folks were being found scattered across the city.

Yet the cutbacks had made his job more of a chore. He'd already reduced hours for part-timers, which was why he was the only one staffing Sentimental Pines Nature Center tonight. He glanced at the clock and was mildly surprised to see that it was already 7:45 p.m. Most of the center closed at 8:00 in the summer. Then the bathrooms remained open for two more hours until the deputies did their rounds and closed for the night.

Hugo stood from his desk and stretched a little. In recent years his muscles had started to groan whenever he spent too long confined to a chair. Such evening aches weren't the only sign of his advancing age. One day he'd woken up and realized the whiskers around his mouth had gone from salt-and-pepper to ghost white. His beard stood in stark contrast to his ebony skin, that seemed to gain a new wrinkle every time he glanced in the mirror.

Hugo began the daily ritual of closing the nature center. He shut off the display lights over the wall of bird taxidermy—Sentimental Pines had a stuffed version of every bird ever witnessed in San Cicaro. He double-checked the UV lights over the indoor turtle pond and snake enclosures before turning off the interactive ecosystem exhibit. The join-our-email-list iPad was the last thing powered off.

It was 7:58 and Hugo was back at his desk, scowling at his smartphone. The HR department had decided last week that all parks employees would be clocking work hours with an app. Hugo had never been savvy with tech to begin with, but this new app seemed to have a personal vendetta against him. He missed the days of scribbling his time in and out on a page in the nature center's logbook. He was about to give up and shoot an apology email to HR when he heard the nature center's front door open and swing shut.

He glanced at the clock. 7:59. Of course someone would walk in now. That was one of the biggest problems working in an urban park system: Not only did the city never sleep, but its citizens viewed closing times as suggestions rather than rules. Hugo creakily stood from his desk and strolled over to the central exhibit room. Maybe he'd give them five minutes to look around the nature center before asking them to leave. It would give him more time to fiddle with the app before turning to HR like an old dog with his tail between his legs.

He found the perpetrator hunched over the turtle pond, apparently getting a closer look at the indifferent reptiles within. Hugo squinted a little in the darkness. His eyesight had been growing poor—he couldn't even tell whether the figure was a man or a woman. As Hugo approached, the figure uncurled and turned towards him.

A flash, like lightning without thunder; an indescribable vision. Before him stood something inhuman. A towering shape, eight feet tall at least, androgynous in figure, with rippled skin the color of polished malachite. Eyes that blazed like a bonfire's last dying embers, and wood-grain patterns adorned the skin like intricate tribal tattoos. The scent of burning leaves filled Hugo's nostrils.

Then Hugo blinked.

Before him stood the decidedly unthreatening figure of Mrs. Esther Aronowitz, a regular park patron who checked every box on the doddering-little-old-lady checklist. She wore her usual thick glasses, two-pound layer of makeup, and garish purple getup. There was a little container of turtle pellets in her hand.

"Oh, Mr. Debois!" she chirped cheerfully. "I was wondering who was working at the center today. Now I know it's a little late, but I had to come and feed my darlings here. You know they start to miss me if I'm gone too long but I couldn't come on Thursday because that was my granddaughter Effie's last soccer game of the season. And she and my daughter hate it when I'm not there. You know my daughter says that she thinks Effie plays worse when she can't see me on the bleachers. And those bleachers at Rackham Park are so hard, you should really have someone take a look at them, I think they're causing me lower back pain… are you alright, Mr. Debois? You look pale! Well, not too pale, of course, I don't think you could ever look too pale, I just don't think your complexion would allow it."

Hugo gulped down air. His heart felt like it would beat straight out of his chest. He blinked several more times, half expecting the strange image to reappear, but all he could see was Mrs. Aronowitz. "No… No. I'm alright, thank you. Just getting a little old, I think."

She frowned at him. "You should go sit down for a little while, Mr. Debois, you do look frightful! Did you have too much dairy today? I know sometimes I have too much dairy and later I feel awful for hours, truly miserable, I really do… But do go sit down, Mr. Debois, I'll only be a few minutes in here, then I'm off on my evening walk."

Hugo nodded mutely. He went back to the office, sat at his desk, and closed his eyes. His head throbbed painfully, and he considered tracking down an ibuprofen somewhere in the office to help, but ultimately decided against it. With his elbows on the solid wood desk, the familiarity of his office helped him to calm his heart rate. Soon the startling image began to fade from his mind. By the time Esther found him, he'd nearly forgotten about it entirely, having written off the lingering, dreamlike image as nothing more than a trick of the light. Esther smiled and gave him a little wave.

"Just checking on you before I go, Mr. Debois. I want to take a nice jaunt around the trails before the deputies close everything up."

Hugo frowned a little. Though he wanted people to enjoy the parks, he hesitated at letting little old Esther Aronowitz wander out alone at this hour. Especially with rumors of killers and kidnappers running rampant as of late. "Are you sure, Mrs. Aronowitz? There's been… a lot going on in the city lately. It might be safer for you to go home and come back in the morning."

Esther laughed. "Oh, don't you worry yourself about me, Mr. Debois. I'm safe so long as I'm with the trees. You get yourself home now, though, you hear me? Tell Margaret that Esther says hello."

Hugo's head suddenly felt strangely blurry. He was having difficulty focusing on his next thought, as though trying to pierce a coastal fog with a laser pointer. "When have you met my wife, Esther?"

Hugo couldn't be certain, but it seemed to him that Esther Aronowitz's smile faltered briefly. "Well I met her during the Winter Bird Count last year, don't you remember Mr. Debois? That was such a horribly cold day, and we were out there for so long. And at such a god-awful hour, I swear my toes felt like icicles for a week!"

"Oh… yes, of course," said Hugo. *That was strange*, he thought—they had to cancel the Winter Bird Count last year because of a snowstorm. Maybe that was two years ago? He really must be getting old. "Well… You enjoy your walk, Mrs. Aronowitz. Be careful out there."

Esther Aronowitz smiled at him. "I will, of course, dearie. You too." Then she left.

Hugo wearily rubbed the bridge of his nose as he drove towards the park's exit. Subconsciously, he kept an eye on the roadside forest for any deer with a death wish. The occasional bat flittering back and forth above served to remind Hugo that the park, like the city, never truly slept. The sunset only began the night shift.

The road meandered like a river through the park, moving with the hills of the forest around it. At the apex of one of these curves, Hugo's headlights illuminated a park police vehicle on the side of the road, apparently abandoned.

Normally, seeing an officer's car in the park at this time wouldn't cause Hugo any alarm. The park police were even more vigilant at night to discourage the vandals, the druggies, and the general ne'er-do-wells from taking advantage of the dark. On this strangest of evenings however, something about the parked car gave Hugo pause.

It was an odd spot for an officer to pick to pull over, even while on the lookout for miscreants. There weren't really any structures in this part of the park—rather, it was part of the preserved natural area. This particular bend of the road was too far from the trailheads for any practical stroll.

Hugo couldn't imagine what would have possessed an officer to stop here. Pulling over, he parked behind the abandoned vehicle, and exited his car.

With some degree of apprehension, Hugo squinted and peered through the driver side window. But the car's interior revealed nothing amiss. Frowning, Hugo walked a circle around the vehicle, yet the exterior didn't give him any hints either. Finally, he fumbled his smartphone out of his pocket and used its flashlight to brighten the ground around the car. At last he found something— the light illuminated a set of vague footprints in the mud. The footprints traced a purposeful line away from the road, leading deeper into the forest.

Hugo frowned and tried to mentally picture where he was on the park's map. The forest here was one of the wildest areas in the park. In fact, it might have been the most undeveloped spot in all of San Cicaro, all due to the fen. This particular marsh happened to be a very rare sort; the gentlemen at the natural features inventory referred to it as a "perched prairie fen."

Hugo was a little vague on what exactly that meant from a hydrological standpoint. As such, the staff had been asked to do what they could to leave it in its untainted, natural state. The surrounding pine forest served as a buffer, protecting it from the road's surface runoff. And all the walking paths and cross-country ski trails that zigzagged their way through the area gave it a wide berth. Most visitors didn't even know the fen existed; the staff had left it off the maps to discourage the curious. The only people who regularly ventured there were natural features surveyors, a few hardcore birdwatchers and wildflower enthusiasts, and the occasional ecology researcher from the local universities.

What on earth would lead park police to the fen at this time of night? Hugo stared into the forest indecisively. The trees seemed to stare back.

He made up his mind. Fetching a pen and notepad from his car, he scribbled his phone number and an explanatory note. If the officer returned before Hugo, he would discover it under his windshield wiper. Hugo then wrestled an ancient high-powered flashlight out of his trunk and smiled. No one would ever be able to say old naturalists weren't prepared, not in his parks.

"Just like a boy scout," Hugo chuckled to himself, and set off into the forest.

As soon as he stepped foot into the woods, Hugo felt more at ease. He was in his element now. The cedar and birch trees around him were widely spaced, enough that he was able to get a good view of the stars. Their soft light was a natural compass that kept him on track. All around him the chorus of the forest played its quiet music. The tiny woodwind noise of the crickets, the vibrant string-like song of the treefrogs, and the occasional deep, booming bass of a bullfrog. It all mixed into a pleasant symphony that soothed Hugo's soul.

Hugo estimated he was about two-thirds of the way to the fen when a bright light flickered between the trees up ahead. A circle of piercing blue hovered in the darkness, perhaps fifty yards away. The officer's flashlight! Funny color, though, that electric blue. Police force must have switched over to some sort of new LED bulb. Hugo shined his own flashlight back in response and started walking towards the bobbing blue light.

Hugo was about to assure the officer he was with park staff when the light blinked off.

Hugo stopped and squinted into the darkness. The afterimages of the blue light still dominated his vision, and he found himself unable to pierce the inky veil of the night. Hugo was suddenly acutely aware of just how vulnerable one old man alone in the woods could be.

"Hello? Officer?"

There was no reply, but the blue light flickered back on, ahead of him and to the left. It was about fifty yards away from him again.

Hugo blinked. His skin crawled. The air around him took on an uncomfortably damp quality, as though he'd plunged headfirst into a cold autumn mist. Almost entranced, he walked towards the new blue light, not even bothering to keep his footsteps quiet or cover up his flashlight. This time he was only about five feet away when the blue light winked out of existence. Another appeared, perhaps thirty yards away this time, hovering in front of a short and spiny tree. Even in the dim light Hugo could identify it as prickly ash.

Hugo frowned. Prickly ash was a strange tree, growing primarily in the transitional zones between wetlands and drier forest soils. A fine plant, except that to Hugo's knowledge it had never been found growing in California. Must be invasive. He'd have to tell the natural resource crew tomorrow.

Hugo stopped halfway to the third light, struck by a sudden burst of rationality. He berated himself for not looking closer at the first and second lights. He suddenly realized they were probably some sort of motion-activated light source, maybe an LED tied to a tree. Clearly someone was using the lights to make themselves a trail, perhaps leading to a hunting blind or a trap line. The parks had issues with poachers before, some fifteen years ago now, and now it would seem they were having issues again.

Hugo shuffled forward with newfound confidence. Everything was making sense now. The officer must have noticed the lights from the road—maybe they'd taken some of them down already—and had been investigating. Just as Hugo was now. Odds were good that the lights led not only to the officer, but evidence of a poacher's den as well. Just as well that Hugo followed this to its conclusion, then. He could give the officer a hand with their investigation.

As Hugo reached the prickly ash, he considered returning to his car and grabbing a bag so that he could start gathering lights. On second thought, maybe the officer had left them on the trees intentionally so that the incident could be properly documented later. The third light blinked out mere steps from the prickly ash, but this time Hugo didn't hesitate. He put his flashlight down, reached out to the tree and ran his hands carefully along the bark, searching the trunk.

"You really shouldn't be here, dearie."

Hugo whipped around, adrenaline coursing through his veins at the unexpected voice. To his astonishment, Esther Aronowitz stood not five feet away from him, frowning softly.

"Esther?" he nearly yelled, but at the last second he managed to choke it back to a whisper. "My god, you gave me a scare! Don't sneak up behind me like that, I told you I'm getting old. What are you doing here? Do you normally walk to the fen? It's a long way away from the nature center, Esther, I'm impressed."

Esther Aronowitz ignored him, but her mouth turned to a grim slash. She glanced into the forest behind him and murmured something he couldn't understand. Whatever she saw clearly didn't please her, and she scowled, murmuring something even longer that he still couldn't quite make out. The words tickled the edge of his brain in a strange way—like hearing a foreign language that he'd long since forgotten how to speak.

The old woman sighed and patted his hand. "You'd best come with me, dearie. You can't go back now."

Hugo pulled his hand away. "Esther, I appreciate your concern, but I think it's best if you and I both get out of here. It's late. My car is back at the road, I'll drop you off at the nature center."

Esther studied Hugo for an uncomfortably long moment, her normally cheery expression replaced by a look of intense concentration. When she next spoke, her voice maintained a carefully neutral tone. "Hugo, I want you to turn around and look at the forest behind you for a moment. Tell me what you see."

Hugo shrugged and smiled at her. "Can't see much in this light, Mrs. Aronowitz, but I'll take a look. You see a bird or something?" Hugo turned around and scanned the forest. "I don't see much moving, Mrs. Aronowitz. Can you give me a hint?"

"It's not moving."

"Hmmm… I give up, Esther. All I can see are the trees, and they… uh…" Hugo trailed off, and squinted more closely at the woods. The tall conifers that had accompanied him to this point were gone. The only variety he could see, all the way back until they faded into the darkness, were dozens upon dozens of prickly ash.

After giving him a few seconds to process, Esther patted Hugo's hand again. "Come along now, dearie. There are things you must see now, I suppose."

Esther Aronowitz refused to entertain any of Hugo's many questions as they traveled deeper in the forest. In fact, she tersely disallowed talking of any sort. So the pair of them walked on in silence as Hugo tried to ignore the questions danced on the tip of his tongue.

Hugo was a man of science, though not the traditional, white-lab-coat-and-beakers sort. Rather, he held a bachelors in ecology and evolutionary biology, even if many years had passed since he earned it. He still clung to the concept that everything might be explained in a way that fits within the boundaries of physical science. The lights he could explain, but the forest of prickly ash was much more difficult, although he hadn't yet completely given up. But somewhere deep in Hugo—underneath any rational thoughts and justifications—a stirring in his bones told him that he was dealing with something else. He'd walked with Esther Aronowitz for perhaps fifteen minutes before a question finally fought free, escaping his lips before he could consider its meaning.

"This has to do with those murders in the city, doesn't it?" he asked quietly. "And the disappearances?"

She ignored him.

"Esther?"

The elderly lady stopped walking and sighed. Hugo took a long, hard look at her as she considered her answer. On the outside, she appeared to be the same Esther Aronowitz that he'd known for—how long now? Several years, at least—yet something had changed about her. She had walked with a limp since Hugo had known her, but now her gait was as sure as a soldier's. The Esther Aronowitz Hugo had known reminded him somewhat of a chicken: aimlessly pecking at the ground beneath her feet, only vaguely knowledgeable of the world around her, but content nonetheless. This Esther Aronowitz was more falcon than chicken, driven and purposeful.

"In a way," she responded eventually. "Not all of them, certainly not, but I can't deny that it has to do with some of them. Now stay quiet, Mr. Debois. We're almost there."

Hugo obeyed and kept his mouth shut for the rest of the walk. He tried in vain to mentally prepare himself for what may lie ahead, but he soon abandoned the attempt. Hugo knew himself. He couldn't prepare himself for the impossible; it just wasn't how his brain was wired. He was so grounded in reality that he practically had roots himself, deep as any forest pine.

Then, with no warning, they were in the fen. Esther placed a gentle hand on his elbow. It was a good thing she did, because what he saw would have driven him to his knees otherwise. As it was, he felt the blood drain from his face, and cold rivulets of sweat ran down his back. He supposed he should thank his lucky stars that his heart didn't give out then and there.

The dragon caught his eye first. Gleaming bronze scales glinted with reflected moonlight, covering a reptilian face that reflected an undeniably intelligent, and even more undeniably sinister, expression. Lurking a safe distance from the dragon was a massive gaunt creature with flint-grey skin that resembled the wendigo of Native American legend.

Other beings were less tangible. They were wavy outlines and transparent figures, shimmering clouds of strange shades, or else colorless black voids that absorbed light. These floated off the ground and hardly moved at all, except occasionally to bob up and down in the moonlight.

At the far side of the fen was a third group of figures that Hugo could barely make out from the corners of his vision. When he tried to focus on them a sustained wave of dread and panic overwhelmed him.

He shut his eyes before he'd gotten more than the vaguest impression. He could look no more. He could barely even stand.

It was a nest. A nest of unimaginable beings. Right here, in his park.

And even worse, right in the middle of his city.

Mrs. Aronowitz steadied him. "Come along now, dearie. They won't see us here so long as I'm with you, but there's nothing else to gain by sitting here and watching them. They're waiting for the night to get a little darker, I think, before they go hunting."

Hugo tried to respond, but his voice failed him, and he only made a hoarse grunt in response. He mechanically trailed behind Esther as she led them back out of the fen. He thought no thoughts. It was as though his brain kept rebooting, trying in vain to load a version of the world in which all those things existed. Hidden, right here in Sentimental Pines Park. In the city. Right here in the city. He brought children to this park.

Esther Aronowitz led him away from the fen but in a different direction than the one they'd come. She seemed less sure of her route this time, occasionally casting her eyes up towards the canopy, muttering and making minute changes in direction. It wasn't long before she stopped in apparent frustration. Without looking at Hugo she strode forward a few paces and gave a cedar tree a quick kick.

"Oh come out, you absolute ass... You trapped him here. The least you can do is give him a proper greeting."

Hugo wanted to ask Esther Aronowitz who she was talking to and why she was kicking a tree. Instead, he found he was still unable to unstick his throat sufficiently to spit the words out. He may have gurgled a little.

For a moment there was silence in the forest. Truly silent, and it suddenly struck Hugo how strange the quietness felt. No crickets sang, no bats fluttered, no frogs sang their chorus to the wind. The silence was broken by was a flurry of wings amongst the needles. A bird flew down from the cedar tree, landing lightly on a nearby fallen log.

Hugo peered into the darkness. It was a grey catbird, a handsome, slate-colored bird about the size of a robin with a black cap covering the top of its head, so named for their strange mewing call. The catbird regarded Hugo nonchalantly for a moment. Hugo stared right back.

A rising noise filled the night. A deep, twinkling laugh, with no apparent source unless the trees themselves were mocking Hugo's plight. The din filled the forest, rattling Hugo's frayed nerves. The catbird had made no further movement, regarding Hugo with the same casual indifference.

"Hugo of the Woods," the voice boomed. It was the strangest, most ethereal voice Hugo had ever heard; it certainly didn't sound like anything organic vocal cords could produce. More like sound clips of flowing streams, creaking trees, and the howling of storms and woven them together into words. It carried in its pronunciations numerous, subtle inflections. Yet none of them seemed to correspond to human emotions, leaving the voice with the distinctly robotic tones of a machine attempting speech. "Welcome to my land."

Hugo's voice suddenly unstuck, and rather to his surprise he found that he felt oddly calm. The rational part of his mind, the flame of science and sense, had finally gone out, leaving nothing but a sense of fatalistic tranquility. "What... pardon me. Who are you?"

The voice laughed again. The catbird cocked its head slightly. "You are polite, Hugo of the Woods. There is no name for a thing like me. But humans try and name everything, don't you? You name the rivers, you name the trees. You name the rocks in the earth and the stars in the sky. No other creature cares for names the way you do. I would have my own name before you invent one for me, so you may call me Quercus."

Hugo decided to try for the friendly approach. Fear threatened to paralyze him, but the monsters in the fen had drained him of that particular emotion. He felt strangely alive, and younger than he had in a decade. "Quercus it is, then. I like it; oaks are wonderful trees. How long have you been in Sentimental Pines, Quercus?"

The voice laughed again, but it didn't bother the naturalist quite as much as the first time. "Longer than you have, Hugo of the Woods. Much longer. But I have not always had a voice. The power of this place grows, no matter how your kind tries to tame it. "

Hugo nodded. He decided to leave that point alone for now. He looked to Esther Aronowitz for help, but she only stared back at him, patterns of shadow dancing on her face, revealing nothing. The catbird hopped along the log a few inches and cocked its head the other way, still staring intently at Hugo.

Hugo thought carefully about his next question. He was starting to get an idea what manner of creature he might be dealing with. And he even thought he might have an inkling why Esther Aronowitz had brought him here. "Tell me, Quercus. Do you care for these woods?"

The voice didn't laugh. For a long time, there was no answer.

"There is nothing else," it said at last.

Although Hugo still had little confidence in his analysis of the voice's words, he thought he detected a hint of wistfulness in the riverlike tone.

"I do too," said Hugo simply. He spread his arms wide, gesturing broadly at the trees all around him. "I have cared for them for most of my life. I have listened to the symphonies of birdsong in the morning in these woods. I have guided kids to look at the frogs in the ponds on the trails through the trees. I have guided adults to the wildflowers and the owl nests. People are fickle, and all of them are different, but I've done my best to make them care about Sentimental Pines the same way that I do. Sometimes it's worked, other times I don't think it has. But nevertheless, I have always ardently defended the presence of this forest in a sea of skyscrapers, for the benefit of people just as much as for the sake of the forest."

Hugo paused and took a furtive look at his audience. The catbird hadn't budged an inch. Esther had sunk back, her face even more covered by shadow, her expression impossible to discern. Hugo took a deep breath and continued. If his gut was right, this was the most important speech of his life. Should he lose his momentum now, he'd never get it back.

"So. Because I care about these woods, you can imagine how aghast I feel. To discover, without my knowledge, that the fen here has become a hive of horrible creatures. Esther said earlier that they're waiting for the darkness to deepen before they go hunting—I don't need either of you to tell me what they're going to hunt. I won't stand for it! They don't belong here, Quercus. Now I don't know what kind of creature you might be, but I'm pretty certain you're not like the monsters from the fen. So how about you and I do something about them?"

There was silence again, for a very, very long moment.

Then the voice started to laugh, but this time there was an edge to it. No more were the tones of flowing water and creaking trees. Now the voice reverberated with the harsh cracking sounds of branches snapping, of crackling wildfire, of torrential storms that tore through the trees.

"They don't belong here?" The voice crashed into Hugo's eardrums, catastrophically loud, sending vibrations rippling down straight to his bones. *"They don't belong here? You would say this? And I suppose you do? You, human* of the city? You do more harm here than they. Those beings... they are new here, but compared to the forest so are you. They live in my home, but they hunt in your city. They disturb little here. Monsters of your 'myths' cause less harm than fire, than axes, than chainsaws and bulldozers and your own monsters of metal! Even the new beings your kind bring to the forest—a beetle maybe, a flower, or a reed—even these seemingly insignificant creatures have the potential to cause more lasting damage than the beings in the fen."

Hugo tried hard not to let the fear show on his face. Standing in the forest with this voice raging all around him was akin to trying to stand tall in the heart of a thundercloud. Around Hugo the ferns had started to ripple subtly, as though reacting to an unseen breeze. He frowned in what he desperately hoped was a nonchalant manner and held unwavering eye contact with the catbird. "I don't think you're giving us quite enough credit."

Quercus laughed again. Two feet to Hugo's left, a branch snapped off a tree and thudded unceremoniously to the ground. "San Cicaro is a world of glass, metal, and stone. What nature remains in these islands of forest are no more than relics—memorials to the natural world that you destroyed to make your presence known. Just as you memorialize the humans that suffer equally meaningless deaths. I feel, in fact, that the appearance of these creatures may be providing a wonderful opportunity for what's left of the natural world in San Cicaro. Perhaps they'll hunt enough of you to free up some of the land you've claimed? It won't be a fast process, with so many of you littered through your world of glass and stone. But the earth is patient. We can wait. And when you're gone, we shall reclaim, and restore.

"But perhaps," the voice suddenly disconcertingly quiet, and Hugo strained to catch it at the very edge of his hearing. "Perhaps I can speed the process along. Your Esther Aronowitz has protected you, sight and smell, from the creatures of the fen thus far. There are a few of her ilk across this city, playing human even as they try to guide and protect your worthless species. But she doesn't trump my power, not here. There are rules, set down before there were words to speak them. In the woods, I can dispel her power with a thought."

Hugo opened his mouth, desperately trying to formulate a reply by the time he had to speak. Before he could, Esther Aronowitz made a strangled noise and keeled over, landing motionless on the ground, hidden among the ferns.

"And now I have," said Quercus. The blood-chilling noise of a wolf howl punctuated the night. "Do you hear that, Hugo of the Woods? They already smell you. You should run, human. There is a chance you could escape the boundaries of my home before they reach you. Your car is northeast from here. Go."

Hugo whipped around, his blood pounding in his ears. His eyes darted through the spaces in the trees, suddenly aware of even the slightest sound of movement. The wolf howled again, somewhere behind him.

He turned his eyes upwards, frantically tracing the stars. Northeast. There was Draco, there the big dipper, so there the north star, so...

A roar, not unlike a movie interpretation of a T-Rex, tore through the forest. He finished his hasty compass of stars and started jogging off into the night.

And then stopped almost immediately. Another wolf howl, followed by what sounded like an elk's bugle, if it were an elk the size of a semi. Hugo still didn't move.

He turned around. The catbird was watching him. It hopped sideways on the log as though to get a better look at him.

Hugo deliberately took off his glasses and cleaned them on his shirt. The catbird watched him. He replaced them on his face. Still, the catbird watched.

Then, very slowly, he sat, cross-legged, on the forest floor. He clasped his hands before him, just as he asked the kids to sit during nature programs for the school groups on a park field trip.

There was silence. The elk bugle rang out from behind him, perhaps a little louder than it had been. Hugo resisted the urge to turn around, and instead kept his eyes fixed on the catbird. It cocked its head at him. Hugo smiled wanly at it in return.

"This is no bluff, Hugo of the Woods. You will die at their hands," said the voice.

Hugo sighed. "I'm already dying, Quercus of the woods, so you'll have to do something better than that." There was no response, so Hugo continued. "Cancer. Prostate. Already spread to other parts of my body. That puts my five-year survival rate at about thirty percent."

He took a deep breath, letting the scent of the pines filling his nostrils reinvigorate him. "Now, thirty percent ain't that bad. And five years is a long time to wrap up my affairs—it's a lot more than most folks get. But you know, I think if I can talk to you for five minutes right now, before the beasts can tear into me, then these last five minutes will be worth much more than five years of dying would have been anyway.

"Now look," he said, in as stern a tone as he could manage, leaning forward in his intensity. "You're right about a lot of what you said, but I still don't think you're giving us enough credit. Now, I'll grant you that humans got a little overeager with the skyscrapers for a few decades—heaven knows. I get a little uneasy downtown when I can't see the horizon—but people have gotten a lot better in recent years. Folks care about the woods again. You say you've always been here, Quercus, and that means you've seen the people who come to the parks. Any of those folks look like they're itching to take a torch to the trees?"

"Islands," Quercus bellowed. "You've left islands of nature, surrounded by a cage of metal and glass and stone."

"And why would we do that?" challenged Hugo. "Hmm? Riddle me that, if you know everything. Why leave the islands if we don't care?"

He waited for a reply, but there was nothing but the sounds of wind and quiet breathing from the still-unresponsive Esther Aronowitz. He heard the bone shuddering roar again, much closer now. Hugo decided to opt for a different tactic.

"Let me ask you a question. I came in here following an officer." No response. "Come now, these are my last few minutes alive. Can't you at least honor a dying creature by satisfying his curiosity?"

"Yes," said Quercus. "Young Officer Ortiz. She followed the will-o'-the-wisps, same as you did."

Hugo nodded. "I figured as much. Where is she?"

"Are you sure you dare ask, Hugo of the Woods? If this is your fate, why should hers be any different?"

Hugo hummed, low and deep in his throat, and leaned back on his hands. He could feel fallen needles tickling at his palms, and he wrapped a hand absentmindedly around a group of them. "Because I don't think you spoke to her the way you're speaking to me. I'm willing to bet those monsters in the fen didn't get her, because Esther Aronowitz wouldn't have taken me to them if she thought I'd be finding an officer's bones. And I certainly don't think you killed her yourself. So that means she's still somewhere in the forest, and she's safe. Because you've kept her safe."

There was a silence again. The catbird mewed at Hugo, and it surprised him so much that he nearly leapt to his feet, but he managed to keep his composure. "I'm right, aren't I? See, I don't think you're quite the kind of nature spirit that you'd like me to believe you are. I've known this park for a very, very long time. It seems to me that you're an ambassador for it. Or maybe it's just a part of you, or maybe you are the park… damned if I know. But if you represent my nature park here, I find it awfully hard to believe that you're some cold-blooded spirit of vengeance. Nature values life. Death, too, but not meaningless death."

A pair of yellow eyes appeared in the trees to Hugo's left, perhaps twenty feet away. Hugo closed his own eyes and continued.

"And revenge itself isn't a very natural concept, is it? The deer doesn't chase down the wolf that killed its brother. You've absorbed that idea from us I think, no matter how much you claim to despise us. You're saying you would harbor these creatures here, keep them safe, but you'll let them eat humans in your forest? That's not very natural either! Nature doesn't favor one side over the others, it lets itself even out. It reaches an equilibrium. But here you are tilting the scales. If the monsters are protected here, then the humans should be too. No favoritism, just keep things fair."

Hugo's voice caught in his throat. Even though he wasn't quite sure that he'd made his points to the best of his ability, it was moot now anyway; Hugo Debois was out of time. He could feel warm breath, rancid with the smell of death and decay, wash over his face. His eyes treacherously slid open just enough gaze upon his death—the silhouette of the wendigo loomed perhaps two feet away—before he slammed them shut again.

He decided to forgo a final breath and tried not to gag. An image flashed through his mind of his wife, his dear sweet Margaret, filing a missing person report alone at the police station in the morning. For the first time since he'd sat cross-legged in front of the catbird, he felt close to tears. Hugo grasped his handful of fallen pine needles so tightly that they dug into his palm.

Goodbye, Sentimental Pines. Good luck.

There were plenty of places to see in San Cicaro.

The Golgonooza, where the weird and the weirdest of San Cicaro's denizens congregated. The annual kite festival over the bay, where fae lights and foo fighters danced between airy rice paper constructions. Restaurants with food so delicious, you'd sell your soul for a second bite, and someone else's for a third. There were places in San Cicaro where the very air felt alive with the colors of indescribable wonder, sublime and terrible in equal measure.

But despite their accessibility, prominent locations, and abundance of pleasant greenery, almost no one talked about the parks of San Cicaro. At least, none of the visitors did.

Among the residents of San Cicaro, whispers began to spread. As the number of mysteries in the city mounted even higher, people spoke with a surprising note of optimism when they discussed the little islets of woodland in the city's heart.

"Nothing mysterious ever happened in the parks," they'd say. No bodies were ever found there, no unidentified pools of blood, no baffling cases that left investigators mystified.

"No," people would say. "The trees are safe. So long as you treat the parks well, you'll be fine there. If you're ever being chased down an alley by an unimaginable horror, go to the nearest park, because the trees are safe."

The trees are safe...

About the Authors

Ichabod Ebenezer has lived in the Pacific Northwest for twenty-four years, making him a virtual native. He writes Mystery, Horror, Sci-fi, and Fantasy. http://theichabodebenezer.com

Evan Purcell is a writer and teacher currently working with students in Kazakhstan. He writes horror and fantasy stories for all ages.

Jonathan Ward has a novel "Into the Blight" published through Amazon, with a second due for release soon. Like all English people, his blood is 90% tea.

Jenn Cavanaugh's poems and stories have appeared in several U.S. journals, including *America*, *Parabola*, and *NonBinary Review*. She lives in Seattle.

Eric Stoveken is an author of strange and unusual tales. More of his unholy scrawling can be found at www.ericstoveken.weebly.com

Leora Spitzer is a queer Jewish bibliophile and writer. She lives in St. Louis, MO, with her pet snake, Princess Buttercup.

JC Hemphill has had more than thirty stories published and was awarded the Writing Downtown Fellowship by Amazon in 2017. He has a terrible memory and often forgets to

Larry C. Kay knows all too well what lurks within the sinkholes of central Florida. Find out more about his succulent skull meat at GoodReads.com or ScribbleNinja.com.

Ian Ableson is an ecologist by training and a writer by choice. When not reading or writing, he can reliably be found scowling at a clipboard while ankle-deep in a marsh somewhere in Michigan.

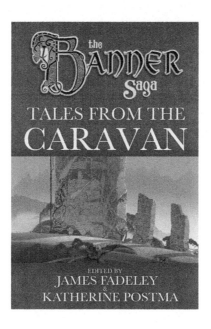

Based on Stoic's sweeping epic, *Banner Saga: Tales from the Caravan* collects ten tales from our fans and our shorter classics. From the First Great War to the exodus of Tistel, the founding of Nautmot to Rugga's rise of power, this anthology is a must for fans of the series and low-fantasy lovers alike!

***Banner Saga: Tales from the Caravan*, from Stoic. Available this July on Amazon and SmashWords!**

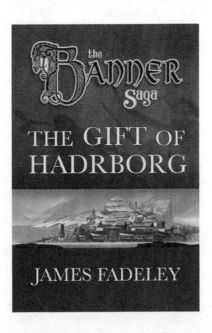

In the troubled city of Strand, Governor's Guardsman Eirik struggles to fend off the criminal empires who rule the streets. But everything changes with the arrival of a powerful relic that belongs to the northern giants, threatening the security of the city itself. The thrilling prequel to Stoic's award-nominated *Banner Saga* trilogy!

Banner Saga: The Gift of Hadrborg, from Stoic. Available now on Amazon and SmashWords!

Made in the USA
Monee, IL
20 July 2020